Remembering Richard

Also by Stephen Smithyman and published by Ginninderra Press
Snapshot in the Dark
Halfway and Back

Stephen Smithyman

Remembering Richard
and Other Tales of Unease

Acknowledgements

'Climbing the Mountain' won second prize in
the William Todhunter Literary Award, 2009.

'Autumn in the Orchard' won first prize in the Short Stories Unlimited
Autumn Story Competition, 2022, and was published in
the subsequent Four Seasons Project Anthology ebook
(https://www.smashbooks.com/books/view/1185870).

'Jack o' Lantern' was published in the *California Poppy Times*,
Halloween edition, October 2022.

Remembering Richard: and Other Tales of Unease
ISBN 978 1 76109 483 5
Copyright © text Stephen Smithyman 2023
Cover image: Ebrahim Hussain, Aotearoa Lakes (https://nzlakes.org/)

First published 2023 by
GINNINDERRA PRESS
PO Box 3461 Port Adelaide 5015
www.ginninderrapress.com.au

Contents

Remembering Richard

The primary school I went to was next to a lake, known by its Maori name, Pupuke – overflowing lake. To us kids, it was simply an expanse of shining water, surrounded by bush and houses, and inhabited by black swans. They built their nests among the toi-toi and raupo on the shore, laid their eggs and raised their young. Our teachers warned us not to go near them. An angry swan could break your arm with a single sweep of its wing, they said. We stayed away, terrified – marvelling that something so beautiful could also be so savage. But this was the world the way we found it.

In Standard Two, when I was seven, I was befriended by a boy nobody else wanted to be friends with. I accepted his friendship – partly because I felt sorry for him and partly because he was bright, interesting and a little bit different, like I was. We used to go to his place, a large, double-storeyed brick house with a peaked roof on the edge of the lake. I'd never been in a house with a staircase and bedrooms upstairs, just like a house in a story. His father was a well-to-do lawyer, which made him different from most of the people my parents knew. Richard – that was my friend's name – showed me his collection of William books, which amused him immensely. After something to eat, we went outside to play. This friendship continued, off and on, for the rest of our time in primary school.

In our final year, I fancied myself as a swimmer. I wanted to see if I could swim across the lake. Richard, who didn't swim, agreed to accompany me in the family rowboat. We set out, I in my togs, and Richard, fully clothed, pulling silently on the rowboat's oars. I swam and swam. It seemed I was tireless, although it also seemed the lake got bigger, all the time. To my disgust, I discovered that the lake didn't appear to get any deeper in the middle, as I'd imagined. Instead, the depth remained more or less the same, all the way across. Far from swimming over deep, dark water, the shallow bottom was covered by a bed of flowing, waving, none-too-clean-looking eel grass, which terrified me, once again, as I swam over it. I imagined myself caught up in it, struggling to free myself, sinking down and drowning.

I don't remember if I swam across the lake. I don't remember what happened to Richard, either. I didn't see him after that. Maybe his family moved away or, more likely, he was enrolled in a private secondary school and I was enrolled in the local state secondary. But I always remember him, his red hair, his freckles, his pale eyelashes, his expression of perpetual hurt and anger, aware the other kids didn't like him, and I remember that grass, reaching up from the bottom of the lake, just below me, extending its muddy, air-bubbled tendrils, its slimy green fingers, to grasp me, trap me, pull me down beneath the shining surface, overwhelming me, like a cold, clammy invitation from the grave…

That Summer

That summer, when I was ten years old, my brothers and I holidayed with our mother at our grandparents' – her parents' – place in Rotorua. My father didn't take part in such excursions. The official explanation was that he was 'staying home to get on with his work'. My grandmother was warm and kind; my grandfather was notoriously cold and mean. But they were always welcoming, in their neat, clean house.

Ignoring the sulphurous smells and the ground shaking beneath our feet, we often went to the Blue Baths, where our mother was treated for her arthritis, while we boys swam. I loved to swim. I dreamed I was setting world records and winning Olympic gold, as I charged up and down the pool, dodging the other kids, who only wanted to play.

One day, we took the ferry to Mokoia Island, in the middle of Lake Rotorua. We lay in the hot pool where Hinemoa rested after her epic swim across the lake to join her lover, Tutanekai (he of the amazingly tuneful wooden flute). Moved, as we were, to be in such a legendary spot, we were even more moved to discover a Coke machine nearby, containing ice-cold, fizzy nectar to counteract the effects of the hot day.

It was while holding a bottle of refreshing Coke and running across wet rocks on the side of Hinemoa's pool that I slipped and fell, cutting my hand badly. I stared in shocked disbelief as the blood welled to the surface and began to flow, then screamed for my mother, who came running. She bandaged my hand, as best she could, and sat with me, for the rest of the afternoon, on the grass beside the pool.

When we arrived back in town, she took me to the local hospital. There, my hand was cleaned, stitched and bandaged again. I was told to stay out of the water for the rest of the holidays, or run the risk of infection. I loved to swim, as I said, and begged repeatedly to be allowed to do so, but it was not until we were at a holiday house owned by friends of my mother, on the shore of Lake Rotoiti, one very hot day, that my mother finally said 'Yes'. She covered my bandaged hand with a plastic bag, tied at the wrist, and I dog-paddled happily around the lake all afternoon, with my hand raised protectively (or so I thought), like a periscope, above the water.

Within the next few days, it became evident the hand was infected. By this time, we'd moved to my uncle's farm, at nearby Whakatane. I was put to bed in the sunroom of the house, with a sore hand and a high temperature. The local doctor came and gave me injections, throwing the hypodermic, like a dart, into my bum. I lay there, reading my way, enthralled, through *The Collected Stories of Sherlock Holmes* for the rest of the holidays. During this time, my father turned up, completely unexpectedly, and gave my mother the one and only driving lesson of her life. She ran off the road, they exchanged words and she never drove again.

Back in Auckland, when the bandages came off, it was obvious there was a problem with the index finger. It wouldn't bend. An operation (experimental at the time) was suggested, to transfer part of a tendon from my wrist into my finger, to make it work again. I was put into a big city hospital, all by myself, for ten days – the longest time that I'd ever spent away from my family, though they came and visited every day. In the next room, an eighteen-year-old boy, who'd broken both his legs in a motorbike accident, kept tearing the bandages off and swearing at the nurses when they tried to stop him. In the room opposite, another boy, the same age as myself, lay dying. He cried continuously in the night, until doctors and nurses came running, curtains were drawn, hushed conferences held, an injection administered, then silence…

I had the operation, vomited my heart out for two days, endured many doctors' conferences around my own bed and eventually went home. But the operation wasn't a success. Whether that was the operation's fault or my own wasn't entirely clear. I was supposed to flex my finger around a piece of dowel I kept with me at all times – even at school. Needless to say, I wasn't able to do that with much consistency, especially in front of my peers. The finger continued to stick out from my hand, stubbornly inflexible, completely useless and potentially dangerous.

And so it has remained, ever since. Not working, it never grew. It's shorter, thinner, less wrinkled than any of my other fingers – a child's finger on an old man's hand, a strange persistence from childhood, reminder of that far-off summer, the child I once was and the man I became.

In My Grandfather's House

It's the 1950s. It's New Zealand. My mother and I catch a taxi from the bus station to my grandparents' house. My father hasn't come with us. He never comes with us on holidays.

The smell of sulphur is everywhere in Rotorua. It smells like rotten eggs. That's the smell I associate with this holiday town where my grandparents live. That and the heat. It always seems to be hot when we go there – hot, baking days of summer. It's not a place where it rains much.

My grandparents' house is made of brick. It's very small and square and neat. It sits in the middle of its block like a little brick box, with steps and a small front porch, leading up to the front door, and a concrete drive down the side. The Venetian blinds are always down and the lacy curtains are always drawn, so you can't see in from the street. It looks very private and quiet.

The tiny patch of front lawn is always immaculately watered and mown, and my grandfather's prize roses sit in tidy beds, with woodchips heaped up around them. There isn't a weed in sight. I'm not allowed to play anywhere near the roses. Like everyone else, I'm in awe of their beauty and terrified of their thorns.

My grandfather and grandmother come out of the house while the taxi driver is unloading our baggage from the boot. They greet my mother. My grandmother gives my mother a warm hug. They embrace and seem to cling to each other, for a moment, for support. My mother gives my grandfather a cold and rather distant peck on the cheek, and he replies in kind. I'm expected to give them both kisses on the cheek. They smell very clean but, at the same time, they have that unmistakable, musty smell of old age.

My mother pays the taxi driver, then we all go inside. Inside the house, it's very cool and dim, after the heat outside. The loudest sound is the ticking of the grandfather clock in the hall. You can hear it everywhere you go. It's my grandfather's clock, given to him when he retired. He's very proud of it. Every morning, he winds the clock and makes sure its pendulum's swinging correctly, before he taps the barometer to check the weather. Every night, he does the same again. Everything in that house runs according to that clock.

We put our bags in our room and go through the house to the kitchen, where my grandmother makes a cup of tea for the adults and pours a lemonade for me. Out the window, above the stove, we can see Mount Ngongataha, which dominates the view for miles around. The mountain is, the adults have explained to me, a dormant volcano, like so many others in this land. I look at it, big and silent and green, and secretly waiting to explode.

'So Kevin didn't come?' enquires my grandmother.

'No, he's at home, working,' my mother replies.

My father's always working. Somehow, I get the impression that no one is very sorry that he hasn't come.

'Oh well, you'll have a nice enough time without him.' says my grandmother.

'Yes,' my mother replies, and there's a look of shared understanding between them.

My grandfather goes out to work in the back garden, and the two women settle in to talk and prepare lunch in the kitchen. I follow my grandfather. There's a concrete path, leading down to a Hills hoist in the centre, and two more strips of green, immaculate grass on either side. On either side of them, again, against the fences, are more beds of my grandfather's prize roses, all blooming. I have my ball with me, so I can play cricket or football for New Zealand all afternoon.

'You be careful of those roses, mind!' calls my grandfather.

'I will!' I promise. I'm too scared of their thorns, anyway, to go anywhere near them.

And that's the way the days pass at my grandparents' house. My grandfather potters in the garden, I score tries and centuries and win test matches single-handed for my country, and the women talk in whispers in the kitchen.

At one stage, I hear my mother saying to my grandmother, 'You could always come and live with us.'

I can tell this is something she really wants, because there's a peculiar urgency to her voice. But I can tell she also knows it's impossible, because there's a sadness there, as well. My grandmother doesn't even bother to reply.

I notice my mother only ever speaks to my grandfather if she absolutely has to, and, when she does, she does so in a remote manner, as if she doesn't really want to make contact with him at all, and this pains him. But, like so many things in the adult world, it seems that's the way it is and there's no changing it. It's like the relationship between my mother and my father. The only time they talk is when they're yelling at each other.

After dinner, my grandfather reads the newspaper in the living room. But he soon drops off and slumps back in his chair, face turned up towards the ceiling, mouth open, snoring, holding the newspaper loosely in his lap, with his legs stretched out in front of him and his slipper-clad feet crossed at the ankles. The women tiptoe around, trying not to wake him, and I read my book, quietly, in a corner. We go to bed early when we're here.

The first night, I'm still trying to cope with the strangeness of sleeping with my mother in the same room. But, eventually, I drop off, only to be woken in the middle of the night by a sensation that the whole room is shaking. The bed moves from side to side. The bedside lamp rattles, slides sideways and teeters on the edge of the bedside table. I lie in the darkness, paralysed with fear, wondering what on earth is going on.

It takes some time before I can go back to sleep. I lie awake, staring into the blackness, listening to the steady ticking of the grandfather clock in the hall. It chimes loudly and increasingly elaborately, every quarter-hour, half-hour and hour. I come to dread the next chime, which always seems to happen just as I am about to close my eyes and drift off into sleep.

In the morning, there's discussion between the adults.

'That was a big tremor last night,' says my mother, though I could have sworn she slept right through it.

'Yes,' replies my grandmother. 'You get used to them after a while. I hardly notice them now.'

'Was there a tremor last night?' asks my grandfather. 'Wait till you get a really big one,' he half-jokes, half-threatens, 'that'll shake you.'

I don't want to imagine it.

To escape from the strained atmosphere in the house, my mother and grandmother take me to the Blue Baths. They're big, white-tiled and echoey, and the water in them is bright blue, like the sky. My grandmother looks after me, while my mother goes and has a hot mineral bath and a massage in the old, Tudor-style spa building next door. My mother is slowly being taken over by chronic arthritis, which means she's often in pain. But nobody really speaks about it. It seems to be something she has to bear on her own.

I swim up and down, winning gold medals for New Zealand, while my grandmother looks on, approvingly. We're surrounded by local kids, playing noisily. They yell and splash and dive-bomb each other, and I'm glad to have her with me. My grandmother is a kindly, comforting presence, always taking care of everyone. I can see why my mother loves her.

We go back to my grandparents' place. I play for a while in the back garden, overlooked by the shadowy, green bulk of the mountain. When I go back inside, I can hear my mother's and my grandfather's voices, raised in argument, in the living room. Worried about my mother, I push through the door from the kitchen just in time to hear her say, 'No! Go away and leave me alone!' and see my grandfather's disappointed face, his hand reaching out in appeal towards her, before my mother leaves the room in tears.

That night is more than usually tense. My grandfather doesn't even go to sleep, in his usual way, after dinner. Instead, he goes to bed very early.

The next day, trying once more to escape the atmosphere in the house and give me a treat, my mother and grandmother take me to the Whakarewarewa thermal reserve and Maori village, on the other side of town. We walk up and down gravel paths, between pools of boiling water and mud. The boiling water is deep green and leaves layers of yellow all over the surrounding rocks. The boiling mud looks exactly like porridge. It makes big bubbles that rise up and burst with a hilarious 'blooping' sound, sending ripples out in solid, heavy rings across the surface of the pool, before collapsing back into the mix, only to rise up and bloop again, somewhere else. Everything is covered in steam and stinks of sulphur, even more strongly than the rest of Rotorua.

My mother is scared and keeps telling me to stay away from the edge of the pools. But I go as close as I can, staring into them, trying to see right down into their depths, fascinated by the thought of all that ferment happening underground.

The earth shakes constantly, underfoot. It feels like we're walking on a very thin crust which might break apart at any moment, to let what it can barely contain come bursting through. As we walk, my mother and grandmother are talking about my grandfather and my father, thinking that I can't hear.

'He's a cold, distant man,' my grandmother is saying. 'He's always been like that. There hasn't been much satisfaction or enjoyment in it for me, I can tell you.'

'I know,' my mother replies. 'That's pretty much what it's like with Kevin and me. He does try, up to a certain point, but he's never there when I really need him. In the end, he's only interested in himself.'

Then they both sigh, as if to say, 'Men are so difficult!'

We stop to stare at a narrow, deep hole in the ground, out of which, it's said, a geyser will erupt. We stare and stare, but nothing happens. In the end, we walk away and come to the Maori village, at the end of the reserve. There are very few men in sight. Women and children stand in front of the traditional raupo whares and the meeting house, posing for photographs. The fronts of the whares and meeting house are beautifully carved, but the women and children look sad. The old women are dressed in mildewy black. There's one very old woman there, who still has the traditional, blue 'moko' tattoo on her chin. Lots of people take photographs of her. The children look a bit scruffy and play in the dust, while the women cook food in flax kits, in the hot pools.

We eat delicious corn, smothered with butter and salt, from one of the hot pools and walk on. We come to the very end of the reserve, where a bridge crosses over a creek, on the way out. Young Maori boys compete at diving from the bridge for small change the tourists throw into the creek below. They leap off the rail of the bridge and plunge into the creek, then resurface, proudly brandishing the glittering coins aloft. My mother doesn't want to throw change for them, because she doesn't feel it's quite right, but I pester and pester her. I want to be like those boys. I want to soar with such ease, plunge beneath the clear, cold surface and come back up, clutching my rescued treasure. Finally, reluctantly, my mother throws a coin. One of the boys dives in.

Just at that moment, some people who are leaving the reserve ahead of us come running back across the bridge, shouting, 'Look! Look!' and pointing over our heads.

We turn and look. Above the trees behind us, the geyser is throwing its fountain of white, steaming water high into the hot, blue sky. There's a rumbling underground like a beast waking, throwing off its sleep and staggering upright. The bridge itself sways with the combined effects of the people running and the earth moving. Up and up, the towering fountain mounts, until it looms above us like something we've always known about, but never seen till now – untamed, dangerous, awesomely beautiful and powerfully exciting. There are more and more people coming from every direction, running towards it. Unable to resist, my mother, my grandmother and I join them. Together, we all start running.

Four Snapshots of a Creek

1 Early morning

That morning, the two brothers woke early. The sun was barely peeking through the gap between the bedroom curtains. The rest of the world was still hushed and sleeping.

They got out of bed and dressed very quietly, their feet freezing on the cold, polished floorboards. They walked the length of the passage, past their parents' bedroom, with its half-open door, across the green kitchen linoleum, down the concrete back steps and out to the washhouse, where they put their gumboots on. They took the string hand line, which was stored behind the washhouse door, and an empty jar to put worms in. Their breath smoked in the early morning air as they walked out of the washhouse and down the path through the orchard which led to the creek.

The fruit trees were just coming into blossom, with tight little buds appearing along every bough. The brothers knew summer was on the way – their favourite time of year. There'd be plenty of time, then, to go fishing for eels and paddling their corrugated-iron canoes on the creek. This was only the merest beginning of it, but even so, they couldn't wait.

They stopped by the place where their father burned rubbish at the bottom of the garden, on the bank of the creek, and scrabbled there in the dank earth for worms. The worms weren't hard to find and the brothers soon had half a jarful of them. They gazed in fascination at the wriggling, pink bodies, crawling all over each other and tying themselves in knots inside the jar. Very soon, they knew, the worms' time would come.

They crossed the creek on the bigger, drier rocks in the rapids, which formed a natural bridge to the other side, where the empty paddock began. They knew that the biggest eels took shelter there, under the bank. They'd been planning this expedition for a long time.

They clambered up the bank on the far side. This bank was covered by weeping willows, like the bank on their side, but the grass was longer under these willows because it was never mown. No one farmed this area any more. It was just vacant land, waiting to be developed.

They lay on their stomachs in the cold, wet, grass, looking into the shadowy, brown water under the bank. The sun had risen a little higher and its rays helped them to see better into the depths of the creek. Sure enough, there they were – the big, black eels, swimming in slow circles, or lethargically finning to hold their place against the gentle pull of the current. They saw some very big eels there – bigger than they'd expected. The older brother was very excited, but the younger one was a bit nervous.

'They won't bite, will they?' he asked.

'No!' said the older brother, sounding more confident than he actually felt. Like the younger brother, he was thinking about those rows of razor-sharp teeth, like little needles. 'Of course they won't.'

'Oh!' said the younger brother, trying to believe him, against his own mounting fear. He was prepared to follow his older brother just about any-where and everywhere in those days, but he still had some reservations.

The older brother wrestled the hook from where had been stuck for safekeeping in the fishing line, which was wound around a short stick. He put several worms onto the hook and lowered the line into the water directly below them, to tempt the eels, swimming under the bank.

The brothers continued to lie on their fronts and observe the eels. The eels sniffed and nudged the baited hook, but none bit for a while. Finally, while neither of the brothers was looking, one did. The effect was imme-diate – it nearly pulled the line right out of the older brother's hand.

'Quick! Quick! We've got one!' he yelled, in a state of mixed panic and excitement.

The younger brother jigged up and down on the spot, in an agony of indecision. He had no idea what to do.

The older brother held on tight, occasionally giving the thrashing eel a little more line, but not so much that it could get away from the bank and tangle the line around any of the rocks, or the debris that gathered round the rocks, in the middle of the creek. The younger brother dashed in and out, peering over the edge at the eel's ferocious struggle down below, then back behind his older brother for protection, in case the eel should suddenly leap out of the water.

Eventually, the eel began to tire.

'We'll pull it up on the bank,' the older brother said.

The younger brother could only nod, wide-eyed.

His older brother began to haul the eel in, hand over hand, winding the wet string back around the stick. 'Be careful of the teeth!' he said.

The eel flew through the air with the force of its own momentum, violently coiling and uncoiling the whole length of its body. The younger brother was terrified. The eel landed on the long, green grass of the bank, thrashing backwards and forwards. The older brother held on, desperately. The frantic lashing of the eel's tail drove both brothers to the edge of the narrow bank, in danger of falling into the creek, themselves.

The eel's red blood was smeared across the grass. The brothers were both horrified and revolted. They'd never seen anything like it in their short lives. It was a very big eel – one of the biggest they'd seen.

'Hit it with that branch there!' yelled the older brother.

There had to be some way to end this struggle, before someone got hurt. The eel's needle teeth were all too apparent, clamped around the piece of string.

The younger brother snapped into action, as if woken from a dream. He seized the solid, sizable length of branch that had fallen from the willow behind them, raised it above his head and brought it down, with all the strength he could summon, on the eel's fragile skull.

More blood spurted across the grass. The brothers felt that they were locked in a battle of life and death – a battle of epic proportions to match any they'd seen at the local movie theatre on Saturday afternoons. The eel continued to thrash, but less violently now. The life was visibly draining out of it onto the grass. The brothers themselves were splashed with little flecks of the dying eel's blood. They felt triumphant, but a bit sick as well.

Finally, the eel stopped moving.

'Phew,' said the older brother. 'I thought it was never going to die!'

'Me, too!' the younger brother rushed, as always, to agree with him. He felt as though he'd witnessed something he was never going to forget. He was amazed at how brave and calm his older brother had been. He was filled with admiration for his brother, and shame at his own fear and helplessness.

But any qualms either of them might have felt were swept away in the rising elation that followed the eel's death.

'We did it! We did it!' they chanted, dancing around on the bank. They saw themselves as heroes, just like in the movies. This was the kind of adventure cowboys might have, out riding the range.

The older brother stripped a small branch off the willow and threaded it through the eel's gills, taking care to avoid those razor teeth. It wasn't easy, because the eel was covered with a jelly-like slime, which made it extremely slippery. He slung the stick, with the dead eel hanging from it, over his shoulder and the two brothers set off home.

It was still early morning when they carried the eel into the house, having first taken off their gumboots at the back door. They carried it, dropping little spots of blood and slime, across the worn linoleum of the kitchen floor, towards their parents' bedroom. The door was open and, though the room was dark, they could clearly see their parents in bed. Their father was snuggling up to their mother as they came marching in.

'Look what we caught!' they announced proudly, more or less in unison.

'Take that thing out of here!' yelled their father, shocked, angry and trying to shield their mother, who hadn't woken up properly yet, from the sight – all at the same time.

The brothers were intensely disappointed with the reaction, which was nothing like they'd expected.

Their father sensed their disappointment. 'It's a very fine eel,' he said, making an effort to calm down and get his voice back under control, 'but it doesn't belong in here. Take it out to the washhouse and leave it in a bucket of water. And well done!' he added, belatedly, to further soften the blow.

The two brothers turned and left the room. They glumly retraced their steps across the kitchen floor, down the back steps and out into the washhouse. The younger brother found a bucket and half-filled it with water. The older brother put the eel in and filled the bucket up to the brim. A long flower of blood came out of the eel's mouth, discolouring the water.

The brothers stood back and watched the eel, the water and the flowering blood. No words were exchanged. They didn't need to speak. Each knew how proud the other was of what they'd achieved. This was a legendary moment that would live forever in both their memories. Then they realised how hungry they were. They quickly washed their hands and faces in ice-cold water from the washhouse tap, then went inside to eat the breakfast which they could hear their father preparing, rather grumpily – banging cupboard doors and muttering to himself – in the kitchen.

2 Winter rain

It rained all day and all night. The rain drummed on the fibrolite roof and slid down the steamed-up windowpanes in fat, round drops, obscuring the view. It turned the ground sodden and the creek – their mild, sweet summer creek of amiable, brown water, slipping gently between the rocks they liked to call 'The Rapids', or sleeping in pools inhabited by eels and dragon flies – had turned into a muddy, raging, winter torrent. And still it rained, right on through the next day and into the night. This was becoming dangerous. It reminded Charlie and Sam of the story of Noah's ark. They half-expected the little wooden house to come loose from its foundations and float away on the current. How amazing that would be – to be sole survivors of the deluge and founders of a new world!

Things hadn't been too good, lately. Mum and Dad were fighting a lot. Almost every night, they heard raised voices from the kitchen after they'd gone to bed.

One night, they heard Mum screaming, 'I hate you! I hate you!' at Dad, and half-a-dozen rashers of bacon she'd been holding in her hand, getting ready to fry them for tomorrow's lunches, came skidding along the passage floorboards and crashed into the blackboard, in the far corner of their bedroom. When Charlie and Sam talked about it in years to come, they always referred to it as 'The Night Mum Threw the Bacon at Dad'. It was clearly a turning point in the life of their family.

But tonight there were no raised voices – only the rain. Heavy and threatening though it may have been, it was also very soothing. Charlie and Sam were soon fast asleep, only to be woken by Dad, torch in hand, in the dark, at midnight.

'Shh!' he whispered, calming their fears. 'I wanted you to come and see. The creek's in flood.'

They got up very quietly, taking care not to wake their younger brother, Garth, who was sleeping in a small cot in their room now, put the raincoats and gumboots Dad held out for them over their pyjamas, and tiptoed out of the room behind him. In the passage, the noise of the flooding creek was louder already. By the time they got to the kitchen, it was like the roaring of a train. Outside, in the dark, lit only by the beam of Dad's torch probing the steady fall of heavy rain, the noise was deafening.

The narrow light of Dad's torch showed them the amazing thing he wanted them to see – the creek was now up over the back lawn, washing around the foundations of the bungalow and the trunks of the fruit trees in the orchard.

'How much more is it going to rise, Dad?' Charlie, the older brother – taking the lead, as usual – asked in an awed, frightened voice.

'I don't know,' said Dad. He sounded excited, but worried too. 'Depends how long it keeps on raining, I suppose. We'll just have to see what it looks like in the morning.'

'I'm cold,' the younger brother, Sam, complained, stamping his boots in the water running over the concrete paving, at the bottom of the steps.

'Yeah.' Dad tried to reassure and placate both boys. 'I just wanted you to see it. You won't see something like this too often.'

The boys stared once more into the unimaginable dark, listening to the roaring monster.

Dad even turned his torch off to increase the effect, but it obviously upset Sam when he did that, so he quickly turned it back on. 'Come on,' he said, 'time to go back inside!'

Charlie turned away with some reluctance, but Sam could hardly wait, dreaming of the warmth and comfort of his bed. The two boys took their boots and raincoats off in the little porch at the top of the steps, and ran quickly, quietly, through the kitchen and down the passage to their bedroom, with that slight feeling of being spooked, of being followed by some scary monster. Sam did his familiar, flying leap into bed, just in case there was anything underneath it.

'Shh,' Dad admonished them, 'don't wake Garth!' indicating their younger brother, still sleeping in his cot. 'Or Mum, either…' he thought, though he didn't say that out loud.

In the morning, it had stopped raining. There was only the steady drip, drip, drip of large water drops from the eaves, the branches of the trees and every available surface where they could gather. A thin, watery sun was even trying to force its way through the uniform, grey cloud cover. The floodwater had retreated from the back lawn, but the creek was still up very high, moving with tremendous speed and force – and the same thunderous roar – especially up close.

The boys stood in the shelter of the spindleberry hedge, which separated the orchard and the end section of the garden, watching the hugely swollen creek fly past. The flood carried large amounts of debris with it – trees which had been torn out of the ground by the roots, building materials, fenceposts and twisted coils of fencing wire, a dead cow from the farmland up at the creek's not-so-distant source, and even the rusted out shell of an old car. It all went tumbling and twisting, borne along by the roaring, leaping, muddy-brown, creamy-foamed torrent, terrifying and exhilarating them, down the creek's normal course and out to the open sea. At least, this was what the brothers assumed. They followed it in their minds' eyes, right down to the summer beach they loved, allowing for what got caught up in the branches of trees, on rocks, in swampland and under bridges along the way, where it would remain in evidence for many months to come. They were in awe of the flood's fierce, destructive power and its ability to transform their world.

Finally, the spell was broken by the growing cold of their extremities and the emptiness of their stomachs. It was time to go inside for breakfast. They could hear Mum's and Dad's voices, as they approached the house, raised in anger once again.

'You did what?' Mum was yelling. 'You took them out in the middle of the night, in the middle of a rainstorm, to take a look at a dangerous flood? You must be out of your mind! What if something had happened?'

'I only took them out to the bottom of the steps, for Christ's sake!' Dad yelled back at her.

'That's so typical of you. You're so irresponsible. When are you going to grow up and start behaving like an adult?'

'Nothing happened. What are you carrying on about? You can't keep them wrapped up in cotton wool the whole of their lives. They're a couple of boys. They like a bit of excitement, a bit of danger.'

'What're you going to do if they catch colds? Are you going to look after them?'

'They won't catch colds!'

'How do you know that? You never think before you do things. It's like living with another kid around. If they do catch colds, you're looking after them. You can ring up work and say you're taking a day off to look after them. How do you think that'll go down?'

'It won't come to that.'

'I'm so disappointed in you.'

'You bitch! When are you going to ease up on me?'

'When you start taking your share of responsibility for this family! When you start acting in a grown-up manner!'

There were the muffled sounds of a scuffle, followed by the sharp, clear sound of crockery breaking. When Charlie and Sam entered the kitchen, Dad let go his grip on Mum's wrist and the two of them stepped rapidly apart, with a broken plate on the floor between them. They looked at the two boys, shamefaced.

'I'll just tidy this up and get on with breakfast,' Mum said. She was close to tears. She knelt down on the floor and started picking up the pieces.

'I'll go and check everything's all right around the place,' Dad said. He started into sudden, uncharacteristically businesslike motion, pushing blindly past the boys and going out the back door, without so much as a backwards glance in anyone's direction.

Charlie and Sam stood stock still, not knowing how to react in the face of their parents' anger.

'Why don't you go and see if Garth's awake?' Mum suggested.

Together, they trailed slowly up the passage to their bedroom. As they went, they could hear the clatter of broken crockery dropping in the bin, and their mother crying softly behind them.

3 Summer heat

That summer, there was a terrible heatwave. It went on for weeks. The parched earth suffered, but for the three brothers it was a piece of heaven, because they went to the beach every day. It wasn't so good in other ways, however, even for them. It seemed to make their parents' usual bad relationship even worse. Mum took to staying late at work, putting off the moment of returning home as long as possible. When she did come home, there were fights between her and Dad, with much recrimination, screamed abuse and sobbing. Finally, Mum would make dinner and they would all eat, in a tense silence, at nine or ten o'clock at night.

Another way it was not so good was that their beloved creek had turned into little more than a stagnant, muddy-brown and green-slimed, dried-up ditch. This hurt them deeply, because it had been the site of so many of their childhood adventures. In their earliest memories, some of the bigger neighbourhood boys still swam in the pool, just before 'The Willows', as the swampy area downstream from their place was called. When they were a bit older, the three of them made tin canoes out of corrugated iron and paddled them down to the Willows. There, they took part in epic battles with other boys from the neighbourhood, throwing stones and firing specially sharpened willow-frond arrows at each other from home-made willow branch bows. They felt sure that Mum would have died if she'd found out, but, of course, she never did.

On quieter days, they made miniature outrigger canoes from the woody shafts that grew out of the middle of flax bushes, and raced them across the pools and down the rapids at the back of their place, until they vanished in the distance. On other days still, when nothing else was happening, they went on massive rambles up and down the creek, as far as the beach where it came out, in one direction, and up to the swampy valley farmland where it had its source, in the other. They liked to walk upright through the huge stormwater pipes and stand under the bridges, while traffic roared overhead, scattering stones past the entrances, and shaking the pipes and bridges till they felt like they would break. And, of course, there was always fishing for eels, though, as time went on and the creek became more and more polluted by the houses being built along its banks, they were actively discouraged by their parents from doing so.

Now the creek was no more than a sad reminder, a ghost of its former self. It survived in the deeper pools under its banks, where it never dried up. But even those pools were stagnant, dark and dirty. The whole thing stank of sadness and decay, which the brothers somehow understood and came to accept as they grew.

In the middle of the heatwave, Mum decided to go and stay for a while with friends of hers in the country. This was something she did from time to time. Dad was obviously not invited. She took Garth with her, because he was still the baby of the family. Charlie had started on his first holiday job, so he was seldom home. That left Dad and Sam, struggling on through the long, hot days together.

At first, Sam filled in the time by continuing to go to the beach every day with his friends. But, gradually, even that palled, and he began to spend more and more time on his own, brooding, dreaming, drifting along in a semi-somnolent combination of adolescent languor and heat exhaustion. Dad, preoccupied by his own concerns, hardly seemed to notice.

One day, Sam dragged himself through the oppressive afternoon heat down the garden path that went past the bungalow, in search of a cool spot to rest, under a shady tree. He found himself standing on the bank of the dried-up creek. He was surprised to see that the dark brown water in the pools under the banks had turned a diseased-looking milky white, covered with a crusty, dirty yellow scum. It didn't look right and it didn't smell right. It smelt, in fact, as if the water itself were rotting.

Then he saw, with horror, that eels had begun to climb up the banks and wriggle across the grass on either side as they sometimes did – in summer, anyway – migrating from pool to pool in an effort to get away from the diseased-looking water. Except they weren't getting very far. They were only getting a few feet from the edges of the banks, where they stopped moving. There, they rolled onto their backs and died. As they died, their stomachs swelled up like semi-transparent, greyish-coloured balloons and burst, spilling the contents of their stomachs onto the grass. These piles of rotting insides stank even more than the creek itself, Sam realised. The whole scene was overcast by a pall of unnatural, almost surreal, disaster.

'Dad! Dad!' Before he knew it, he was running up the garden path like a little child. 'Dad! Something's wrong with the creek! It's poisoning the eels! They're coming up out of the water and dying!' The words came tumbling out of him, in panic and confusion.

Dad looked at him, nonplussed. This wasn't something he wanted to deal with on such a hot afternoon. 'Where? What's happening?' he spluttered.

'Come and see!' Sam practically pulled Dad along with him by the hand, down to the bank of the creek.

'Hmm…' said Dad, confronted by the carnage. He ran a hand through his thinning hair, both puzzled and appalled. In his way, Dad was as fond and protective of the creek as the boys were. He liked to take specimens out of it and look at them through the microscope he'd bought, fancying himself as a bit of a scientist lately. 'Someone's put something in the creek – the bastards! We'll have to tidy the mess up, I suppose. We can't leave these eels out here to rot. They're a health hazard. The flies are gathering already.'

So, surrounded by clouds of flies, in the hottest part of the day, they hauled eels up from the bank of the creek to the vegetable garden, where they dug a mass grave for them. Some of the eels were enormous – four to six feet long and as thick as a man's thigh. Sam had no idea, after all the years he'd lived there, that eels as big as that lived in the creek. It wasn't easy, lugging them in the heat.

Halfway through, Dad suddenly decided he had something more urgent to do and left Sam to finish the job by himself. Sam laboured on until late afternoon, when he covered the last of the stinking, fly-ridden pile with rich, black earth and patted it flat. He felt, as he was doing so, that he was burying the last of his childhood.

It turned out that a paint factory in the industrial estate which now occupied the swampy valley where the creek had its source had emptied cyanide waste into the creek. There was a great fuss about it in the local paper; the paint manufacturers were fined; the creek was cleaned up. Dad followed it all with outraged fascination, as if the degradation of the creek were somehow a direct attack on him. Mum, when she returned, felt he was taking it too personally and responding in a typically immature fashion, when he had more important things he should be giving his attention to. The three brothers just felt disillusioned, sick. None of them ever had much to do with the creek again.

4 Autumnal

The leaves were falling from the plane trees around the park at the bottom of the hill where Sam caught the bus to go home. The bus went under the overpass, along the freeway which ran past the marina, and over the bridge to the other side of the harbour. From the top of the bridge's arc, there was a magnificent view of the harbour spread out below, with the whitecaps and white sails of the yachts flying. Further out, the big ships – tankers, freighters and liners – made their way slowly along the channel between the island and the mainland to the docks.

Sam sat back, trying to enjoy it, but inside he was nervous. He hadn't been home, hadn't seen Dad, for some time. He'd heard his younger brother, Garth, describe the situation, last time he'd seen him.

'He's changed,' Garth said. 'He's living there by himself, but I don't think he really knows what to do with the place. He's living out the back, in the bungalow, and only comes into the house to cook and watch TV. It's like he doesn't really want to live there any more, but he doesn't know how to give it up. He's just clinging onto it because he doesn't know anything else – although why you'd want to hold onto those memories, I really don't know. I think he should just sell it, get rid of it. Who cares, anyhow? Mum's gone…we've gone…none of us is ever coming back. I think he's quite deeply depressed.'

The bus drove through the nearby town, which had been ramshackle and run-down when Sam was young, but was now the thriving centre of a large city. He could hardly recognise it. Progress was coming, at last, to this side of the harbour. The bus went round the lake, past the footy ground where he'd played so many games in childhood, past the girls' school which had been the site of so many teenage fantasies, and along the main road, until it came to the stop, which he nearly missed, so engrossed was he in his memories. But he pulled the cord at the last moment, and the bus deposited him by the familiar, weather-worn and graffitied wooden shelter which stood on the side of the road.

He walked down the side road opposite, over the bridge, round the corner, where a block of flats had been built on the drained ground of the old willow swamp, and up the hill towards home. He wondered if any of the people in the new houses knew about him or his claim on the place. Only home itself seemed not to have changed. It was still tiny, still ugly. It seemed, if anything, to have grown smaller with the years, standing forlornly in the middle of its large, rather unruly block. Dad evidently wasn't making much of an effort to keep up the garden in Mum's absence.

He walked up the concrete path to the front door. The house was oddly silent, with a definite air of abandonment. There was clearly no one in the front part of the house, so he continued to the back. There, the back door was open and the familiar smell of coffee was coming from the kitchen stove. But, once again, when he climbed the back steps and peered round the door into the kitchen, there was no one there. He actually called 'Hello!' this time, but only his own voice came back to him, faintly disturbing the emptiness.

Not wanting to intrude, he was temporarily at a loss what to do. He stood for a moment at the top of the steps, taking in the overgrown orchard, which was a tangle of unpruned branches and falling leaves, then proceeded down the garden path, calling tentatively ahead of him, 'Hello-o! Hello-o!'

To his relief, there were noises from the bungalow and Dad's head peered around the door. He rubbed his eyes and rumpled the curly, greying hair on either side of his bald dome. He'd obviously been asleep. Sam couldn't believe how small he looked, or how vulnerable. But his face, which was sad, at first, lit up when he saw Sam.

'Sam,' he cried out, 'how good to see you! We haven't seen each other in such a long time. How are you keeping?'

'I'm well, Dad, thank you. And how are you?'

'I'm well.' (Even though he didn't particularly look it.) 'Here, let me have a look at you!' He seized Sam by the shoulders, in an unfamiliar gesture, and looked at him appraisingly. 'You know, you remind me so much of your mother…'

'How is Mum, Dad?'

'I don't know. She never communicates with me. You mean you haven't heard from her?'

'Not for a while.'

Dad abruptly lost interest in the subject. He dropped his hands from Sam's shoulders. 'Well, come and have a coffee!' he said, moving around him in the direction of the house. 'Or, better still, a beer.'

They took a beer each from the fridge and sat around the kitchen table, talking. Dad seemed obsessed with the subject of the creek. He described a legal battle he'd had with the local council. The council wanted to concrete the bed of the creek – to turn it into a conduit, as they called it, to counteract the effects of the winter flooding. A conduit, they calculated, would better conduct the volume of water and save damage to property, on either side. But Dad hated the idea.

'I fought them tooth and nail.' he said. 'I waged a propaganda war in the local paper. I wrote letters. I commissioned articles. I gave them no rest. Finally, I had them on the ropes. And then came the *coup de grâce.*'

'What was that, Dad?' Sam tried to appear a bit more interested as he started to feel the relaxing effects of the beer.

'No, no. Come and see!' said Dad. He suddenly rose up, taking his beer with him, and headed down the back steps.

Sam followed him dutifully. The orchard and the vegetable garden were revealed as even more sadly overgrown, given time to examine them. When he passed the garden bed where he'd buried the eels, that hot summer day, Sam winced.

'Here, have a look at this!' said Dad, proudly.

Sam looked. He gaped.

'They wanted to take everything out and have it smooth, just like a ditch.' said Dad. 'But I refused to let them. I loved those rapids. I didn't want to lose them. The sound of them in the night is magical. Apart from anything else, they remind me of your childhood. Do you remember how you boys used to play in them?'

Sam could only nod, dumbly.

'I did some research. I consulted lawyers. I found out that our property rights actually extend to halfway across the creek. I threatened to take the council to court. I threatened to sue them if they tampered with my property. In the end, we reached a compromise. They agreed to remove the rocks before putting their ditch through, then set them back in the concrete, exactly as they were.'

And that was just what they'd done. The evidence was laid out, in plain view, before Sam's incredulous eyes. There was no water in the creek at that time of year. The original creek bed had completely vanished, transformed into a perfectly flat, concrete-bottomed conduit with angled concrete sides. But there, set into the concrete bottom, carefully preserved in their original order, were the familiar childhood rapids. The whole thing was so bizarre, it made Sam want to laugh and cry at the same time. But, in the event, he did nothing.

He didn't need to. Dad did it for him. Immensely pleased with his own success, Dad threw his head back and roared with laughter. He waved his arms about and broke into a little jig of victory. It was the first time Sam had ever seen him dance.

Sam watched his dad caper like a happy child. He thought about his mum, sharing a house with one of her sisters, who was also divorced. He thought about Charlie, pursuing his career overseas, and Garth, working on a farm in a remote part of the country. He thought about himself, staggering on half-heartedly with his studies, unable to fully engage with them but at the same time unable to give them up. Part of him always seemed to be preoccupied with something else.

'What is the truth about our family?' he wondered. 'What is the balance in this complicated combination of love and loathing that simultaneously draws us together and drives us apart?' After all the years of their being together, he was no nearer to an answer; in fact, he felt further away than ever.

He and Dad shared a desultory meal that night. Dad seemed to have retreated into himself again after his brief moment of happiness down by the creek. They ate mostly in silence. Sam helped with the dishes, then said he had to go.

'Not so soon!' Dad pleaded, with something like desperation in his eyes.

'I have to.' Sam didn't sound very convinced, even to himself. 'I've got uni tomorrow.'

'Have another drink before you go.'

So they had another drink, with all the memories jostling at the windows, like the leafless branches of the trees out there in the dark. Then Sam caught the bus back to the city and the life that he knew, from now on, he'd have to live more or less on his own.

The Longest Swim

That was the summer Sam went to the beach every day of the holidays. He was twelve years old and had just finished primary school. He met up with a group of his friends there. They'd all been friends in primary school, but they were splitting up now. Most of the boys and girls in the group would be going their separate ways to the local single-sex state secondary schools. There was a sense of something finishing as much as there was a sense of something else beginning.

They all lay around in a big group on the sand. They fooled around, went swimming, occasionally went out in friends' boats, turned red or tan all over, according to their differing complexions, and, if they had the right kind of hair, it turned surfer blond – with or without the aid of lemon juice. They hit the beach just after breakfast, went home for lunch, returned to the beach in the afternoon and stayed till late, long after most of the other beachgoers had picked up their towels and gone. The beach was like a way of life for the group, almost a religion.

They were old enough to start being interested in the opposite sex as more than just friends, too, though not very seriously. A bit of fairly innocent experimentation went on. For instance, Sam was supposed to be in love with Veronica, a busty, black-haired English girl with very pale skin, who'd arrived at their primary school during the year. Veronica was a bit older and considerably more sophisticated than most of the others. She wore winklepicker shoes, lipstick and perfume, smoked and taught the group how to do the Twist, which had just become popular in England. She'd take Sam off from time to time and give him lessons in kissing, but would never go further than that. Veronica was a good girl really.

But Veronica, out of all the group, didn't come to the beach very often. Sam didn't mind that, actually, because he had a secret. Secretly, he was in love with Sharon Parsons. Sharon Parsons, by contrast with Veronica, was blonde. She was small, with a small, pretty, sharp face, and a small, pink body that was just starting to develop, unlike Veronica, whose body was already well and truly mature. She was also smart. She was Sam's main rival for academic honours in the class and she looked at him in a sceptical, almost mocking, way, as if she knew something about him he didn't yet know himself. He found her utterly irresistible and always had. They'd been in the same class all the way through primary school. Sam was always trying to find ways to impress her. If he wasn't impressing her with his superiority in class, he'd be down at the beach, taking his top off and walking around with his chest puffed out and his muscles tensed, so she could see how manly and good-looking he was.

Sam was greatly preoccupied with his hair in those days. Getting his hair just right – for Sharon, especially – was a major challenge. He wore his hair in a swishback with a kiss-curl. It had to be sculpted and locked in place with the aid of generous amounts of hair oil. If it wouldn't work out, it was the cause of endless frustration and quite a bit of bad feeling. For instance, one day, a hank of Sam's fringe, which should have been part of his kiss-curl, just wouldn't cooperate. It refused to lie down smoothly. The more he oiled it and combed it, the more it stood out. In desperation, he seized a pair of scissors and cut it. This left him in a terrible situation, because now his fringe had a very obvious gap in it. It looked exactly like somebody's smile when they've lost a front tooth, but up on top of his head, rather than down the bottom of it. He was devastated. He knew he couldn't go to the beach like that. Most of all, he couldn't appear in front of Sharon like that. She'd know how vain he was and how he'd created, then tried to fix that problem, all by himself. Her knowing eye would miss nothing.

Sam thought, perhaps, if he tried to cut the whole fringe, to shape it from the gap – which was over on his part side – around his forehead in a smooth, semicircular sweep, he might just get away with it and still have some left for a kiss-curl. So he cut away, but the more he cut, the worse it got. He simply couldn't disguise the original gap and he was rapidly ruining what remained of the fringe. He was also ruining his future. He wasn't going to be able to appear at the beach until he'd rectified the damage. In the end, he cut the lot off. He had no fringe, no kiss-curl, just a short, spiky hedge at the top of his forehead, a bit like the front of a 'flat-top', as the Americans called it, except nothing else in his hairstyle went with it. And he couldn't stay away from the beach. He just had to go.

When Sam turned up at the beach, the girls, in particular, thought it was hysterical. They broke out in fits of giggles, which they tried to hide behind their hands. 'What happened, Sam?' they called out. 'Did you have an accident with a pair of scissors? Were you trying to cut your hair?'

'I burned it leaning over a fire, actually.' Sam mumbled. This was the story he'd decided to tell, when the matter come up.

'Burned it over a fire, did you? Oh, yeah!' the girls chorused, and burst into gales of unrestrained laughter.

Sam kept a very low profile for the rest of the afternoon.

Sharon, curiously, didn't join in with the others. She kept herself, as she often did, a little apart from the others, looking on with that same sharply observant, slightly sceptical expression she always wore. It became more important to Sam than ever to impress her, to show her he wasn't really as much of a fool as the other girls were making out.

The summer progressed; Sam's fringe grew back; he continued to go to the beach every day. But he was still no closer to Sharon, or finding any way to impress her.

Finally, one afternoon, as they were all lying around, torpid in the heat, Sam hit on a plan. The beach where they lay looked out on an island. It was the same triangular-shaped island, the two roughly symmetrical sides leading up from the base to a triple peak, that dominated the view from any beach on that inner harbour. It was the first thing they saw when they arrived in the morning, and the last thing they saw when they left at night. It had always been there and always would be. It was a gateway to their past, present and future.

Legend had it that people had swum to it from time to time, most probably with a boat beside them. It was a good long swim, across at least a mile of inner-harbour water, with marker buoys for the yachts and, further out, a deep channel where the big boats – the tankers, freighters and ocean liners – came in. Sam decided he would swim to the island. Surely, Sharon Parsons would be impressed by that!

The others were joking, laughing and throwing sand over each other, irritating the people around them. Sam felt suddenly bored by them – by all of them, himself included – and the way they turned up at the beach and did the same thing every day. It was time to move on, to do something different. He felt like he'd had enough.

He quietly left the group and made his way down to the water. There was a gentle, low surf rolling in to the beach. The water itself was quite warm. He felt no particular shock when he eased himself into it. He began to swim through the first line of bathers, who were standing or paddling around, trying to catch the extremely tame surf. A few other bathers, like him, preferred to swim further out. But those others soon stopped to rest, breathing hard and treading water, and he rapidly left them behind too.

He was swimming in open water now, as far out as he'd ever been. Sometimes, he and the other boys dared each other to swim out beyond the line of the other bathers, as a way of asserting their superiority, their natural right of ownership to the beach. But he'd never before been this far out by himself. This was definitely scary. He had to forcefully remind himself he had a long way to go.

The water was dark green around him. Small but regular waves surged past him, with white foam breaking from their crests. He rose and fell with each one, trying hard not to breathe the brackish water in. He was terrified of choking and losing control. He didn't like to think about how deep the water might be under him, or the fact that it was increasingly cold. His arms and legs looked very frail and white just under the surface.

He swam to the first marker buoy, which was several hundred yards offshore, and clung to the buoy, panting. The shore was already fading with the distance. His friends were reduced to the size of ants, though he could still just make them out. He wondered if any of them missed him, or if they were at all concerned he was swimming so far out on his own. But no one stirred onshore. Out here, there was only him and the task he'd set himself to do.

He swam on. He was swimming more slowly now, pacing himself. He tried to swim a bit of freestyle, a bit of breaststroke, a bit of sidestroke, in turn, to save his energy. His progress slowed, but he made it to the second buoy. An occasional yacht or launch would pass him by, and the people on board gaped to see a young boy so far out from shore. He was sure they wanted to pick him up or tell him to go back, but, in the event, they left him alone. Everyone on the beach had shrunk to dot size. He could no longer distinguish his friends. The island, by contrast, looked much closer. He could make out individual trees on its slopes.

He swam on. There were many more yachts and launches now. From each one, faces would look down, surprised, incredulous or alarmed. He began to worry that something – particularly a launch with a vicious-looking outboard on the back – would run into him, knocking him out or chopping him into little pieces. How would he cope when he came to the main shipping lane, he wondered. Already, the big ships he could see from there looked enormous, not the bathtub toys they resembled from the beach. When they hooted, they nearly blasted him out of the water. He was terrified.

He began to reconsider his decision to swim the whole way across to the island. Maybe he'd proved his point. Maybe he'd come far enough. It wasn't so much that he was tired. He still had plenty of energy, thanks to the way he'd been swimming, but he needed to know he had enough for the whole of the return swim. Halfway back wouldn't be good enough. That thought, combined with the complicated calculations about the threats posed by yachts, launches and swimming into the shipping lane, proved too much for him to handle. He turned around.

The way back seemed much slower and harder, from the start. Was the tide running against him now, or was he finally starting to get tired? Would he run out of energy much sooner than he'd thought? As he began to tire, he became much more fearful. The wonderful confidence he'd felt, setting out from the beach, evaporated. He saw himself sinking down through green depths. He saw the grey shapes of sharks barrelling up towards him from below. He took longer and more frequent rests, treading water desperately, trying to suppress his growing feeling of panic. If he waved and shouted, would anyone launch a rescue party from the shore? They wouldn't, he concluded. He was still too far out. It was his own stupid fault.

He swam on. Gradually – infinitesimally slowly, it seemed now – the shoreline edged closer. He could make out his friends again. They were still laughing, clowning around. Did any of them have any idea about the life and death drama that was occurring to him out there, he wondered. That thought – and the vague resentment that came with it – gave him energy to keep swimming.

He reached the first buoy again. He could see Sharon Parsons from there. She was sitting separately from the rest of the group, quietly reading a book. As he looked at her, he understood something about her he'd never understood before. There was a new word which had recently entered his vocabulary – inviolable. Sharon Parsons was in some way inviolable, he saw that now. He wasn't really sure what it meant, but he could see it quite clearly as he looked at her. Inviolable – he turned the word over in his mind as he prepared himself for the final push back to shore.

Eventually, to his immense relief, after many more stops and starts he coasted into the shallows on the back of one of those timid waves and lay, absolutely exhausted, on the wet sand. It was all he could do, after some minutes, to haul himself to his feet and stagger, rubber-legged, up the beach to collapse on his towel. His chest rose and fell, gulping air; the world spun around him. He buried his head on his arms, burrowing into darkness until the spinning stopped. When he raised his head, Sharon Parsons was looking at him quizzically.

'What've you been doing?' she asked, in a kindly but disinterested manner, a bit like his mother.

'I've just been on an enormous swim,' Sam told her, as factually as possible. He felt he didn't have to boast. He'd actually done it. 'Didn't you see me? I went way out, beyond the buoys, practically into the shipping lanes. Then I had to turn round and come back again.' He felt the glow of that accomplishment, right through his body. Surely the pleasure, the pride he took in what he'd done, would communicate itself to her?

'Oh!' said Sharon Parsons, a slightly mystified look on her face, as she returned her attention to her book. 'No, I never even noticed you were gone.'

Higginbottom's Leap

Sam rode his bike into the car park at the northern end of the beach. The other boys were there already, waiting for him. There was Harry – big, gentle Harry, or Hercules, as they sometimes called him, on account of his almost unnatural size and strength – but who, unfortunately, for all his other good qualities, wasn't very bright. That's why he was still in his last year of primary school at the age of fourteen. Then there was Jezza, who was younger, smaller and smarter than Harry – and tougher, if anything. Jezza's father was rumoured to drink and beat him, and Jezza had a reputation as a mean fighter. Most of the time, he was fine, but he could suddenly turn on people without warning, so it paid to be careful around him. And, finally, there was Sam. He was the son of a couple of local teachers, who didn't really like him hanging out with these rough boys, but, given the amount of time they spent fighting each other at home, they left themselves little opportunity to do anything about it. Sam was in his last year at the local primary school and spent most of his time with his mates, down here at the beach, well beyond the limits of their control. That is, until next year, when he and the other boys would go their separate ways. Harry and Jezza would be in the lower, technical classes and he'd be in the top academic class at the local high school, and they already knew they wouldn't have much more to do with each other from then on. In the meantime, they were making the most of this brief period of freedom before the next stage of their lives began.

'Hi!' Harry and Jezza greeted him.

'Hi!' Sam replied, panting from his ride.

'Did you bring the money?' asked Harry.

'Yeah.' Sam gave the money to Harry, who was big enough and old-enough looking (he shaved, regularly, and always had a dark five o'clock shadow by this time of day), to go into the little store beside the car park and buy their cigarettes. Jezza and Sam stood around in awkward silence looking at the view. They looked across the grassy area of the reserve to the burnt out remains of the Pirate Ship nightclub and restaurant, and the silted-up, saltwater swimming pool, which, town legend had it, used to be the biggest in the southern hemisphere back in the town's heyday, when it was a popular leisure spot for people coming over from the city. But those days were long gone. It was just a backwater now, with a strong smell of decay, which might have been coming from the creek running under a spindly-looking, old wooden bridge at the far end of the beach.

Kids were swimming in the creek, even though they weren't supposed to. All kinds of local waste ended up in the creek and it wasn't very healthy. It was a bit like swimming in an open drain. Sam and Jezza could hear the kids' voices and water, splashing faintly, in the distance. The bridge, which teetered high above the kids' heads, led over the creek to a patch of bush at the top of the cliff on the other side. That's where they'd be heading later on that afternoon, they hoped.

Harry came out of the shop with the packet of cigarettes. Sam chained his bike to the rack, and they went down onto the beach and sat in the shadow of the car park wall. Harry took three cigarettes from the packet and handed one each to Jezza and Sam with a clumsy sense of ceremony. The boys lit up and sat back against the wall, looking out at the sea, which was dark blue in the late afternoon light. Tiny waves broke, almost sound-lessly, on the golden-brown sand. The smoke from their cigarettes drifted up, to mingle with the bright blue of the cloudless sky. There was a slight chill in the shadow of the wall, and Sam shivered, although whether that was from the unexpected cold, or the slight nausea brought on by the un-accustomed cigarette, was hard to tell.

In the distance, they saw the girls coming along the beach. The girls – Val and Rachel and Veronica – were in their class at school. Even from a distance, they were quite recognisable. Val was tall and thin, with her blonde hair swept back in a ponytail and quite pretty in a sharp-featured way. But, unfortunately, like Harry, she wasn't very bright. There was never much in the way of interesting conversation to be had with Val.

Rachel was shorter than Val. She had an attractive, freckled face under a brunette, beehive hairdo, with a cute turned-up nose and a broad smile. She had quite a well-developed body, too, for her age. In fact, Rachel had already acquired a reputation for being a bit fast. She sometimes went for rides with older boys in their V8 cars, or so rumour had it.

Then there was Veronica. She was smaller than the other two, with thick, glossy black hair that fell straight down her back. She'd recently arrived from England and her skin was extremely white, which made a startling contrast with her hair. She may have been small, but her figure was very well-developed for her age. Coming from England, she'd brought a whole world of pop music and dance crazes like the Twist with her, which were brand-new to Sam and the others. They thought she was very sophisticated and beautiful, even though her accent and some of her ideas seemed a bit strange to them.

The girls stopped in front of them. They were wearing swimming togs and carrying towels, as if they were intending to go for a swim, which was probably what they'd told their mothers. Veronica, in particular, looked stunning in a pink bikini with white flower patterns which showed off her shapely body to advantage.

'Hi!' the girls said.

'Hi!' the boys replied.

Everybody tried to act very nonchalant, as if they'd forgotten the reason they'd arranged to meet each other here.

'Would you like a cigarette?' Harry asked.

'Yeah,' the girls replied, together.

They lit up their cigarettes, trying, like the boys, not to choke on the harsh smoke. The boys stood around and waited, while the girls smoked their cigarettes.

'What's going on over there?' Rachel asked, between puffs, pointing to the creek.

'Just some kids swimming,' Jezza said.

Sam was still feeling nervous and a bit dizzy after his cigarette. He couldn't, for the life of him, think of anything clever or interesting to contribute to the conversation.

'Anyone from our school?' Rachel enquired further, taking another drag on her cigarette.

'Probably,' Jezza said, and they all laughed, thinking about who might be there.

'Why don't we go and take a look?' Rachel suggested.

'Yeah, why not?' they all agreed, glad that somebody finally had the courage to break the ice.

The girls threw their cigarette butts down on the sand and they all headed in the direction of the bridge. Rachel and Jezza paired off, as did Val and Harry. These four led the way, in a group. Veronica and Sam followed, a short distance behind. They were keen on each other, but they hadn't had much of a chance to talk yet.

Sam found it strange being close to Veronica like this. Her skin was very soft, and her lips were moist and full. From time to time, the little pink tip of her tongue poked out from between her strong, white teeth. Her eyes were beautiful, but they were half-hidden by their long, dark lashes and he could only catch glimpses of them.

She was talking about England. 'In England, we don't have beaches like this,' she said, looking around her. 'You're so lucky you grew up here.'

Sam was a bit surprised by her remark. 'I hadn't really thought about it,' he replied, which was true enough.

'If I told my friends back home about this, they wouldn't believe it.'

Sam walked along, trying to imagine a world which didn't have beaches and sun and summers, like the one he'd always known.

He and Veronica stopped at the foot of the bridge, just behind the others. They all recognised some of the boys playing in the water, though most of them were younger than they were. One, however, was a boy from their class. Nobody liked him. He was an ugly, scrawny little kid called Higginbottom. Everyone in their class made fun of his name, of course. He called out to them as they went past and tried to act like he was their friend, but they ignored him.

They walked up several flights of rickety wooden steps which led to the top of the bridge, about thirty or forty feet above the muddy brown water of the creek. The bridge was getting old, and people were starting to say it was unsafe and should be pulled down. The steps were cracked, splintering and warped in places. Many of the boards on top of the bridge were worn and loose, and there were wide gaps between some of them. From the top of the bridge, the water looked a long way down. The figures of the boys looked tiny and their voices sounded faint as they splashed about in the shallows. Sam was privately glad there was a guard rail when they stopped and looked over. Harry goobed, thoughtfully, in the direction of the boys below.

The other reason people thought the bridge was unsafe was because some older boys – the same kind of older boys it was said Rachel sometimes rode around with, in their V8s – dared each other to dive off the top of the bridge, even though there was a notice which said, quite plainly, in large, fading letters, 'No Diving'. The dive was dangerous, not so much because of the height, but because there was only a narrow channel in the middle of the creek which was deep enough to dive into, surrounded by much shallower water on either side. If someone dived and missed the channel, they ran the risk of breaking their neck. For that reason, the younger boys were terrified of the dive and in awe of the older boys who competed with each other to do it to prove how big and tough they were.

None of them said anything about that as they stood there, but they were all thinking about it.

'Ha! I nearly got Higginbottom,' Harry exclaimed, breaking the silence.

They all laughed and walked the rest of the way across the bridge.

On the other side, the couples divided up and went their separate ways into the bush. Veronica and Sam could hear the others making a bit of noise in the undergrowth, then everyone settled down in silence. Veronica lay down in a smooth hollow in the ground, which made a small clearing among the thickly clumped tea trees surrounding them, and Sam followed her. They lay together awkwardly, side by side. This was the closest Sam had ever been to a girl. His nostrils filled with her delicate, musky girl-smells.

They began to kiss. To Sam, Veronica's lips felt fleshy, strange and delicious. They seemed to lead a life of their own, alternately softening and spreading beneath the pressure from his mouth, then contracting and solidifying to nibble at his upper or lower lip. From time to time, their teeth clashed, in hard enamel contrast to the softness elsewhere. He was aware of the saliva from her mouth and hoped he wasn't dribbling into hers.

After he thought a suitable time had passed, he put his hand on one of her bikini-top-clad breasts and give it a tentative squeeze. Veronica didn't seem to mind; in fact, she responded more fiercely, if anything. She pressed her body against his and kissed him harder. Sam felt like he might be swallowed up by the intensity of her kisses.

He squeezed first one breast, then the other, trying to give them equal attention. Her breasts felt deliciously squashy, yet firm, like squeezing ripe oranges. The hardening tips of her nipples pushed up through the material of her bikini top against his palm.

Emboldened by his apparent success there, he slid his hand down over her soft, white stomach and under the tight-drawn top of her bikini bottom. The drawstring scraped his knuckles and the muscles of her lower stomach fluttered excitedly under his fingertips. In spite of the difficulties posed by the tight drawstring, he moved his hand even further down and encountered, for the first time, the coarse curls of a girl's pubic hair against the smoothness of her skin. He was astonished by the tough wiriness of it, then realised how similar it was to his own very recent growth. As he was finding with so many things, real life was nothing like his fantasies.

He was about to move his hand even further down, in pursuit of the ultimate mystery, when Veronica suddenly cried out, 'No, don't, please!'

He stopped, shocked, frustrated, torn between the unexpected urgency of her demand and his strong – almost overwhelming – desire to go further.

'Please!' Veronica pleaded.

'Why not?' he asked, managing to sound peeved, but withdrawing his hand, like his fingertips fingers were burning all the same. To tell the truth, he felt relieved. He really wasn't sure how far they were going to go, or what he was supposed to do from that point on.

'When I was nine years old…' Veronica explained, slowly, with great difficulty, 'some older boys I knew invited me into their room. When I went in there…they took my clothes off…held me down…and raped me.'

Sam felt appalled by what she said, but guilty too – as if he were somehow complicit with those boys and their actions. He felt deeply ashamed of himself, for wanting Veronica in that way.

'It's all right.' Veronica reached out a cool hand to console him. 'Kissing's fine. It's lovely. I just don't want to do anything more than that.'

He snuggled back up to her, doubly grateful that she forgave him and that he didn't have to take responsibility for going any further. They kissed a bit – in a more gentle, relaxed way – until they heard the others starting to move around again and it was time to go.

They met up with the others where the track came out on the other side of the bush, next to the road that ran around the cliff. It was early evening now. The girls were going home by the road, so the boys said goodbye to them there, in the growing shadows. Their goodbyes were brief and no one looked anybody else in the eye.

'Whoo! How did you go?' Jezza burst out, as soon as the girls had vanished around the corner.

'Aaargh, that bitch, Val!' Harry scuffed his big, hairy toes in the sandy dirt by the side of the road. 'She wouldn't let me do anything.'

'Aw, too bad!' Jezza crowed. 'Rachel let me do everything!'

Sam and Harry stared at him, dumbfounded. This was way beyond their comprehension – someone their age actually doing it.

'What about you, Sam?' Jezza put the pressure on him. 'Did you get a hand on?'

'Yeah, yeah, she let me…' he replied, sketching it in with an airy gesture that left the rest to their imaginations. Jezza and Harry gave him a quizzical look. He looked defiantly back at them, hoping they'd be convinced. They seemed to be impressed with him. He couldn't tell whether the heat in his cheeks was the heat of the day, or embarrassment at being caught out lying.

They swaggered back across the bridge as the sun sank lower in the sky, with their chests puffed out like the big, tough men they wanted to be taken for. To their surprise, Higginbottom was standing in the middle of the bridge, staring over the guardrail into the water with an expression of intense concentration on his face.

'Aah, you little turd, why don't you jump?' Jezza challenged him.

'Yeah, jump, why don't you?' Harry kicked the guardrail with one bare foot.

Sam realised he was still quite angry after his encounter with Val.

'Yeah, come on, jump!' Jezza challenged Higginbottom again.

Higginbottom looked right at Sam, out of his misery, his small size, his ugliness, his desperate desire to belong to someone, somewhere – anywhere else, but where he was…

Sam's head swam with everything he'd experienced that afternoon. 'Yeah, jump!' he called out, following Jezza and Harry's lead.

And jump Higginbottom did. In a sudden flurry of activity, he leapt up onto the guardrail, stood there for a brief moment, like a king surveying his domain, then let himself fall, feet first, into the water below. Sam and the others watched, stunned, disbelieving, as Higginbottom's tiny body fell through all that space and hit the surface of the water like a bomb. The water exploded upwards in a fountain of white foam, then subsided, spreading out from the point of impact in brown rings which washed to the banks, on either side. Higginbottom himself completely disappeared.

Five…ten…fifteen seconds passed, which seemed to take forever. Sam and the others leaned over the guardrail and stared at that patch of furiously disturbed water where the bubbles continued to boil up, in a silent agony of suspense. Was Higginbottom dead? Had he hit his head on the rocks and drowned? Had he broken his neck and was lying, paralysed, at the bottom of the creek? Their imaginations filled with unspeakable horrors. More to the point, would they be blamed for encouraging him to do it? What kind of new, more serious, grown-up trouble would they be in, for having failed to stop him?

Twenty seconds…and the dark crown of Higginbottom's head – a tiny, hardly discernible black oval, at that distance – broke through the cloud of bubbles on the surface, succeeded rapidly by his familiar, ugly face.

'I did it! I did it!' he screamed ecstatically, raising both hands above his head in celebration, and nearly choking on a large mouthful of the rank, muddy brown creek water, as he did so.

Sam, Jezza and Harry looked at each other, uneasily. They felt suddenly mean-spirited and ashamed. There was no way they'd ever wanted him in their gang – they still didn't – but they hadn't wanted him to die either. On the other hand, they did feel shown up by him, somehow, on what should have been their afternoon.

'Dickhead!' they said to each other, scornfully, reassuringly. 'Yeah… dickhead!' they yelled at him, laughing among themselves as they turned away from the rail and continued to walk across the bridge, down the rickety steps and back, along the beach, to the car park.

In Country Dark

'Would you like to go to the beach with me this weekend?' asked Penny. Her voice was very light and breezy over the phone, as if she were hardly aware of the excitement she was stirring up in Sam.

'Yes…yes, I would.' Sam managed to reply, his tongue thick and his mouth dry, but trying to sound calm all the same.

'Good! A guy I know – he's really a friend of a friend of mine – has a shack out at the beach that he says we can stay at any time we want. All we have to do is ring him up and let him know.'

'Sounds great.'

'I thought we might go out there Friday night and come back Sunday afternoon. What do you say?'

'I say, yes, let's do it!'

'Good. I'll call round for you about four, Friday. How would that be?'

'That would be fantastic.'

And so it was, about four on Friday night, Penny called around and picked Sam up in her old bomb of a car. The two of them drove a long way out of the city, past the suburbs and the city fringe, then over heavily bush-covered ranges, to the wild ocean beach.

They pulled up in the car park in the middle of the main beach, where they got out and tramped the rest of the way across black sand to the shack at the isolated, secluded, southern end of the beach. On their backs, they carried packs full of food, a change of clothes, sleeping bags and pillows.

The shack was located in a little half-moon bay, almost completely en-closed by a headland which curved protectively around it, leaving only a very small entrance for the open sea at the far end. A notorious tunnel ran right through the middle of the headland, created, presumably, by the ac-tion of the sea over thousands of years. Pounding waves surged through the tunnel, filling it up with terrifying speed and power, then emptying it out again in a ferocious undertow. It was said that anyone who got caught in there stood a very good chance of being sucked straight out to sea and drowned.

The bay was fine for swimming, though. In fact, protected by the headland from the full force of the waves, it was quite calm by comparison with the rest of the beach, except where the water came out of the tunnel.

There was no one else around, so Penny and Sam dumped their packs on the sand, stripped down to their underwear and went for a swim in the shallows before they headed up the beach to the shack. The water was cold and bracing. It made Sam's cock shrivel and Penny's nipples stand out in a most beguiling way.

The shack stood right where the beach met the steep, bush-covered hillside behind it. It was tiny – hardly more than a boathouse – with a plank door and a salt- and sand-encrusted window on the front wall, and another similarly encrusted window on each of the side walls. Inside, the front half was filled with fishing and boating equipment. The back half was filled with a table and chairs, a sink bench against the back wall, with a tap that supplied rainwater from a tank, and a single bed along the southern wall.

It was quite dim inside the shack, in spite of the windows, because the daylight was already failing as late afternoon turned to evening. They towelled off and changed into warmer clothes. Penny lit a hurricane lamp and cooked a couple of steaks on a Primus stove. They ate the steaks and drank a bottle of red wine they'd brought with them as it got even darker outside.

They were both astonished by the speed with which the darkness fell. It was that absolute, primeval, country darkness which can still be experienced in remote places. There was no moon that night. The sky was clouded over and there wasn't another light for miles. They felt completely alone at the end of the universe, as it were. They might have been the last people left in existence – just them and the distant roar of the waves.

They were happy to be that way. Sam and Penny were old school friends, but they'd only recently become lovers. It was less than a week ago, in fact, that Penny had taken Sam, quite literally, by the hand and led him to her black-painted bedroom, with its one fluorescent poster of Jimi Hendrix on the wall above the bed, where she took his virginity.

Sam was uncircumcised, so the first time had been quite painful for him and he'd come very quickly, in an excruciating, exquisite combination of pleasure and pain. This time, he was hoping it would be less painful for him and he would last for longer. He wasn't sure he loved Penny, but he did genuinely like her and wanted to give her pleasure, too.

Penny was a jolly girl with a solid, well-rounded figure. She didn't have the stick figure of current fashion at all, but she was very satisfying to hold onto in bed for just that reason, he'd discovered. Older men liked her too, he'd noticed, because she was sweet, funny and had interesting views on a whole range of topics. Best of all, she appeared to be as fond of him as he was of her – even fonder, perhaps. She took the lead in this, as she did in so many other things. Sam often felt himself to be younger, less experienced, more naive – almost an innocent – compared to her.

They moved rapidly from the table to the bed, shedding their clothes along the way. Penny lay back on the narrow bed, naked, and Sam lowered himself on top of her. He was relieved to find the pain was far less intense this time, and he was able to make love for much longer without coming. Penny really started to enjoy it as well, and they were making love with great enthusiasm when Sam felt her body stiffen under him. He thought she must be approaching orgasm and was about to redouble his own efforts, when he suddenly realised her look was one of terror, rather than ecstasy.

'There's a face!' she gasped.

Sam could hardly understand what she was saying. 'A what?'

'A face!'

'Where?'

'At the window!'

'What window?'

'Behind you!'

Sam felt his exposed back go cold. He twisted himself to look back over his shoulder, and saw that what she said was true. There was, indeed, a ghostly, white face pressed up against the cobwebbed, heavily encrusted glass of the shack's northern window, peering in. A hand on either side framed the face's dark eyes as they tried to focus on what was happening in the shadowy, lamplit interior.

'It's Graham!' Penny exclaimed, in an undertone of mingled shock and embarrassment.

'Graham?'

'Yes!'

'Why the hell would he be here?'

'I don't know. Maybe he's come to check up on us or something.'

Graham's face disappeared from the window.

'Quick, he's going round to the front door! Get off me – get some clothes on!'

They scrambled for their clothes on the floor, while Graham went round to the front of the shack. Penny put Sam's shirt over the top of her head, so it covered her body like a sack dress, and Sam pulled his jeans up hastily, nearly zippering himself in the process. They'd just finished dressing in this way when they heard Graham's knock at the front door. Penny went to the door while Sam hovered in the background.

'Graham!' Penny exclaimed, acting surprised but, at the same time, as casual as possible.

'Yeah, sorry to disturb you,' Sam heard Graham's plainspoken farmer's tones reply.

He couldn't really see Graham past Penny, as Graham was still standing in the half-dark, outside the doorway. He wondered if Graham could see him and how much he'd seen, through the dirty windowpane.

'I just came by to see if everything's OK.'

'Yeah, it is, thank you.' Penny responded, enthusiastically. 'The shack's fantastic.' She managed to sound somehow convincingly appreciative – not a tremor in her voice – as if this conversation were being conducted under entirely normal circumstances.

Sam marvelled at her coolness under pressure.

'Well, if there's anything you need…you've got my number, haven't you?'

'Yes, I have.'

'Well, good then…you call me if you need anything.'

'Yes, I will.'

'Make sure you do then… I have to say it worries me a little, a young woman like yourself on her own at night. It's a long way from anywhere.'

'I'm not on my own,' Penny said 'I've got a friend with me.'

'Oh?' Graham sounded as if this were not exactly the most welcome news he'd ever heard.

'Yes.' Penny gestured over her shoulder. 'This is my friend, Sam.'

Sam stepped into the clear, by the door.

'Hello, Sam.' Graham looked a little grim-faced, but made the best of it.

'Hello, Graham.' Sam was interested to see Graham, at last.

In the half-light, Graham looked to be in his mid-thirties, maybe forty, at the most. Big, bluff face, check flannel working shirt, faded khaki work shorts, boots…he had every appearance of being a typical farmer, a man from another generation, another culture – completely – as incomprehensible to him and Penny as they were to him. They shook hands, Graham's big, hard hand enclosing Sam's smaller, softer one and squeezing it, painfully.

'It's very kind of you to let us use your shack.' Sam's voice came out at a higher pitch than he would have liked.

'Ah, that's nothing.' Graham looked more shamefaced than anything now, perhaps realising what he'd interrupted. 'I've known Karen' – referring to Penny's friend – 'for years. Anything for a friend.'

'Would you like to come in for a cup of tea, Graham?' asked Penny.

'No, look, I won't, thanks. I'd better get back. I hope I didn't frighten you. I'm glad everything's OK. Remember to call me if you need anything.'

'We will. Goodbye!' said Penny, as Graham began to move off into the dark.

'Goodbye!' echoed Sam.

'Bye!' Graham's voice floated back to them, though they could hardly see him already, as he became lost in the blackness, beyond the faint light from the shack.

Sam and Penny waited, in silence, for a long time after Graham went, just in case he came back for any reason. Then they exploded into laughter.

'He must have seen us screwing!' screamed Penny. 'Did you see his face?'

'Yeah, I reckon he came by to put the hard word on you!' crowed Sam. He felt he needed, somehow, to prove his superiority over Graham, especially after that handshake.

'Do you think so?' Penny asked, with an air of doubt, as if this genuinely hadn't occurred to her.

'Yeah, I think so,' said Sam.

'Yeah, I think you might be right. Gee, thank you for saving me!'

And they both exploded into laughter once more. They stood in the darkened area just inside the door, leaning on each other for support, laughing till the tears literally ran down their cheeks. Then they turned round and Graham was behind them…

No, he wasn't. This is not a horror story and Graham was really a very nice man, if a bit lonely. But the thought that he might be out there somewhere, lurking on the bushline, watching, was still quite unsettling for them. They were left with a slight, persistent uneasiness they just couldn't shake.

They turned off the hurricane lamp and climbed back into bed, where they finished making love, to the intense pleasure and ultimate satisfaction of them both. Then they went to sleep with their arms around each other, because the night was enormous, dark, full of dangers, and they were – when all is said and done – only very small.

The Visit

It was about this time that Sam decided his life had to change. He took a job working as a sales assistant in a shoe shop in a country town on the banks of a large river. His girlfriend, Penny, drove him up there in her purple Austin Seven and left him there. He moved into a three-storey rooming house on the bank of the river, on the other side and a bit along from the town business and shopping centre. He'd never lived in a place like it before. Everything was made of concrete – the stairs, the corridors, the tiny, boxlike kitchen and bedroom of his flat, the shared bathroom along the end of the corridor…the place was like a gigantic, cold, echo-ing, concrete bunker, left over from some long-forgotten war.

He spent all day on his knees in front of locals trying on new shoes. Being a country town, a lot of the shoes were work boots and gumboots, and some of the socks were none too fragrant. But there were shapely women's feet to admire too. The work wasn't bad, it was just boring. He had to keep reminding himself that, with the economy the way it was, he was lucky to have any job and he was trying to turn his life around. He'd dropped out of university twice already, he'd changed cities, he'd dabbled in acting…nothing seemed to stick. The job made him known around town – any newcomer was a centre of interest – and he soon had a small circle of vaguely compatible friends.

Penny continued to come up and see him from time to time, when she'd finished work in the city. They weren't really in love with each other – at least, he wasn't with her – they were more like good companions who also shared sex. And the sex was good. Penny was a good, reliable fuck, as far as Sam was concerned, which stopped him from looking in other places. Love wasn't high on his list of priorities, especially not when he was in love with someone else he couldn't get to see any more.

This Friday night, Penny arrived with food, drink and a tab of orange-coloured, California Sunshine LSD. Sam was trying to give acid up. He thought it was one more thing – like his constant smoking and drinking – that held him back, that stopped his life from changing. But he decided to take it one last time anyway.

They sat in the concrete box kitchen, eating the food and drinking the wine that Penny had brought with her from the city. They had music playing on a tape deck that echoed loudly around the space. It made them feel a little less lonely in this strange place, and a little less awkward around each other after the time they'd spent apart.

Penny was catching him up on the lives of their friends back in the city – the trendy architect who was in love with her, but she wasn't the least bit interested in, the dopehead moron they'd shared a house with, who did the lighting for a well-known rock band, and his two speed-freak girlfriends, the three of whom were always being hassled by the cops…it all seemed far away to Sam, not part of the life he wanted to be living now.

But the wine warmed and relaxed him. He took the acid for old times' sake and because Penny wanted him to. The acid was cut with a lot of speed and it came on very fast, very intensely, like a jet plane, taking off inside his skull. He wasn't sure he was going to be able to take it. It felt like it would blow the top right off his head. He looked down and his hands were balled up, in fists, on the kitchen table, the knuckles white with pressure.

Penny saw that he wasn't feeling very comfortable. 'Are you all right?' she asked.

'Yeah,' he mumbled, 'it's very strong.'

'Yeah, it is at the beginning, isn't it? But that'll soon pass.'

The feeling of extreme pressure did eventually pass, though not nearly soon enough as far as Sam was concerned. Then the walls of the tiny room moved back. He was able to relax and breathe again, entering the immense space and timeless wonder of acid tripping.

Penny saw that his mood had changed. 'Let's go for a drive.' she suggested.

'Yeah,' he mumbled. That was all he was ever able to do in this state, mumble and follow along. Penny was his guide and protector. He just had to let go, abandon himself to it and trust her to take him safely through the long, unpredictable journey.

'Where do you want to go?' Penny asked.

'Let's go to Pete's.' The words were thick in his mouth. Soon he wouldn't be able to speak at all. The words would echo and re-echo, hundreds of times, on their way from his brain to his mouth, making speech impossible. What did any of them mean?

Pete was one of the locals with whom Sam had become friendly. He knew, from conversations with him, that Pete had also taken acid and he'd understand. Pete's place was nearby and easy to find. He could help Penny find the way there, before everything became too confusing and difficult. Penny had already met Pete as well.

Penny drove the purple Austin through the dark country night. The moon had not yet risen. The streetlights were few and far between on this side of the river. First, a little random starlight, then the lights of the town twinkled off the surface of the river. Each point of light was an inestimable, jewelled treasure, dazzling his eyeballs. The blacks in between sank into terrifying depths, pulling him after them. The ageing, constricted interior of the Austin had expanded to become huge and rich, like a Rolls-Royce's. He lolled in it like a king.

Luckily, Pete was at home. He seemed amused by Sam's condition. 'Come in!' he said, opening the door wide. 'Barry's gone away for the weekend,' he added, by way of explanation, referring to his housemate and lover, a local dentist.

They entered a warm, comfortable interior. There were big couches, shelves of books and paintings on the walls. One painting – an abstract – had a light-coloured circle on a dark-coloured ground. Sam looked at it. The circle immediately multiplied, filling up the room, blocking out his vision. There were circles everywhere he looked. He stood in a world of multicoloured circles.

Pete laughed. His laughter boomed inside Sam's skull like a PA system with a thousand speakers. 'He's far gone, isn't he?'

Pete and Penny sat in the living room and talked while Sam roamed around, looking at the many decorative objects Pete and Barry had on display – touching them, picking them up and marvelling at them. He was having great trouble working out what most of them were, even though they were probably quite ordinary. They transformed as soon as he picked them up. Right in front of his eyes, they became something different, then something different again…

Eventually, he tired of the endless changes and ran himself a bubble bath. Penny and Pete came and sat on the side of it, talking to him, while he played with the bubbles, childishly. Pete started to look at him in a strange, more calculating way, but Penny was there to protect him.

They had a few drinks and a late meal with Pete. They finally left him in the early hours of the morning. The moon had risen. Penny stopped the car on the bank of the river, upstream from the reflection of the town's lights. The moon's disc was fractured by the ripples on the surface of the river into a million fragments that seemed to detach themselves from the surface and blinded Sam. They rose up out of the water like a glittering wall of light. The river was a moving wall of light!

Then his attention was taken by the immensity of the blackness all around them, and the tiny pinholes of the stars, their brightness dimmed by the moon. He felt the hugeness of it all and understood how the earth was just another pinprick of light in the immensity of space. Time and space faded away. There truly was only infinity and eternity… He more than knew it; he felt it, he lived it.

Penny just managed to restrain Sam from throwing himself in the river. He wanted to bathe in the light, to merge himself with infinity and eternity. Penny herself seemed more than a little affected by his condition. Maybe she'd smoked some dope with Pete while they were talking and he was moving round the house unaware. She seemed somehow linked to him, to understand everything he was going through.

It was very late when they finally made it back to the rooming house, where they fell in bed, exhausted, and went straight to sleep.

Sam woke some time later from a horrifying dream where he was an inmate in a concentration camp. He was being tortured, beaten and starved, along with the other inmates. Like them, he was reduced to a skeleton, a skerrick of his former self. When Sam woke, he was still in the grip of the dream. The concrete bedroom around him was like a cell in the camp. When he looked at the window, he saw bars.

Ignoring Penny, who was asleep beside him, he got out of bed, left the flat and went down the cold, dark corridor to the shared bathroom at the far end. The corridor was still part of the concentration camp, patrolled by guards with sub-machine guns who gestured threateningly at him out of the darkness. When he turned on the light in the bathroom, his hand and arm in front of him were like sticks. He could see the bones through the thin layer of skin. The mirror showed his face like a skull. Pain and death were all around him. He peed in a state of absolute terror and ran all the way back down the corridor to his bed in the flat.

Jumping into bed, panic-stricken and freezing, he woke Penny. They cuddled, briefly, for warmth and reassurance. The cuddle turned into caresses and the caresses into sex. Penny responded eagerly. To Sam, still tripping, the early stages of sex were completely unrecognisable. The mechanics of his body had become a total mystery to him. Then the feeling of pleasure struck him with an overwhelming intensity. He didn't need to know what he was doing any more, he just did it. Penny matched him, perfectly, every step of the way.

Because of his condition, the fucking seemed to go on forever. Penny gave a long drawn-out orgasmic gasp beneath him. When he heard her cry of extreme pleasure, he started racing towards orgasm himself. As he approached orgasm, he felt that he was flying through outer space, that he'd become part of the universe. Galaxies exploded inside him as he came. They died and were reborn in immense cycles of creation and destruction. The universe was inside and outside him. He understood that he himself was part of those endless cycles of creation and destruction, as everything else was, that this was the very essence of his being, dying and being reborn, eternally…

When he came back to himself, he was lying in bed and it was daylight.

Penny was lying beside him, long hair tousled, eyes firmly closed, a look of quiet contentment on her sleeping face. He got out of bed and went to the window. The sun was coming up over the river. The early morning rowers were out, sculling up and down. He was no longer tripping. He had that hollow, let-down feeling that comes after intense experience.

He knew there was something familiar about that day, something he ought to remember. Then he remembered what it was. It was his birthday. He'd been so involved with his new life, changing his old habits, trying to be somebody different – until last night with Penny – that he'd completely forgotten, not only that it was his birthday, but that it was also his twenty-first birthday. It was the day he was supposed to have finished growing up, when – theoretically – he became a man.

He thought about his family, whom he hadn't seen for a long time. He thought about his brothers, one of whom was studying overseas and the other of whom was working on a farm in a remote location. He thought about his parents, separated now, but the memory of their constant bickering and frequent, blazing rows persisted. He thought about the girl he'd lost, who was now married to someone else. He thought about all the chances he'd been given and thrown away, so that he'd ended up here, in this two-bit country town, burned-out, desperate, trying to put his life together again.

He looked back at Penny, asleep. He wouldn't – couldn't – wake her up to tell her this. Instead, he leaned even further out, across the sill, into the crisp, blue morning air and cried bitter, useless tears for his life, which had gone so wrong.

Brother's Keeper

Sam was living at his parents' place after he'd lost – or failed to stick with – a succession of jobs and his latest relationship had broken up. He was deeply depressed, just lying round the house all day listening to his parents, who were making one last attempt to get back together, bickering with each other. Sam was supposed to be helping them with the process of getting back together. He was supposed to get between them, somehow, and stop them from tearing each other apart. At the very least, he was supposed to be supporting his mother, who was now quite seriously ill, especially as his father, who was still working part-time, was drinking heavily when he was home. Sam had no money, no plans and he had nowhere else to go. He'd run out of options.

Then Sam's younger brother, Garth, turned up. He was working on a farm in a very remote location, so he didn't often come to town. Their parents were comparatively happy with the way Garth had turned out, unlike Sam. He didn't have a wife, or a home of his own, like their older brother, Charlie, but he was earning money and he was off their hands. They could be proud of him to that extent. He'd grown up and Sam hadn't; he'd succeeded at something, even if he wasn't doing exactly what they would've liked him to be doing, where Sam had been dogged by failure – though nobody actually came out and said that in so many words.

Sam and Garth sat on their old beds, in the bedroom they'd shared as kids, years before, listening to the familiar sound of their parents bickering in the kitchen on the other side of the wall.

'Jeez,' Garth said, 'they haven't got any better, have they?'

'Nuh,' Sam said. 'If anything, they've got worse. They do that all the time now. They never stop. That's how they get on, full time.'

'You can't go on living like this.'

'What else am I going to do?' Sam could see nothing but emptiness yawning ahead of him. It was a problem he couldn't solve by himself.

'You'll have to come with me,.' Garth said.

'What?' Sam was shocked. 'Come and live in the country with you?'

'Yeah. There's any amount of work there. Paul'll take you on.'

Paul was the farmer Garth worked for – a hard but fair boss, from Garth's description. Sam didn't know if he was ready for the hard but fair treatment right then. He wasn't a country boy. He'd always lived and worked in the city. He didn't even like the country. He didn't feel at home there. He missed the crowds, the pubs, the movie theatres and all the things there were to do in the city. What did people in the country do after dark? Nothing. On the other hand, when did he ever go into the city now? It wasn't like the old days. His last girlfriend was always complaining, 'We never do anything. Don't you ever wanna go out and do stuff?' But he'd tried to pretend they were happier just being homebodies, hanging around together in the flat they'd shared, briefly.

'Yeah,' he said, after some deliberation. 'I might as well. I'm not achieving a whole lot here, that's for sure.'

'Great! Pack your stuff tonight – we'll leave tomorrow.'

'That won't take long… I haven't got much.' Part of Sam wanted to cry. It was the ultimate defeat, being rescued by his younger brother. Could he fall any lower? At the same time, another part of him was feeling lighter already, like this was an adventure they were setting out on, part of some game he and Garth might have played when they were kids. Maybe he really could leave the past behind, and go to some place where no one knew about him and what a failure he was.

They discussed it that night with their parents over dinner.

'I think that's a great idea,' Dad said. In spite of having spent most of his adult life in the city, Dad still thought of himself as a country boy. It seemed like Garth was living out fantasies for him which he'd had to put aside himself long ago. 'It'll make a man of you,' he said to Sam. 'That's what you need – a bit of a challenge.'

'I wish you wouldn't go,' Mum put in. 'It's so far away and the work's so dangerous. I'll worry about you.'

Dad put his knife and fork down, raised his eyebrows and rolled his eyes towards the ceiling. 'Will you let me talk to my son for once without interrupting me?'

'He's my son, too, you know. And I worry about him. You will take care, won't you?' Mum said to Sam.

'Yes, Mum,' Sam replied, dutifully. How old was he? Hadn't he been out of home for years before he came back here? Hadn't he had a whole lot of jobs and relationships of his own?

'You mollycoddle the boy,' Dad said to Mum. 'He's got to get out on his own again. He's got to stand on his own two feet.'

'You just want him out of the house so you can have your own way in everything. You bastard, you've ruined my life!' Mum shot back.

And so Mum and Dad started their fight for that night. Sam and Garth closed their ears to them and exchanged looks over the table. This was what they'd grown up with. They knew it had nothing to do with them. Sam was glad to be getting out of there. He'd been acting as a buffer between his parents for far too long. He'd come to the end of it. From now on, his parents would have to sort their own mess out without him intervening.

Sam and Garth slept in their old beds that night, which was pretty strange, considering that they were both grown-up now and made a lot more noise – snoring, tossing and turning, muttering, farting – than either of them remembered. Sam fervently hoped they'd have separate bedrooms in the country.

In the morning, he put on the work clothes and boots from his job in the concrete factory, grabbed his old backpack, stuffed his few, meagre belongings into it, and he was ready to leave. They had breakfast, said goodbye to their parents, who were sitting in frosty silence after last night's fight, and set off.

They drove for most of the day in Garth's rattling, smoky old truck to get to Paul's farm. They soon left the city far behind. They went down the highway, through gradually thinning suburbs, until they were surrounded by farmland. Then the farmland ran out. There was just bush and the occasional farmhouse, with a bit of cleared land around it. Then there was just bush. They stopped on the way for lunch, beers and a few games of pool in a country pub close to the sea.

An alarmingly narrow gravel road rose up from the coastal flat. It wound around sheer cliff faces several hundred feet high. Though Garth carefully sounded the truck's scratchy horn before every bend, Sam was still terrified they'd run into some vehicle coming the other way. Fortunately, they were the only ones on the road.

Late in the afternoon, they came around a final bend and saw a perfect half-moon bay spread out below them. A freshly painted white Victorian farmhouse stood on the flat down by the beach, surrounded by empty paddocks. Steep, bush-covered hills climbed rapidly from the back of the flat towards a mountain range, blue with distance. A sizable creek flowed between the hills, past the farmhouse and out to sea. A rocky, potholed farm track ran along its near bank. At the start of the track, beside a farm gate, they could just make out the figure of someone waiting.

In the the half-light at the end of the day, they pulled up by the gate down on the flat. The figure they'd seen in the distance turned out to be a stocky, amiable-looking, middle-aged farmer in a work singlet, shorts and boots, with a battered hat scrunched on top of his head.

'G'day,' he said, with a smile, as he came up alongside the open driver's window. He was obviously happy to see Garth.

'G'day, Paul. This is Sam.' Garth gestured in Sam's direction.

'G'day, Sam.' Paul stuck a big, friendly mitt across the truck's cab in front of Garth.

Sam shook it. Paul's hand was enormous – very dry and hard. The bones of Sam's hand cracked when Paul squeezed it.

'I've heard Garth talk about you.'

'All good, I hope,' Sam said, trying not to wince.

'Sam's looking for work, at the moment.' Garth continued his introduction. 'I said he could come and stay with me for a while and have a go at scrub-cutting. Is that all right with you?'

'Sure,' Paul replied, without any hesitation. 'We're starting tomorrow on that hill opposite your place. Are you up for that?'

'Sure,' said Garth.

'Sure,' said Sam, without any idea what he was getting himself into.

'I'll see you then, bright and early.' Paul grinned.

'See you then.' Garth grinned back at him, like some secret sign passing between the two of them.

Paul opened the gate for them and they drove up the bumpy, dusty track. It led, eventually, to a slightly incongruous-looking, Swiss chalet-style farmhouse, with multi-paned windows, weatherboard walls and stone foundations, sitting on a rise above the creek, surrounded by bush.

'This house was built by some out of work bushies during the Great Depression, with timber felled in the gully out the back and stones from the creek,' Garth told Sam, proudly, as it came in sight.

It was a beautiful old house – a bit magical, like something out of a fairy tale – even if it was very rundown because it hadn't been lived in for years.

They arrived at the house right on nightfall. Garth left the truck's headlights on while they got out and went into the house. In the shadowy, timber-panelled kitchen, Garth fumbled round with some Tilley lamps and got them going. 'The house has got tank water but no electricity,' he said. 'Paul's promised me he'll help me do the place up if I stay. There's a generator down by the creek, but it's not working at the moment. That woodstove's not working, either, so we have to heat water and cook over the fire in the living room.'

They walked down the corridor from the kitchen to the living room. Garth put the lamp he was carrying down on the timber mantelpiece above the river-stone fireplace which occupied most of the end wall adjacent to the kitchen. Sam could see a blackened kettle and a camp oven sitting on the hearth. There was a fire already laid, which Garth crouched down to light. Then he stood up and walked over to the set of multi-paned windows, which extended right along the outside wall of the room. 'That's the hill where we'll be cutting tomorrow.' he said, pointing through one of the panes at the darkened hillside before he went out to turn off the truck's headlights. They were in.

For dinner that night, they had tea and toast made over the fire before going to bed. Sam unrolled his sleeping bag on the mattress in the spare bedroom, used his jacket for a pillow and slept like a log after the long day's travelling.

In the morning, Garth woke him just as it was getting light. 'Hurry up!' he said. 'Paul'll be here any minute.'

Sam got out of bed, stiff and cold in the morning chill. He put yesterday's clothes back on, splashed some freezing water on his face in the bathroom, and went into the living room. Garth had revived last night's fire there and was making more tea and toast for breakfast.

Within minutes, they heard Paul's four-wheel drive pull up outside. He came straight into the house, without knocking. 'Are you guys ready yet?' he yelled out over the clatter of his hobnails as he strode up the corridor from the front door.

He sounded very gung-ho for that time of the morning, but Sam noticed he did stop to drink a hot cup of tea when Garth offered it to him.

'Come on, you guys, we've got work to do!' he announced loudly, banging his cup down on the mantelpiece and heading for the door as soon as he'd finished.

Sam and Garth threw the dregs of their cups on the ashes of the fire, where they sizzled and steamed, and trooped out after him.

They took a chainsaw each from the back of Paul's four-wheel drive, and crossed the creek on some stones that made a bit of a rapids below the house. On the far side, the bush – mostly tea tree and a bit of regrowth – came right down to the water.

'We'll start here,' said Paul, looking up the long, steep slope ahead of them. He showed Sam how to use his chainsaw and they started.

To say it was hard work – even for Paul and Garth, who were familiar with it – would be a major understatement. They had to find a firm footing on the slippery slope, bend over, scarf the trunk of the tree or bush low down on one side, cut through it from the other, hoping it wouldn't fall on them, then move as quickly as possible to the next one. They had to stay in continuous motion, bending over much of the time, bracing themselves against the slope, breathing in smoky petrol fumes, covered in a mix of grease, dirt and woodchips, with the deafening roar of the heavy chainsaw filling their ears. Although the morning was still cold, it wasn't long before they were all dripping sweat.

They cut in a line, strung out along the edge of the bush, making what Paul called a 'face'. The other two were much faster than Sam was, so they were soon far ahead of him. Their sections of the face progressed cleanly up the slope, side by side. Sam stumbled after them, tripping over stumps, dodging falling trees, tired and sore. His section of the face was like a dog's breakfast. It didn't look like he'd done anything, compared with the others. But they were generous with their comments when they stopped for a short, mid-morning break.

'We'll make a scrub-cutter of him yet,' Paul said to Garth, surveying the mess Sam had made, and they both laughed – not that Sam cared, really. He had other, more important things on his mind which made it hard for him to give all his attention to the work in hand. All too soon, they were back into it.

They stopped again for lunch, which they ate sitting down amongst the cut scrub. Paul had a small mountain of sandwiches, made by his wife, and a hot cup of tea from his thermos. Sam and Garth had one sandwich each, which they'd made the previous night before they went to bed, and some water in a couple of old soft drink bottles Garth had found. It felt good to be sitting down, resting their tired limbs. Paul and Garth talked while Sam listened. Paul's political views, as Garth had warned Sam, were somewhere to the right of Genghis Khan.

'These bloody dole-bludgers,' he was saying, between mouthfuls of sandwich, 'they ought to be made to take the first job they're offered, wherever, whenever… Bloody parasites! They think they can live off other people's hard work…or the taxes the government makes us pay! Then the government spends a whole lot of our hard-earned money putting them in those fancy so-called employment training programs. Talk about a holiday at the taxpayers' expense! At least they're not spending all their time drinking and taking drugs, I suppose. But the government'd be better off cutting them off without a cent and forcing them to take any work they can find, don't you think?'

Paul looked at Garth expectantly. It seemed he was saying this in order to get some sort of response out of Garth. He obviously liked to check his ideas out against other people's. Sam suspected he didn't actually talk to many people, living in such an isolated place, and he wanted to find out what people thought, in the outside world. He seemed genuinely interested in what Garth had to say. For all that Paul was trying to sound so tough and mean, Sam could tell that he really liked Garth. In spite of how different they were, in age, background and experience, there was a real bond of friendship between them.

'No, I don't,' Garth said, looking straight back at him. 'I think we should support them and give them the chance to find a job that suits their abilities and other important stuff they've got going on in their lives.'

'Do you really think that?' Paul asked, like it was the last thing he'd expected to hear.

'Yes, I do,' Garth said. He looked at Sam. His expression was serious, but Sam could tell he was laughing inside.

Sam felt like laughing himself, for reasons he wasn't completely sure about. It was a bit like provoking one of their parents in an argument.

'Am I my brother's keeper?' Garth went on. 'Yes, I think I am. I think people should look after other people, take care of them – not make their lives more difficult, or punish them for something that's not their fault.'

'Oh!' was all Paul said. It wasn't clear whether he was surprised by that, or agreed with it. He chewed his way through some more of his sandwiches in silence for a while.

And that was how things went for the next couple of weeks. They finished that block, although Paul and Garth finished their sections long before Sam, and had to come back to help him finish his. Then they started on a second block while they waited for the cut scrub to dry on the first so they could burn it. Sam did get a bit better at what he was doing – he learned to cut his share of the face in more of a straight line, for instance – though he was never anything like as fast as Paul or Garth. But Paul didn't seem to mind that Sam was so slow. He seemed happy enough to keep Sam on, probably out of consideration for Garth.

It was heading into summer. The weather was warm and dry, so the scrub on the first block was soon ready to burn. Paul turned up at the house one morning and announced this was the day they were going to do it. To start the fire, he gave Sam and Garth torches made from sticks wrapped with kerosene-soaked rags, plus sacks which had been soaked in water, to stop the fire spreading, if they needed, and they followed him across the creek, one more time.

Sam was surprised to see Garth had brought his .22 rifle with him, even though he'd got used to seeing him with it over the last few weeks. They'd been out hunting after work quite a few nights, to add to their fortnightly deliveries of food supplies. Garth shot goats and rabbits. He skinned and butchered them, and cooked them up as roasts or stews on the living room fire.

He winked at Sam when he saw him looking. 'You never know what'll come crawling out of that scrub when we light it up.' he said, laughing.

Paul laughed with him. It appeared he enjoyed the way Garth was living, almost as much as Garth enjoyed it himself.

They moved along the bottom of the slope, poking their lit torches in amongst the dried branches, which burst into flame on contact. The fire spread rapidly. It raced away up the slope like a wild animal, completely beyond their control, with a roaring, crackling sound. Clouds of white smoke poured out of it and rose up in the air. The smoke must've been visible for miles, not that there was anyone, other than Paul's wife, Gail – in the house down by the beach – to see it. They were yelling, screaming and whooping with excitement. Even Paul joined in, though not quite as loudly and enthusiastically as Sam and Garth.

They followed the fire up the slope with their wet sacks, putting out any spot fires that started on the sides. But they'd done their job well – even Sam – and there wasn't really much of a problem. Eventually, they headed back down the bottom, tired, hot, smelling of smoke and very thirsty. That was all the work they were going to do that day. Sam and Garth were looking forward to having some of the beers they'd been keeping cold in the bath back at the house, specially for the occasion. Paul, who didn't drink, was looking forward to a hot cup of tea.

They were at the bottom, close to where they'd started from, when Garth suddenly grabbed Sam's arm. 'Look!' he said.

Sam looked where he was pointing. A fat, young wild turkey hen came waddling out of the bush, her feathers slightly singed and covered in soot, very put out by the inconvenience of it all. She sniffed at them as if they were picking on her deliberately, and continued on her way.

Garth's eyes were round and shining, in spite of being red with smoke. Sam could practically see the saliva dripping from his mouth. He ran to where he'd left the .22, down by the creek. He picked the rifle up, loaded it, took the safety catch off and aimed it. Paul and Sam stood well back. They watched while Garth shot the hen once in the chest. It fell over, got up, staggered a few more steps, then fell over again, dead. Paul and Sam cheered.

'That's very impressive – one shot!' Paul was all admiration. 'It'll be delicious,' he continued, looking at the fat hen lying at their feet. 'I almost wish I could join you. But I'm glad you'll be plucking it and not me.'

They all laughed. It was a good way to end the day's work.

Garth and Sam took the turkey home and plucked it while they were having a beer. Paul wasn't wrong – it was a horrible job. Even though they took turns, it still hurt their hands. The bigger feathers were surprisingly hard to pull out, and the little, fluffy ones stuck to their fingers and got in the way all the time. When they finished, Garth gutted and butchered it. They browned it in the camp oven, made a stew with it and cooked it on the fire for several hours. They ate it with slabs of bread slathered with butter, and plenty of salt, pepper and beer. It was delicious, just like Paul had said.

It was night outside by this time, and they were both quite drunk. They were sitting in the living room by the light of the fire. Neither of them could be bothered lighting the lamps. It was like a cave in there, with the fire sinking low in front of them, and their shadows rising up behind them in the growing dark. They ate till they couldn't eat any more and sat back, stuffed.

'Look,' said Garth, 'you can see the Southern Cross!'

'Can you? Where?' Sam asked. Stars had never been his specialty.

'Out the window, you mug! High up.'

Sam looked. The windows were black with the night, except for a little reflected firelight along their end. The hillside opposite was largely black again now, with small pockets where some embers still glowed. But the stars in the clear night sky above it were enormous and bright, like Sam had never seen them in the city.

Garth took him over to the window and pointed upwards, to the roof of the sky. 'You see there?' he said. 'Those are the pointers.'

When Garth pointed directly to them like that, Sam could see them standing out from all the other stars around them. 'And that's the Southern Cross,' Garth said.

Sam saw it really clearly for the first time – those five stars, laid out in the southern sky. He'd heard people talk about the Southern Cross but it wasn't until he saw it shining down on them like that that he realised how amazing it really was.

They sat back down and had another beer. It was almost time to go to bed. Sam was sure Paul would have another job for them tomorrow. He was thinking about him and Garth. He was thinking how Garth was really just cheap labour for Paul in that remote location, but nonetheless Garth was clearly getting something out of it which made it worthwhile for him – like Paul was getting something more than just the cheap labour out of having him there. Sam knew it wasn't the place for him in the long run. It was Garth's scene and he was just passing through. But he was getting something out of it too. He realised, with a bit of a shock, that this was the first time in a long time when he'd spent the entire day without thinking, even once, about his life and what a failure he was. That made him feel very light-headed…almost like he was flying. He didn't know where he was going from here, or how he'd end up, but Garth had taken him in and got him moving – given him a future to look forward to once again – and for that, he'd always be grateful.

Coming to Australia

They set up camp on the bank of a creek on Lisa's father's property at Maylesville, up in the mountains. There were five of them in all – Lisa, Sam, Lisa's daughter Isobel, Lisa's friend Jenny, and Jenny's son Eric. They had three tents – two for the adults and one which, it was hoped, the kids might share. Lisa's father owned five hundred acres there, so there was plenty of room for the kids to run around in. It was incredibly hot in the mountains in midsummer, and the creek would provide welcome respite from the heat.

They had to be careful of snakes, however. For Sam, who'd recently arrived from New Zealand, this was a novel experience. There was nothing more dangerous in New Zealand than the katipo – the redback spider – which people rummaging through woodpiles had to be careful about. There were certainly no deadly creatures lying in wait in the long grass, or swimming up silently behind bathers while they were basking in a cool creek on a boiling hot day.

'You have to watch for their heads and the V of water spreading out behind them,' Lisa warned them when they arrived. 'You have to bang on the water with your hands and make lots of noise to drive them away.'

Sam found that very disturbing. But then, he found Australian wildlife disturbing generally. He remembered the first time he'd encountered a kangaroo in the bush and realised there were creatures that size running – or bouncing – freely across the countryside. It was an altogether different experience of nature and not one he was entirely sure he liked. But he persisted with it for Lisa's sake. They'd left New Zealand so she could be closer to Isobel, who lived with her father in Melbourne, and he'd just have to stick it out.

He had trouble coming to terms with the Australian landscape too.

Sam had always been interested in painting. He'd done a lot in New Zealand – especially landscapes – but he struggled with the comparative dryness and sparseness of the Australian landscape, and the harshness of the light. He had to change his accustomed palette and almost, it seemed, his way of seeing.

But by far the most important adjustment he'd had to make was in his relationship with Lisa. Isobel completely upset the balance between them. Back in New Zealand, he'd had Lisa all to himself. He'd been the centre of her attention. Then suddenly, in Australia, he had to compete for Lisa's attention with Isobel. In fact, he found he no longer came first, but only second, in Lisa's consideration – and quite a long way second at that. To add to his problems, Isobel, who was very young – just turned six – didn't like him very much. This created all sorts of difficulties between them, when Isobel, who spent the week at her father's place, and weekends and holidays with Lisa, came over.

'You just have to try!' Lisa said.

And he did try, but it made no difference. Isobel seemed genuinely set against him. In particular, Isobel hated any time that he and Lisa might spend together which didn't involve her. Every time that he and Lisa were alone and had a chance to have sex, which Sam was desperate for, Isobel would come along and interrupt them.

'Oh, grow up!' Lisa said. 'This is what it's like around kids.'

But he couldn't get used to it. In fact, it made him extremely bad-tempered, which made his relationships with Lisa and Isobel even worse. He wasn't looking forward to spending a whole week camping with the two of them together.

He wasn't looking forward to camping with Jenny and Eric either. Jenny was incredibly shy and uncertain, and clung to Lisa like she was some sort of security blanket for her. She was always wanting attention and reassurance from Lisa, in rather the same way Isobel did.

'Oh, Lisa, I don't know what I'm doing with my life!' Jenny would wail, then carry on for what seemed to Sam like hours, when he had what he thought were much better things he could be doing with Lisa.

He wondered how aware Jenny was of the problem she was causing, or if she even knew that it existed. As for Eric, he was simply a more painful extension of his mother – super-sensitive, continually complaining and impossible to please. Sam didn't know how he was going to cope.

After lunch on the first day, he set himself up to paint on the bank of the creek. He had a little outdoor easel, complete with stool, palette and a box of paints. But a wind came up in the afternoon which shook his easel and threatened to blow it over. This didn't make for easy painting, or improve his temper either. So, when first Jenny, and then Eric, came over to where he was struggling to get something down on canvas (Lisa was busy and Isobel never showed any interest in anything he did), he was just about ready to crack.

'It must be so difficult, painting under these conditions!' Jenny said. 'But I envy you. I wish I had your artistic talent. It must be wonderful to have something like that to give some meaning to your life…or even just to have something you enjoy doing with your time.'

'Is it finished yet?' Eric wanted to know. Then, when he walked around and saw it, 'What is it?' he asked, without trying to hide his disappointment.

But Sam persisted. He was starting to get his palette right and it was a good composition, with the creek winding through the middle, between bush-clad hills, taking the viewer's eye deep into the painting – something he'd learned from his study of Cézanne. There were other subjects he had in mind, too, like the rusting sheds and rickety hay barns scattered around the property. He was fascinated by the whole subject of rural decay. The more farmers tried to control things, it seemed to him, the more they fell apart.

That night, Lisa and Sam were invited to dinner at the farmhouse with Lisa's father, Roy, a wealthy surgeon in his previous life back in Melbourne, and his fourth wife, Margaret, who'd been principal of a snobby girls' school in South Yarra. Lisa had warned Sam that Roy was eccentric, but he rapidly realised that was a considerable understatement. Lisa had also warned him that Roy and Margaret drank.

'Look, it's all in the hips!' Roy was saying as Margaret ushered them into the living room. He was standing in the middle of the floor, drink in one hand, cigarette in the other, imitating the actions of skiing, of which he was a mad enthusiast. He swayed gently, seductively, from side to side, like a Tahitian vahine doing the hula, without spilling a bit of ash, or a drop of whisky.

'Keep the skis hip-width apart and parallel!' he intoned. 'Bend your ankles, knees and hips equally! Isn't that right, love?' This last was addressed to Lisa coming into the room – also, herself, an expert skier.

'Yes,' Lisa replied, as if she'd learned it by rote, which she probably had. 'Put your bodyweight on the downhill ski.'

Roy roared approval and skied even harder across the living room floor.

'Sit down!' cried Margaret gaily, waving an arm set in a plaster cast, which she'd broken in a recent fall. There'd been no official comment about her condition at the time of the fall, but Lisa seemed in no doubt. 'She was pissed!' she'd told Sam scathingly.

As Roy did, Margaret carried a cigarette in the other hand, which she also waved freely, sprinkling ash like fine powder snow over the carpet. She spoke with an absurdly refined, cut-glass accent, which must have struck terror into the hearts and minds of innocent young girls at her exclusive school. She was the only person Sam had ever heard refer to South Yarra as 'South Yarrah'. But for all that, she did seem determined, as Roy was, to be kind.

They sat down for drinks and chit-chat before dinner. Most of it was about Lisa's skiing, at which she'd once been junior state champion. Did she think she'd be coming up this winter?

'I don't know. I don't think so…but I really would like Isobel to learn how to ski.'

'You must!' cried Roy. 'You were such a good skier, you mustn't let it slip.'

'And what about you, Sam?' inquired Margaret. 'I hear you're a painter.'

'Well, I try,' Sam replied, with what he hoped was appropriate modesty.

'You should meet my Rory,' Margaret said, with evident pride. 'He's a painter too. He painted that landscape over there.'

She indicated on the wall opposite what seemed to Sam a small, fairly ordinary landscape of a river flat, a river, trees and hills – not dissimilar to the one that Sam had been painting himself that afternoon.

'Oh, that's good!' he said – convincingly, he hoped.

'Yes,' said Margaret, 'but he's a naughty boy. He doesn't do it enough, you know. I always say you have to do it a lot if you want to be really good at it. He has too much of a good time with his mates, living in that house of his in Carterton, and he doesn't take anything very seriously that I can see. I often wonder how he'll survive.'

This was news to Sam, who had a pretty fair idea of how Rory survived life in the country, based on what Lisa had told him.

'I say to him, if you have talent, you must use it!' said Margaret, as much to herself as to anyone else, while taking a puff on a fresh cigarette, lit off the butt of the previous one. 'Do you do it a lot?' she asked, sharply, giving him an appraising look from under her drunken, slightly dishevelled fringe.

'Yes, I do.' Sam tried, once again, to look and sound as convincing as he possibly could.

Over dinner, Roy warmed to another of his favourite themes, which Lisa had also warned Sam about. 'Stalin was a great man!' he declared, hand on whisky glass, which he'd brought to the table and topped up with milk – the first time Sam had ever seen anyone do that. 'He saved us, you know. He won the war for us. If he hadn't stood up to Hitler, we wouldn't be free today. He was brilliant. He organised the Russian war effort and led the Russians to victory. He was a hero and that's how he should be remembered in the West. We couldn't have survived without him and we owe him a debt of gratitude, much greater than the one we owe to the Americans.'

Sam thought briefly about arguing for a more balanced view, but decided against it. Better, he thought – for Lisa's sake as much as anybody else's – to let the night pass peacefully.

When they left, Roy was standing in the middle of the living room, once again, reciting his favourite poem:

They lie, the men who tell us in a loud decisive tone
That want is here a stranger, and that misery's unknown;
For where the nearest suburb and the city proper meet
My windowsill is level with the faces in the street...

He declaimed it loudly, swaying ruddy-faced and twinkle-eyed in time, cigarette, as always, in one hand, whisky and milk in the other.

Margaret, meanwhile, had collapsed in sleep, head rolled to one side, mouth hanging open, snoring lightly, in an armchair in a corner of the room. Sam and Lisa muttered their excuses and let themselves out.

Back in their tent, in the dark, Lisa refused to make love with Sam, even though Isobel was sleeping in the kids' tent with Eric. 'No! You'll wake the others up,' she whispered, putting him off, yet again.

The next day was hot, with the same wind blowing as the day before.

Sam struggled to paint the old farm buildings on the other side of the creek. 'Decay and death,' he reflected, as he painted, 'this is an expression of what waits for all of us.'

The subject was also very romantic, in a ruined kind of way – the old timbers and warped, rusted tin against the brown of the Australian hills, a colour in which which he was starting to find great subtlety...but he couldn't make anything of it. The heat, the wind, Lisa's apparent indifference and the pestering voices of the others all conspired against him. That, and the grogginess he still felt after last night's extraordinary meal, made him feel tired and irritated. In the end, he gave it away. It was a subject he was sure he'd return to. In the meantime, he retired to his and Lisa's sweltering little dome tent, for what he assumed would be a couple of hours of feverish, discontented rest.

To his surprise, Lisa appeared at the tent entrance, a mischievous twinkle in her eye. 'Shhh!' she cautioned, finger to her lips. 'Jenny's watching Isobel and Eric while they swim in the creek.'

He could hear the two kids splashing and calling out in the distance. Quick as a flash, Lisa burrowed beneath the light sheet which he'd pulled over himself and gave him relief, as only she could, taking him deep inside her mouth, until he came, with a suppressed moan, against the back of her throat. They both lay quietly for a moment, then Lisa crawled up his body to kiss him passionately, as was her habit, with her lips and tongue still tasting of his semen.

After that, he slept for a while – the sudden, swooning sleep of the sexually satisfied – magnified in its effect by the heat. When he woke, Lisa was gone, though he could hear her voice, with the voices of the others, down by the creek. He was aware of a sudden pressure in his stomach, an urgent need to go to the toilet.

The arrangement they'd made was that each person would take a small spade, together with a roll of toilet paper, and head for a clump of tea tree just over the fence in the next paddock upstream. There, they'd dig a shallow hole in the soft earth, above the waterline, and do their business. It was a primitive arrangement, but it was the best they could manage under the circumstances. Sam took paper and spade and set off.

When he came to the fence, he threw the spade and the paper into the next paddock. He bent down, separated the middle strands and went to step through. Some instinct much faster than thought, however, made him withdraw his foot, suddenly and violently, before it even touched the ground, as if he'd experienced an electric shock. The ground beneath the sole of his bare foot appeared to be moving. Then he realised what it was. He'd disturbed a snake on the other side of the fence – presumably, had been about to step on it – and now it was moving down the fence line towards the water.

'Good,' he thought, 'let it go!' since it didn't appear to be moving towards him.

The snake was dusky green, with reddish-brown stripes, and was about two feet long. It slid with frightening, fluid ease over the rough surface of the ground, from which it could hardly be distinguished, in the shade. It paused momentarily when it came to the edge of the water, then bowed its head almost submissively and slid in. It did make a V as it swam, and the only thing that could be seen was its little, dark head above the water, just as Lisa had said.

'Now go away and stay away!' Sam commanded it, mentally. He could see Lisa and Jenny talking, and hear the sounds of the kids wimming downstream.

The snake reached a shelf of grey rock in the middle of the creek. Slowly, lazily, it hauled itself up out of the water and onto the rock.

'Don't stay there!' Sam tried to will it. 'Keep going!' He wanted to see it plunge into the water on the other side of the rock and keep going till it reached the far bank and disappeared. He moved closer to the bank on his side to get a better view.

'Look at Sam!' he heard Eric saying to Isobel, in the distance. 'What's he looking at?'

'I don't know,' Isobel answered. 'Let's go and see!'

They both began to run along the bank, towards Sam.

'Stay away…for God's sake!' Sam eyed the snake, intensely, pleading with it. He was close to praying – not a thing to which he was accustomed. To the kids, he called out, 'Don't come near!'

'Why not?' Isobel asked, all innocence.

'It's a snake,' Sam told her.

'I want to see!' Eric demanded.

Slowly – almost inevitably, it seemed to Sam – the snake slid off the rock and re-entered the water, swimming back towards them.

'Stay where you are!' Sam yelled at the kids.

He felt the snake and he were connected, as if this were all fated somehow, as if the two of them were locked in primordial battle with each other. He looked around for anything he could defend himself with. He bent down rapidly and picked up a largish rock to one side of him. The rock had a fair weight, even in two hands.

The snake paused again at the trampled, muddy edge of the bank where sheep and cattle went down to drink.

'If you come any closer,' Sam warned, convinced he and the snake were communicating directly with each other now by some strange telepathy they shared, 'I'll throw this!'

As if accepting the challenge, the snake started up the bank, straight towards Sam. Sam knew he had just one chance. He took aim and threw.

The rock hit the snake in the head, snapping the head off the body and driving it deep into the mud. The severed body remained on the surface, coiling and uncoiling, writhing frantically, smearing blood of a surprising, bright scarlet across the dark brown of the mud. It was still shocking – and even terrifying – but there was no doubt the situation had been saved. Sam heaved a huge sigh of relief.

Behind him, Eric burst loudly into tears.

'What are you crying for?' Sam asked, irritated almost beyond endurance. He was never going to understand Eric. The snake was dead. What more did he want?

'The snake!' Eric howled inconsolably, as Lisa and Jenny came running towards them, wondering what was wrong. 'It was so beautiful!'

Step in the River

That morning, Sam woke to the smell of coffee and the sound of Garth banging around the kitchen making breakfast in the house Garth and his girlfriend, Roberta, were renting in the city. Sam opened his eyes and looked across to where his wife Judith was lying with the baby, Maya, between them. The two of them were still fast asleep. A pungent pee smell came from Maya, mingling with that of the coffee, indicating Judith would have to change her when she gave Maya her morning feed.

Sam rolled out of their bed, which was an inflatable double mattress on the floor of the otherwise empty spare bedroom. He stood up beside the pile of clothes he'd dropped on the floor last night, and put them back on as quietly as he could. He padded barefoot to the door, opened it and went out into the hall, closing the door softly behind him.

He went up the hall and out into the sunlit kitchen at the back of the house, where he found Garth buttering pieces of toast and preparing to pour the coffee. 'Morning!' he said to Garth, in that slightly kidding around tone they always used when they were together.

'Morning!' Garth greeted him, heartily. He was always noisy and energetic in the morning, a bit like their father, Kevin, had been.

Kevin had apparently seen it as his task to wake the entire family with his rather aggressive brand of morning cheer – not that Garth was anything like in Kevin's league as far as that was concerned.

'Good night?' Garth enquired, lowering the volume a little.

'Yeah,' Sam answered. 'We slept right through. Even Maya didn't wake. We must all have been very tired.'

They'd arrived in Auckland by plane from Melbourne the afternoon of the day before – Maya's first time in a plane, at the age of one – to an enthusiastic welcome from Garth and Roberta which had gone on till quite late.

'We're just having a light breakfast this morning,' Garth told him. 'We're going to see the old man later in the morning – you remember? – and he likes a generous lunch, as you know.'

Sam did, indeed, know what Garth was talking about. Kevin's cook-ups had been the stuff of legend during their growing up. And he hadn't forgotten they were going to see Kevin and his new wife, Marilyn, this morning. How could he? That was the point of the whole trip – to show Maya to her New Zealand relatives, however difficult that might be for him, returning to the scenes of his own confused, protracted growing up to do so.

He took a cup of coffee and a couple of pieces of toast back up to the bedroom for Judith. She'd woken by this time and was sitting up in bed, with her back against the wall and one breast exposed, giving Maya her morning feed. Maya was guzzling greedily, as he walked in.

'Everything OK?' he asked, putting the coffee and toast down beside the bed.

'Yes,' Judith replied, with a grateful air. 'She's feeding just fine. I'll change her and put her down again, and she might even sleep for a bit longer.'

'Remember we're going to see my old man later on this morning. Don't get too comfortable!'

'I won't. But it might give me a chance to have a shower and some time to myself before we go.'

'Good luck with that!' he chuckled, ironically.

He went back out to the kitchen, to rejoin Garth. 'Yeah, I'll be interested to see his new place,' he said, picking up the conversation at the point they'd left it when he walked out of the room.

'It's all right,' Garth allowed, a touch grudgingly.

What, they both paused to reflect, could possibly bear comparison with the wonders of playing with their older brother in their beautiful, expansive childhood garden, or, for that matter, the never-ending war that went on between their parents inside the the ugly little box of their childhood home?

'We can go to some other places, if you want,' said Garth. 'We could, for instance, go and take a look at what's left of the old place.'

'That'd be good,' Sam replied, though he wasn't sure at this point how much he really wanted to do that.

'You have a think about it and let me know.'

'There might be some places Judith would like to see too – not to mention Maya. She should at least see the old place, I suppose, even if she doesn't remember it.'

'Yeah,' Garth agreed, and turned on the radio so they could catch the morning news.

Later that morning, the five of them, including baby Maya, packed themselves into Garth and Roberta's ageing station wagon for the trip over to the North Shore. They went down to the freeway, past the marina and over the bridge. It was a beautiful morning of early summer, with a clear blue sky and brilliant sunshine. The harbour looked absolutely stunning. Sam was reminded, once again, of the beauty he'd given up, going to live in Melbourne – not that Melbourne was without its own attractions. Being a much larger city, it made Auckland look almost provincial.

But Auckland, too, had grown in the meantime. On the other side of the bridge, much had changed. There was a whole complex of freeways, heading in all directions, where there'd just been one, last time he was here. The stand of kahikatea pines on the side of the bridge freeway remained, presumably protected by some heritage order, but the old dairy farm, which had been such a feature of his childhood and growing up – the last in the area – was now gone, converted into yet another real estate development.

Kevin's new house was situated most of the way up the Northcote hill. They turned off the main road and drove round the side of the hill, up and down twisting little streets, until they came to a driveway at the bottom of one of the dips.

'Here we are!' Garth announced, tour guide style, as he pulled the car up, just past the driveway.

They all got out – a considerable exercise in itself, which involving getting Maya out of her travelling pod and organising her bag of essential items for the day – and stood at the foot of the drive. The drive led straight up the hill, with a number of houses running off it at various points along the way. They trudged up the drive, with Judith carrying the sleepy Maya on her hip, and Sam carrying the overflowing baby bag. The view as they ascended the drive was remarkably spacious. It seemed like a sizable slice of the Shore lay at their feet.

'And this is it!' Garth declared, in his best grandiloquent tone, accompanied by an appropriately dramatic gesture, about halfway up the drive.

They all stopped and looked. A house, like a small double-storeyed bungalow, was tucked into a pocket on the side of the hill, just off the drive. There was barely room to turn a car round in front of it. A path led from the drive to a deck and the entrance to an upper storey, while the pocket had been excavated underneath to make room for a one-car garage and what looked like a basement study.

'Well, it's small…but definitely an improvement on the old place,' Sam muttered to Garth, when he'd recovered from his initial shock.

They didn't have to go up to the front door to knock. Kevin and Marilyn must have seen them through one of the living room windows, which overlooked the drive. They came bustling out.

Kevin was all hearty cheer, as usual. 'Hello, hello!' he called out, while Marilyn waited, more quietly, behind him.

In a group, they moved up to the front door, where handshakes and cheek kisses were exchanged. Even though Kevin and Marilyn weren't really baby people, they still exclaimed about how beautiful Maya was.

'I think she looks like you, Judith,' Marilyn said.

'I think she looks more like Sam,' Kevin disagreed.

They took turns stroking her cheek and holding her tiny hand before everyone moved inside.

'This is nice!' Sam declared, stepping through the front door and admiring the view out the picture window opposite.

'Yes.' Kevin bustled in around him. 'It's small, but it's comfortable. Sit down, sit down!' He gestured in the direction of the tidy, clean, decorously formal living room – much more Marilyn's style than anything Kevin had ever been used to, Sam noted.

Marilyn herself stood, beaming proudly, while they installed themselves.

'We're having mussels for lunch,' Kevin informed them in his familiar, booming baritone. 'Does everyone like mussels?'

This was for Judith and Roberta's benefit, because Kevin knew very well, from long experience, that the two brothers loved mussels.

'Oh, yes!' Judith and Roberta both responded enthusiastically, as they were clearly meant to.

'That's good!' Kevin looked very pleased.

Sam couldn't help noticing how small he was, this figure who'd dominated his childhood, like a giant, and how fat he'd grown. 'Life with Marilyn must really suit him,' Sam thought, remembering the incessant conflicts between Kevin and his and Garth's mother, Marion. The strange coincidence of the two wives' names struck him, not for the first time. It was followed by a momentary, intense pang for the sadness and disappointment of Marion's life, compared with this new-found happiness of Kevin's.

'I'm just going to clean the mussels,' Kevin said, tying a ridiculous, frilly maid's apron around his ample waistline. 'I'll be in the kitchen. Relax! Lunch won't be long.'

Everybody tried to follow his injunction, sitting around in the living room, making small talk with Marilyn, while he disappeared into the kitchen.

He reappeared almost immediately, however, brandishing a long-neck bottle of beer and some beer glasses. 'Beer, anyone?' he enquired.

'Yes. Why not?' Sam and Garth chorused.

Just as he was a big eater, so Kevin had always been a big drinker. He was seldom without a glass and a cigarette in either hand. He had the constitution of an ox. How he'd survived this long was a minor miracle. Family social events floated on a sea of alcohol. He'd taught his boys well. They reached for their drinks gratefully, as did Roberta.

Even Judith said, 'I'll just have one,' though she was trying very hard not to drink while breastfeeding Maya.

The mussels were soon cleaned, steamed and ready to be served up at the highly polished antique dinner table in the dining area of the living room. They ate them very simply (and somewhat messily), dipping the mussels in vinegar, placing them on big slabs of wholemeal bread, with lashings of butter, and a generous grind of salt and pepper over the top, plus an oddly contrasting, dainty little salad, prepared by Marilyn, on the side. The men drank more beer with theirs, while the women switched to white wine.

Kevin and Marilyn gossiped about people they worked with, as they ate. They taught at the same school, which was how they'd met. They'd known each other for years – long before they were married – and were both now approaching the end of their careers. They seemed to think this gossip was of great interest to outsiders, though it really served to show how small their world was.

'Do people's worlds shrink – like their bodies – as they grow older?" Sam questioned, observing them. Still, it was easier listening to them than having to explain the complications of his own life.

Then Kevin and Marilyn began to talk about a colleague of theirs, named Michael, of more or less their own age, who'd got in trouble at work for making inappropriate comments to younger women teachers. The young women had complained to the principal, who'd done nothing about it, so the young women had gone public, and now it was all over the media.

'All he did was call them "dear" and "love"!' Kevin said, indignantly.

'He did a bit more than that,' Marilyn, rather surprisingly, replied.

'Like what?' Kevin demanded.

'Well, he made comments about various parts of their bodies…and he may even have gone a bit further than that.'

'It seems highly likely he did,' Roberta, who was a fervent feminist and had been following the case in the news, put in.

'What? He kissed them? I think it was all pretty innocent,' Kevin said. 'Those women should never have gone to the media. It should've been kept in-house.'

'But that's just the way things like that have been hushed up for centuries. And women don't like being treated that way. They're tired of it. How else are they going to put an end to it?' Roberta countered.

'Roberta…' Garth attempted to intervene, obviously uncomfortable with the way the discussion was developing, with all of the women ranged on one side and Kevin on the other.

'Anyway, who should be on trial here…Michael, for doing whatever it was he was supposed to have done, or the principal, for doing nothing about it? There are too many unknowns. A lot more should have happened in-house, before it went to the public,' Kevin blundered onwards.

'Maybe it's the system that's at fault,' Judith volunteered from the couch, where she'd gone to change Maya's nappy and give her a midday feed. She would have liked to feed her at the table, but she wasn't sure how Kevin and Marilyn would react.

'It certainly is,' Roberta concluded, 'and that's because it's a male system.'

Kevin looked like he might have wanted to take the bait, but Marilyn forestalled him as she tidied up the lunch dishes, with her politely poised enquiry, 'Coffee, anyone?'

'Yes, please.' Sam was glad of the break. Not knowing about the case, he didn't really have a strong view either way, but he'd been interested to observe this interaction between the sexes and the generations. Kevin, who'd always treated women in a bit of an old-fashioned, patronising way, seemed to be getting more hidebound with age. 'Does this hardening of attitudes go along with diminishing height and a shrinking world?' Sam wondered. This Kevin was both old and new to him.

The coffee did stem the flow of alcohol, however, which was a good thing. Sam was starting to worry about Garth and the drive home. Over coffee, the talk reverted to non-controversial catch-up about people and places from long ago. The dividing lines between the sexes and generations blurred once more, and family bonhomie prevailed.

To Sam, unused as he was to this kind of contact with Kevin and Marilyn, there was one major gap in the conversation – Marion. There was no evidence of her anywhere in the house that he could see, and no mention of her at all in the conversation. It was like she'd completely vanished from everyone's lives. He felt the loss keenly, but what could he do or say about it?

After coffee, Kevin offered to show Sam around the new house, while Garth and Roberta helped Marilyn with cleaning up in the kitchen, and Judith prepared Maya for their return to the city. Kevin whisked him quickly around the rest of the upstairs living area, then took him downstairs to what, he explained, was a study that he and Marilyn shared. Once again, the room showed much more of Marilyn's influence than it did of Kevin's. It was very well organised and clean, but Sam did recognise Kevin's books, which he'd brought from the old house, stacked with unusual care on shelves behind Kevin's desk in one corner of the room.

'This is where we do our work.' Kevin sounded a note of pride, standing beside his desk.

Sam imagined the two of them bent over their marking and preparation after dinner, the way, in childhood, he'd often seen Kevin in breaks between quarrelling with Marion.

'You know I've gone back to university to finish my degree?' He was unsure whether he'd actually mentioned it to Kevin yet, or if Kevin had taken any notice of it.

'Yes, yes, you told me.' Kevin's tone was almost dismissive. He was always a bit put out when the conversation moved away from himself and his concerns. 'What are you thinking of doing with it?' he asked, as if to atone.

'I'm thinking of teaching. I have to do something to earn a regular income now that we've got the baby and the house and all. If I finish my degree, I could do secondary teaching. That couldn't be too bad, could it?'

This was a mild thrust at Kevin, who only had a diploma, and had spent his career primary teaching.

'I'm sick of cleaning and waitering and all those other useless jobs I've been doing for years. There must be something more worthwhile I can do with my life.'

'What about your painting?' Kevin was aware that Sam had harboured artistic ambitions, of one kind or another, for many years, even if they'd never come to anything much.

Sam deliberately downplayed the issue, though in reality it had caused him considerable anguish. 'I don't have time to do that any more. There's no money in it anyway. It was just something I was interested in. But I have been doing a bit of writing recently. My major's in English, so there's a natural connection there. I enjoy it. I feel like it could really take me somewhere.'

He ended feeling exposed and more than a little fatuous, as he often did with Kevin. It seemed nothing he did ever impressed him.

The two of them were standing on either side of Kevin's desk, staring out the window at the small patch of neatly mown lawn in front of the house, fringed by a pretty, decorative flower bed and one large, rather incongruous-looking cabbage tree.

'You know, Charlie's OK…' Kevin started up, suddenly, out of the blue. 'He's got a very good job and he's happily settled down with his family. Garth's happily settled with Roberta and his new job, after all that time he spent in the country. But I never thought anything of that sort would ever happen to you…' He lapsed back into silence as suddenly as he'd emerged from it.

'What did you think was going to happen to me?' Sam wanted to know, but was rendered temporarily speechless by the apparent implications of Kevin's remark.

Kevin offered nothing more himself by way of explanation. Instead, he turned away from Sam and plodded, heavily, wearily, back up the stairs. Sam followed, experiencing some of the same frustration and anger Marion had obviously felt with him so many times over the years.

There was the usual post-visit release of tension and general hilarity as they drove away.

After the laughter, exclamations and the loud exhalations of disbelieving breath had subsided, Garth asked, 'Is there anywhere else you'd like to go?'

'I wouldn't mind going to the beach…' Sam replied, though he was aware of a certain amount of silent resistance from Judith, who was doing most of the looking after Maya. 'Just to see it. I need to clear my head.'

They drove past the entrance to the bridge freeway, past the old farm, now completely flattened and featureless, ready for its new development, and pulled up at the lights beside the girls' high school – companion to the boys' high which he and Garth had attended. Needless to say, it had been the site of many of Sam and Garth's teenage fantasies.

'Do they still have to wear hat and gloves?' Sam wondered out loud.

'Yeah, and dresses down below the knee,' Garth laughed. 'The less you saw, the more exciting it was.'

Sam laughed in response, remembering his own teenage passions and agonies, most of them entirely unrecognised, let alone consummated, except in his imagination. The women laughed as well, if slightly less enthusiastically than Garth and Sam.

The local hospital, where Marion had spent the last years of her life, too physically wasted to get out of bed, stood on the opposite corner. The hospital was considerably bigger now than Sam remembered it – a real hospital, rather than a glorified clinic. He recalled what he'd been told about the peace Marion had supposedly found there, separated, except for visiting hours, from Kevin. He felt grateful she'd been able to experience at least some degree of relief from a lifetime of conflict and pain before the end.

They turned onto the long, straight stretch of road that led to the nearby town and shopping centre. They went round the roundabout, at the far end, and drove up the main street of the town. Sam was surprised and a bit embarrassed – humiliated, even – to see on the sign outside the local real estate office the names of a couple of boys he remembered from his schooldays. It made him think about those who'd stayed and done well, who were accepted and admired by the local community, unlike himself, returning under a cloud of failure and subsequent, self-imposed exile. He began to wonder what would happen if they met someone he knew from those days. How would he begin to explain himself – what he'd made, or not made, of his life? He'd be even more at a loss than he'd been with Kevin.

At the top of the main street, they turned again onto another long, straight road that led down to the beach. They passed the Picturedrome, where he and Garth had spent so many memorable Saturday afternoons, rolling Jaffas down the aisles, drumming their heels on the floorboards to cheer the cavalry, arriving in the nick of time to save the wagon train, and playing chasey around the darkened cinema. At least they'd never thrown ice creams and Coke bottles at the screen, as some of the other kids had.

The Picturedrome had been converted into some kind of shopping mall, with shops on either side of the entrance and, presumably, more inside. But the fish 'n' chip shop next door was still there. On cold days, Sam remembered, they used to buy sixpence-worth of burning-hot chips wrapped in newsprint, tear the top off the package, extract the greasy, salty chips between the pincers of index finger and thumb, blow on them to cool them down, bite chunks off and chew them, very carefully, so as not to blister their mouths, as they walked along…

Sam's reverie was interrupted by their arrival at the beach. Garth parked the car in one of the spaces provided at the end of the road. Judith wanted to stay in the car and give Maya a feed, so the other three got out and walked down the ramp between the piled granite retaining walls that led to the beach.

'It's pretty much the same,' said Garth, by way of introduction, as much for Roberta's benefit as for Sam's.

And so it was – at least, superficially. On one side of the ramp was the building which once housed the Surf Club and, on the other, the kiosk overshadowed by a towering Norfolk pine where they used to buy ice creams and milkshakes to cool themselves down. This was the part of the beach where Sam had spent every day of his twelfth summer holidays, swimming in the lukewarm, sluggish water and lying around on the hot sand with a group of his primary school friends. That was the summer before the group broke up, going on to their different high schools. It was the summer of discovering girls, of the first, extremely tentative experiments with sex, before that all went into abeyance again for most of his high school years. If Sam concentrated hard enough, he could almost see the group there, lying on their towels, talking, laughing, fooling around and flirting among the sandflies and the drying bunches of seaweed…

But the beach was different in other ways. There were a lot more houses along the beachfront, and they were bigger and more expensive-looking than the old ones used to be. The beach had much less of that decaying, leftover air it had, when he was young. It had been a major destination for day-trippers from the city, decades before, but the party had long since moved on. Now it looked like the party was back, with a lot more money... and to stay this time.

'At least the bridge is still standing,' Sam said to Garth, looking along the beach to the far end, where the rickety old structure teetered above the creek mouth.

'Only just,' Garth replied. 'It's condemned. You can't even walk over it any more. They're going to tear it down.'

Back in the car, Judith and Maya had both seized the opportunity for a snooze. The others, returning, woke Judith – but not Maya, fortunately.

'How was it?' Judith enquired, showing admirable powers of control. Though she resented being woken up like that when she was so short of sleep herself, she was very well aware how much Sam needed gentle, sympathetic treatment just at the moment.

'Oh, pretty much the same,' he said, affecting an outward indifference. Inside, however, he was struggling with the changes he'd seen and having to tear himself away, after such a brief glimpse, from a place which had been so important in his growing up.

'Where would you like to go next?' Garth asked.

'How about the school?' Sam suggested, a little diffidently. 'Do you think we could take a look at that?'

'Yeah, a quick look.'

Garth was even more conscious than Sam of the roundabout route they were taking home and the effect it was having on the women. Roberta, in particular, wasn't saying much, but he could tell she was already tiring of this sentimental excursion through their boyhood memories.

They drove back the way they'd come, up the road to the beach and through the shopping centre. Halfway along the main road, they came to Sam and Garth's old primary school. Only Sam and Garth got out of the car this time. They walked nervously through the open gates and up the driveway, feeling like they might be trespassing – even though it was the weekend – to stand outside the principal's office. Much of the school was still the same. The infant block at the far end had a new wing, but the rest of the school was unchanged, including the play area that ran alongside the two main blocks, with the same old courts for netball and four square, marked in white paint on the black tarseal.

'Do you remember the duels we used to have in four square?' Garth asked.

'Yeah,' Sam laughed, 'they were serious affairs. That big, heavy rubber ball we played with would hit you in the stomach and knock you off your feet if you weren't careful.'

On the other side of the tarseal lay a grassy playing field. In summer, there were cricket nets down the bottom end, but in winter they were removed, so the boys could play rugby – the national religion, as it was known. This was an elaborate exercise, because the different age groups all played together, at the same time, in the same jam-packed space, but somehow they worked it out between them.

'Do you remember those games of British Bulldog the whole school used to play?' Sam asked.

'Yeah,' Garth chuckled, 'when the catchers called out British Bulldog, all hell would break loose. It's a wonder nobody got killed in the rush – specially the little kids.'

Sam shook his head and grinned. 'It used to be banned, periodically, but it always came back…'

The playing field was bordered on the far side by trees, which again were pretty much as they'd always been – with one exception. An enormous oak which had dominated the view for many years was gone. The whole school looked smaller without it, reduced in scale…or was that the same difference, Sam wondered, between childhood memory and adult perception he'd noticed earlier, at Kevin's place?

'Service with Honour – what the hell did that ever mean?' Garth pointed to the motto emblazoned above the entrance to the main block, where the steep wooden steps ran up to the principal's office. 'Apart from the freedom to get yourself killed in the war.'

'I was never very sure about that myself,' Sam replied.

Both brothers knew their names appeared on the Honours Board outside the headmaster's office, but, unlike others on the board, they hadn't served anyone, or anything, with much distinction since.

'It certainly didn't apply to us. We got off to a good beginning, but something happened along the way…'

'Are you two going to be much longer?' they heard Roberta calling.

The sound snapped them out of their increasingly melancholy musing. They hurried back to the car.

'What took you so long?' Roberta wanted to know. 'Was there much to see?'

'Not really,' said Garth, 'just a lot to think about.'

'I would've liked to see the lake,' said Sam, knowing there was no way that was going to happen now.

The lake lay, concealed from sight, down a steep slope, to the rear of the infant block, right at the far end of the school.

'Another time,' Garth replied, with a nervous look in Roberta's direction.

'Will there be another time? Do I really want to come back here again?' Sam found himself asking as he settled into the back seat of the car beside Judith and Maya.

They turned off the main road at the battered wooden shelter where Sam and Garth had spent so many of their childhood and teenage hours checking the graffiti and the peeling posters while waiting for their buses to arrive. They went down the familiar side road, across the bridge over the creek, and round the corner, now occupied by a block of flats, which had been a willow swamp in their earliest recollections. This was home territory for the brothers. They knew every inch of it like the back of their hands. Except, Sam rapidly realised, he didn't any more. He cried out in surprise as they pulled up outside the place where the family home had been.

The only thing left was a distinctively spiky, pale green Swedish spruce which grew in the top corner of the front garden. Everything else was gone.

Gone was the falling down, concrete block wall out the front of the whole property. Gone was the phoenix palm, with its deadly, needle-sharp fronds, which balanced on its base, in the middle of the front lawn, like an enormous, malevolent pineapple. Gone was the ugly, green, box-like house, with the ramparts round the roof. 'Truly,' thought Sam, 'if ever there was a house made for fighting…' Gone was the prettily decorative side-garden, with its flower beds and shrubs. Gone were the super-abundant vegetable garden and orchard behind the house. Gone was the sprawling wilderness area, with its willow trees and flax bushes beyond that again…

The whole lot was gone. In its place, a high, white-painted, rendered-brick wall, obscuring a block of similarly white, rendered-brick, single-storey flats, stretched the whole length of the property to Sam and Garth's beloved childhood creek at the rear – or rather, what was left of the creek, after the council had replaced it with a concrete conduit to guard against winter flooding. A driveway ran alongside the wall most of the way down to the creek, ending with a right-angle turn into a parking area for the flats. Beyond that, access to the creek was blocked by yet another white, rendered-brick wall and a thick screen of leafy, green bamboo. It was as if their childhood had been taken away in a single, sweeping gesture. Sam felt the impact of it physically, like a blow to the chest. His mouth fell open, but no words came out.

'It's pretty amazing, isn't it?' said Garth, in what appeared to Sam to be a massive understatement. 'They bulldozed everything…the whole garden…that wonderful orchard…everything. Ironically, the one thing they didn't bulldoze was the house. They put that on a trailer and transported it up north, where it's made a nice house for someone else.'

'Jeez,' Sam responded, with a pained laugh, 'the one thing not worth keeping, they kept! Hope the new owners don't have bad dreams.'

'Yeah, they keep thinking they hear a man and a woman screaming at each other.' Garth laughed, in his own, equally pained way. 'You want to get out and take a look?'

Unlike the school, Sam felt this was something he really had to see. 'Yeah. Do you want to come, Judith? Maybe we could take Maya and show her what's left of the creek.'

'Yes,' Judith agreed, somewhat to his surprise.

Maya was now awake, lying there quietly, in her protective pod, eyes open, smiling contentedly.

'Do you want to come?' Garth asked Roberta.

'No, thanks,' she said. 'I'll stay in the car.' She'd clearly had enough heavily male-dominated nostalgia for one day.

The other three adults set off down the driveway, with Judith carrying Maya in the familiar, comfortable position on her hip.

The flats were all the same design. Each had a gate set into the middle of the wall, with a concrete path leading from the gate through a small front garden to the door. The wall was just over head height, effectively blocking any further view from the driveway.

They walked down the driveway to the wall at the far end. Faint sounds of creek water running downstream from their old family property came from behind the screen of bamboo. Sam was the first to haul himself up to the top of the wall and hang there, trying to peek between the clusters of bamboo trunks for any familiar sights.

'Can you see those rocks the old man made the council put in the bottom of the conduit?' Garth asked.

'No, you can see a bit of the conduit, but nothing much of interest,' Sam replied. 'We should be able to get a better view of it from here.' He dropped down and crossed to the section of wall in front of the last flat. He hauled himself up it and strained to hold himself there, peering over. 'You can see them!' he called out, genuinely thrilled.

There they were…over the top of the wall, on the far side of the parking area, the bottom of the conduit could clearly be seen. There was very little water in it – the merest trickle, running between half a dozen rocks. Kevin had discovered, in the course of a prolonged dispute with the council, that his property rights extended halfway across the creek. He'd threatened legal action if the council didn't remove the rocks when the conduit was excavated, then set them back in the concrete when it was poured, in exactly the same order as before.

Sam roared with laughter. He felt triumphant, as Kevin had when he first showed him, all those years ago. But he couldn't hold himself up any longer, so he dropped down again, and Garth took his place.

Garth, too, roared with laughter – and appeared to share in the feeling of triumph – at what he saw. Then he dropped down. 'How amazing!' he said, shaking his head. 'Who would've believed it?'

The sight tended to confirm, in both of them, an instinctive belief in their continued ownership of the property, in spite of everything that had happened in the meantime.

'I'll lift Maya up, so she can at least have seen the rocks, even if she doesn't actually remember them,' Sam told Judith. He took Maya out of Judith's arms and carried her across to the wall. He raised her up and spoke to her, as if she understood. 'Look there, baby! Can you see them? Can you see those rocks? Your grandfather made the council take them out, then put them back in.'

As if in response to what he was saying, the gate to the last flat swung open and a tiny, skinny, wrinkled old woman with white hair and glasses came charging out, in full, furious cry. 'What do you think you're doing?' she screamed at them.

Sam, shocked, snatched Maya back – reflexively – into the safety of his arms. 'We just wanted to see the creek,' he answered her, a little shame-faced.

'We used to live here.' Garth rushed to back Sam up.

'If you don't leave here, immediately, I'll call the police!' the woman threatened. Apparently, she was in no mood to consider their claim to prior ownership. She saw them as trespassers, maybe even as thieves casing the joint. She stood there, eyes ablaze, hand raised in warning, shaking with righteous indignation.

The two brothers, along with Maya and Judith, could do nothing but turn away and begin to walk, slowly, reluctantly, back up the drive. Sam and Garth, in particular, were caught between their desire to laugh at the irony of what had just happened to them, and a desire to cry, as the genuine sadness of being thrown out of their childhood home overtook them.

'What the hell…?

'Can you believe that?' they spluttered to each other, as they retraced their steps.

Sam felt he'd travelled the distance from Melbourne to Auckland, across a sea of time between childhood and now, with the many false starts and reversals he'd experienced in his struggle to make something of himself, to finally start his adult life, only to be…what? Rejected? To be told his past, which he'd clung to for so long, which was such an important part of his identity, regardless of how much pain it caused him, was no longer his possession? He realised, finally and definitively, that he no longer had a home here in New Zealand, which somewhere in his mind he'd always seen as his backstop – a place he could return to, if all else failed. His home was in Australia now, with Judith and this precious baby he carried in his arms, against all expectations – his own, if truth were told, as well as Kevin's. He wouldn't be coming back to live here, though he might continue to visit from time to time. The centre of his being had moved; his future lay over there.

A Month in the Rain

Always, it rained. That's what Phillip remembered – the rain outside Helen's bedroom window. It dripped on the pane, luminously green with the light through the leaves. Inside her bedroom, by comparison, it was always dark. It was a dark bedroom – high-ceilinged, cavernous, gloomy, filled with dark oak furniture of a heaviness and ugliness that astonished him. For some reason, she refused to have a double bed. She had, instead, two single beds of the kind one sees in hotels or old-fashioned movies, divided by a dresser with a large mirror. The dresser was covered with her private things, spread in untidy profusion – her jewellery, her make-up, books, brushes and combs. She said it was because she had difficulty sleeping with other people, but he didn't believe her. She lay in his arms quite comfortably all night long (on the rare nights they had together), and certainly she never had any difficulty sleeping in the afternoons.

It was that kind of affair – brief moments snatched here and there, she from her studies and he from his thesis, tutoring, wife and child. They'd met on the campus, though both were involved in different subjects. He was working on his thesis and tutoring in English, and she was finishing a music degree. They met, quite by chance, in a coffee shop, introduced by a mutual friend, and, before long, were feeling that strange attraction which overtakes the hopelessly infatuated. It was only a matter of time before they ended up in bed (at her place, of course – his was out of the question, impossible) and there they continued to meet, all through that long, rainy August, mainly in the afternoons, while his wife, Anita, came and went on family business, which left him feeling slightly guilty and not entirely free.

Though, of course, he'd like to have been. He told himself he and Anita had an amicable agreement, that they were sensible, grown-up people. He reasoned it out with himself as he drove over to Helen's place, the windscreen wipers splashing in the rain. 'We're grown-up, we have an agreement, we recognise these things will happen, there's no reason why they should threaten the marriage. It's better that we should acknowledge them and get them out of the way. Then there's no bitterness, no frustration and we can relate to each other honestly.' He was naïve enough to think about his situation in these simplistic terms – terms he would have queried, seriously, in any essay he was marking.

But always, when he saw Helen, his heart would fold up in his chest with a convulsive motion, his legs would buckle under him and he'd know that he was fated, doomed by desire – or some such other term he would similarly have marked down in a professional capacity. Was it something about her body, so white against the green of the window, or the way she teased him, laughing at him, as she led him to her bed? He never knew, could never find the answer, not even in the intense heat he found between her legs (she showed him once, on a particularly dank afternoon, how it steamed there, in the aftermath). In this way, the struggle grew inside him, all through that cold, rainy month, while cars swished and hummed on the road outside, and he and Helen hid in her dark, heavy room.

There was a struggle between the two of them, too. With the caution of those who know they're bound to hurt each other, they didn't give themselves to each other entirely willingly – rather, with a strange mixture of love and loathing, to broadly paraphrase a Richard Eberhart poem he'd once had to teach.

So it was that they came to wake up one afternoon, in the green light through the window, while the rain still dripped monotonously on the leaves outside. His head ached, he felt disgusted with himself, he wanted to leave. Helen stretched herself out, languorous in sleep, the whole side of her body white – the colour to him, curiously, of desire. He fumbled for his socks on the floor. Somehow his wristwatch got tangled up in them; he could smell his socks, slightly malodorous after Anita had been several days away.

He wanted to say, 'I've had enough. Let's end this now. Why are we doing this to each other, why are we going on, when we know we'll only hurt each other? My wife can sense there's something wrong…she's unhappy, though I haven't actually told her yet. I can only see pain in this. I don't want to leave her and I know I have to lose you, sooner or later.' But something he didn't understand kept him there. Was it the quietly contented look on Helen's face, as she slept, or the peculiarly defenceless look of her body, so white, so open, so drowsily trusting, as she stirred and reached for him?

Instead, he said, 'I have to go.' And louder, so that she'd understand, 'I have a tutorial at four.'

She opened her eyes, which were a soft, sooty grey that was almost black, and blinked at him. 'What time is it?' she asked, in a querulous, slightly babyish tone.

'It's half-past three,' he said.

The watch slipped through his fingers and fell on the floor. Her face bore the same frank look of disappointment as a child's. Sometimes, what he regarded as her immaturity irritated him.

'Some of us do have obligations,' he added, with quite unnecessary cruelty, forgetting that she'd cut classes to be with him.

'Will I see you tomorrow?' she asked, turning her face to look out the window.

His heart went out to her, bracing herself against hurt.

'Fuck this everlasting rain!' she said, in the tones, suddenly, of an adult.

'Maybe. My wife's coming back tonight.' He pulled his underpants over a member still warm and sticky after lovemaking. Later, he knew, it would be cracked and dry. He'd have to shower before he confronted Anita. 'We'll see,' he said. He finished dressing, including the malodorous socks, which he kept as far away from her as possible, like a secret, an emblem of his guilt. He kissed her and went out the door. He left her lying there, silently staring at the rain.

Anita was already home when he got back, several hours later, after two tutorials in a row. She was in the kitchen, rinsing and chopping beans for Amanda's dinner. Light gleamed on the stainless steel bench of their recently renovated kitchen. Outside, it was still raining.

'Hello,' she said. 'I was wondering when you'd be in.'

'I had two tutorials this afternoon.' he said. 'Rolfe's sick. I'm standing in for him.' There was something about her air of innocence, her apparent lack of suspicion in this situation, which maddened him. 'How was your mother?'

'No better, no worse.' Her mother was sick, might even be dying. She drove up every day to see her, in the hospital, and often stayed overnight, in the family home.

'How's Amanda?' he asked.

Anita preferred to take Amanda, who was four, with her, rather than leave her at home.

'She's all right.' Anita paused, knife in hand. 'She finds it a strain, all this travelling backwards and forwards.'

'I'm not surprised,' he said. They were so strangely formal in their greeting, he thought, it tended to confirm Anita was aware (on some unconscious level, at least) that something was wrong between them.

'Come here!' Anita said, as if she could read his thoughts. 'Give me a hug!'

They held onto each other tentatively, awkwardly, for two people who'd been together as long as they had. To Phillip's surprise, Anita began to cry.

'It's awful! It's awful!' she said. She put the knife down on the cutting board. 'I hate it! I hate the travelling, I hate the constant fear. Will she die before I get there? If you knew what it's like, every day… I hate the atmosphere of gloom. My father doesn't know what to do with himself. He sits around, uselessly…' She broke off, wiping her face carelessly with her sleeve. 'Most of all, I hate this bloody rain!' She picked up the knife again and went on chopping beans.

Upstairs, Phillip ran himself a bath and relaxed into it. 'How can I tell her,' he wondered, carefully wiping away the evidence of his guilt, 'at a time like this?' The rain and steam made patterns on the window. It was growing dark. He lay for a long time in the bath, thinking, 'I must tell her soon. This is getting ridiculous, not to mention potentially dam-

aging to all of us, including Amanda.' His heart clenched suddenly, fe-
rociously, at the thought of his daughter, at the risk he was taking. But
he knew he wouldn't, couldn't tell Anita. Something was preventing
him. What? He'd had affairs with students before and they'd survived
them.

The bath was getting cold; he ran some more hot water. Was he in love
with Helen? Ridiculous! She was nineteen, he was thirty-two. There were
too many years between them, too much experience they didn't have in
common. Besides, Helen was adamant it wasn't a serious affair. She wanted
a life of her own. What then? What was he doing, why was he turning it
into such an issue? He couldn't give her up, he knew, any more than he
could give up Anita and Amanda.

He heard Anita's voice calling him to dinner. He shivered for a moment
in the bathwater, though it was now quite warm again, thinking it was
someone else's voice – Helen's…

Fogbound

That morning, Trevor and Karen woke to find their house in the country completely surrounded by fog. It was very dense fog. They couldn't see the paddock in front of the house, or the road behind them. They could still hear an occasional car pass on the road, but it sounded muffled, remote. Occasionally, also, a cow appeared out of the fog at the side fenceline of the paddock, then disappeared back into the fog. The fog was milky-white and intensely cold. There was no apparent likelihood of the sun breaking through. The only thing they could see was the tiny area immediately surrounding their house. They were completely cut off, islanded in the fog.

'Gee, this is going to make driving difficult,' Trevor said, looking out the living room window at the fog. 'What are we going to do?'

'We have to go back today,' Karen reminded him. 'The kids are expecting us.'

Brigid and Quentin were waiting for them back in the city. Brigid was nineteen and Quentin was sixteen. They could survive on their own now, but Trevor and Karen – particularly Karen – still missed them and didn't like to spend too long away from them.

'There are other people on the road,' Karen pointed out. 'We can make it.'

'Yeah,' Trevor responded dubiously, while continuing to peer out the window, 'but that fog's very thick. We'll have to go slowly.' He was, as usual, more than a little reluctant to leave their holiday home and the fog provided a very convenient excuse to stay for another day.

Karen made the decision for both of them, as she often did. 'I'll start packing,' she said, with an air of finality.

But the packing took them longer than they expected, due to one reason and another – in particular, that Trevor didn't see any reason for them to hurry – and they didn't leave until after midday. The fog was still very thick and they drove very slowly. In the fog, it was easy to miss signs and turn-offs, which they did several times. They hadn't had their house in the country very long, and they weren't overly familiar with the routes to and from their home in the city yet. Even Google Maps was useless with such low visibility. By the middle of the afternoon, the fog hadn't lifted at all and they were completely lost.

'Where the hell are we?' Trevor asked, exasperated.

'I'm not sure,' Karen replied. 'I don't recognise any of this.'

'It would be easier if there were some landmarks, but I can't see anything.'

'Why don't we ask at that farmhouse over there?'

Trevor peered through the windscreen and, sure enough, he could just make out – appearing and disappearing through swirling waves of fog – an old farmhouse set some way back from the road, half-hidden behind a tall hedge. The house had an air of neglect, but was evidently still lived in, judging by a light they could see shining round the edges of a ragged blind in the front window.

'Well, I'm game for anything at this stage,' Trevor declared. 'There's obviously someone there.'

They pulled over to the side of the road and left the car with its emergency lights flashing. They walked through a gap in the dark, unruly hedge, where a rusty iron gate hung off its hinges, permanently half-open, and up the cracked, uneven concrete path to the front door. It was very dark now, like twilight in the middle of the afternoon. The touch of the fog on their cheeks was icy.

Trevor tried the doorbell, but it didn't work. He knocked firmly, but briefly, trying not to alarm anyone who might be inside. A long silence followed. Then they heard the sound of shuffling feet slowly approaching the door. The door opened slightly and an old woman, her bone-white hair tied back in a bun, poked her wrinkled face through the gap. Trevor and Karen could hear a radio playing softly, somewhere in the background.

'Hello.' Trevor tried to sound as agreeable and harmless as possible. 'We're sorry to disturb you, but we're wondering if you could help us. We're lost.'

'Oh?' The woman paused, as if evaluating the situation. 'Where are you trying to get to?' she asked at length.

'We're trying to get back to the city.' Karen intervened, thinking a woman-to-woman approach might help at this point. 'We own a farmhouse down Longbridge way…'

Longbridge?' The old woman seemed surprised. 'You're a long way out of your way here.'

'We were hoping to make it home tonight.'

'Tonight?' the old woman's tone didn't sound encouraging. 'I don't think you've got much chance of that. As I said, you're a long way from anywhere here and the weather's going to get worse. My husband and I have just been listening to the forecast on the radio.'

As if on cue, an old man's voice came from further back inside the house. 'Who's there, dear?'

'It's just some travellers, dear, saying they've lost their way.'

'Well, bring them in!' Her husband – stooped, white-haired and wrinkled, like herself – came shuffling at an even slower rate up the hallway towards them with the aid of a stick.

'Won't you come in?' the old woman asked.

Trevor and Karen looked at each other. Karen gave a short, decisive nod.

'You're sure it's not inconvenient?' Trevor checked.

'Not at all,' the old man assured him. 'Park your car in the side drive and come on in!'

Trevor and Karen went to park the car together.

'Are you sure we're doing the right thing?' Trevor took care to double-check with Karen while they did so.

'We only have to stay until the fog lifts,' Karen said. 'It doesn't really matter what time we make it home tonight.'

'My name's Maurice and this is Edna.' The old man introduced himself and his wife at the door when they came back.

Trevor returned the introductions, then Maurice ushered them inside. Trevor and Karen followed the old couple as they made their slow way up the dark, cold hall, smelling of damp and neglect. A closed door at the far end, however, opened onto a surprisingly cosy, well-lit living room at the rear of the house, warmed by an open fire.

'This is very kind of you,' Karen remarked, as they all stood at the door, surveying the welcoming comfort of the room.

'Sit down!' Maurice waved them in the direction of a couch in front of the fire. 'Make yourselves at home!'

'Would you like a cup of tea?' Edna enquired.

'Yes, please,' Karen replied. 'But I need to call our children first.'

'Of course, dear.' Edna beamed at her, understandingly, then shuffled off into the kitchen, through another door on the far side of the room.

Karen called Brigid from one end of the couch, while Trevor sat down at the other. He felt unexpectedly tired after the day they'd had, and the warmth of the fire relaxed him. He felt a strong urge to sleep as soon as he sat down.

'Tired?' Maurice asked, observing him from one of two armchairs on either side of the couch.

'Yes,' Trevor replied, stretching himself and yawning. 'It's been a long day.'

'Well, don't feel you have to get up and rush off. You're quite welcome to stay the night, if you wish. The weather forecast is truly awful.'

Karen, meanwhile, was waiting and waiting for Brigid to answer her phone. Finally, Brigid did answer, sounding tired and a bit grumpy. Karen wondered what she'd been up to, the previous night.

'Hello, darling…'

'Hello, Mum.' Brigid spoke in typically guarded fashion, as if she had some secret she was keeping from her parents. 'Where are you?'

'Well, we got a late start, darling, and the weather's terrible. There's a heavy fog down here and we got lost. So we stopped at the house of some really nice people who've offered us a cup of tea and say we can stay for the night, if we need to. It sounds like the weather's going to get worse.'

'Yes, they said on the weather forecast that there's going to be torrential rain.'

'Did they? It might be better if we do stay the night here then, and drive back early tomorrow morning. Will that be all right with you?'

'Oh, Mum! What do you think?' Brigid responded, scathingly.

'Truly, she's grown beyond us. She doesn't need us any more,' Karen thought.'And how's Quentin?' she asked, smothering her qualms.

'He's fine.'

'Is he doing his homework?'

'Yes.'

'I wonder how true that is,' Karen thought, but decided to leave it. 'There's plenty of food in the fridge.'

'We'll send out for pizza.'

'I love you, darling.'

'I love you, Mum.'

'Bye.'

'Bye.'

'Is everything all right?' asked Edna, shuffling in from the kitchen with a steaming pot of tea and tea things on a tray.

'Yes, thank you,' said Karen. She looked at Edna's kindly, wrinkled old face and wondered how she'd coped with her children, assuming she'd had any.

Edna poured the tea on the coffee table in front of the couch, sat in the other chair and they all chatted, getting to know each other a little. As they talked, a wind picked up and began to howl around the old wooden house, which shuddered at each blast. Then it began to rain heavily, drumming on the corrugated-iron roof. Isolated drops of rain came plopping down the chimney and hissed on the open fire. Edna stood up to pull the curtains. It was now quite dark outside. The drumming of the rain reached such an intensity that Trevor and Karen seriously wondered if the roof could withstand it.

'I think you better had stay tonight,' Edna advised, kindly enough, but with a slight, rather strange edge on her voice, as if challenging them to defy her.

'If that's all right with you,' Trevor and Karen chorused gratefully, feeling like a couple of kids trying to please their mother.

'Then I'll start on dinner,' Edna announced, apparently satisfied.

Over dinner, which was served around the table in the kitchen, Maurice and Edna began to talk about their children. They had two – a son and daughter, just like Trevor and Karen – who'd both grown up and left home.

'They live in the city now,' Edna said, mournfully. 'Unfortunately, we don't see a lot of them.'

'Do they have children?' Karen asked, sympathetically.

'Yes, they do. But it's so far away, it's difficult for both of them.'

'We should probably have shifted closer to the city ourselves, years ago,' sighed Maurice, 'but we didn't…and now it's too late.'

Karen, in particular, found Maurice and Edna's fatalistic air in talking about their kids a bit hard to to take, but she didn't want to make an issue of it, as Maurice and Edna had been so generous. 'Surely they come and see you sometimes?' she said, trying to lighten the tone.

'Yes, they do,' Edna responded, dolefully, 'but their visits are few and far between. It's a hard thing to face about your kids…that they don't really need you any more.'

Karen was strongly reminded of her own recent experience with Brigid, but, when she checked Trevor for his reaction, surreptitiously, he hardly seemed to have noticed Edna's remark. The conversation passed on rapidly, if somewhat uneasily, to other topics.

After dinner, they made themselves comfortable on the couch and chairs in the living room once again and watched a movie on a big old TV, to one side of the fire. Appropriately enough, Trevor noted, with some amusement, Channel 9 was showing a grainy, black and white 1930s horror movie, in which a group of travellers ended up having to take shelter on a stormy night in a spooky-looking, rundown country house far from anywhere. It was funny, but also genuinely scary – especially when the mad younger brother suddenly appeared on the landing of the stair and had to be sent back to his room by the older brother. The carefully controlled calmness of the older brother's tone only accentuated the urgency of the situation. Karen, in particular, found that scene quite disturbing. She wondered for what terrifying reasons the younger brother was being kept confined in his room. The movie fed her already existing fears about the night, the slight, but growing strangeness of their hosts, the kids at home on their own…

Outside, it continued to rain unceasingly, though the wind had now died down. During an ad break, Trevor went to the bathroom, out in the hall, to do a pee. On the way back, he ran into Maurice, heading down the hall, evidently with the same intention.

'Bloody woman!' Maurice moaned, as he came up to Trevor. 'I don't feel so good. How do you feel?'

'I feel all right,' Trevor answered, somewhat mystified. 'You're not feeling so good yourself?'

'I never do, these days. She puts stuff in my food, I'm sure of it. She's trying to poison me.'

'You think…she's trying to poison you?' Trevor couldn't believe what he was hearing. 'Do you have any actual evidence of that?'

'I don't have any evidence at the moment. She's smart…much too smart for that. But I know she's doing it. I haven't been feeling well – haven't been feeling myself – for a long time. I know she's at the bottom of it. She doesn't say anything, but I can tell. It's in the way she looks at me. She's changed. She hasn't been the same since the kids left. She spends a long time fussing with my food and I'm sure she's putting things in it. It just doesn't taste right. I have stomach aches, headaches, like I never had before – really bad ones. I haven't had a sick day in my life and suddenly… How was your meal?'

Trevor looked at Maurice. He really did look bad. His hands were shaking, his eyes were bulging and bloodshot, his mouth was obviously very dry and he had thick, white flecks of saliva in both corners of his mouth.

'Mine tasted fine,' Trevor tried to reassure him.

'Oh, good!' Maurice muttered. He lapsed into a vague, preoccupied silence, pushed past Trevor as if he wasn't there, and entered the bathroom.

Trevor returned to the living room, feeling seriously disturbed. He didn't mind staying another night in the country – in fact, he was quite keen on

the idea – but if these people weren't getting on very well, or even crazy…
He wanted to discuss it with Karen, but she was still engrossed in the movie
and Edna was there, sitting in the armchair right next to her. Any discussion
would have to wait for later.

The movie eventually finished, the younger brother having done his
worst.

Edna rose shakily to her feet and announced, 'I'm going to make a nice
cup of tea for us all to go to bed with.'

Karen, somewhat shaken, went out into the kitchen to help her.

The men stayed talking in the living room. Maurice had come back in
after his pee looking like he'd recovered from whatever was affecting him
out in the hall. The two men chatted as if nothing out of the ordinary had
happened between them.

As soon as she put the kettle on, Edna turned to Karen and said, in a
ferocious undertone, 'You must help me! I'm so afraid of Maurice. Ever
since the kids left, we've had problems. He hates me. I think he wants to
kill me. I woke up the other night in bed and found his hands round my
throat. If I hadn't screamed… I don't know if he knew what he was doing.
I don't know if he even remembers it. I haven't had the courage to discuss
it with him yet. What can I do?'

'I don't know,' Karen responded truthfully, shocked by this sudden rev-
elation.

Edna was looking at her with a mixture of pleading and something that
looked dangerously like hatred in her eyes. She had red spots on her cheeks,
her pupils were narrowed down to black pinholes and white hair sprang
from her bun at all angles.

'Have you talked to anyone else about it?'

'No. There's no one I can talk to out this way, and I don't want to burden the kids with it.'

'What about the police?'

'Would they believe me? I'm not even sure it happened myself. I was
half-asleep at the time. It seems more like a bad dream than anything else
And you know the police hate to intervene in domestic disputes.'

'Or a psychologist?'

'Maurice wouldn't agree to go. He thinks there's nothing wrong with him.'

'Or even your GP?'

'The same thing. Maurice is never sick. He hasn't had a sick day in years. What can I do?'

Again, Karen wanted to say, 'I don't know,' but she had the good sense to ask instead, 'Do you think you're in any immediate danger?'

'I don't think so,' Edna answered. 'But I don't know when he might do something like that again and it terrifies me…'

They were interrupted by the kettle whistling. Edna made the tea and the moment passed. They walked back into the living room, to rejoin the men. Like Trevor, Karen felt profoundly disturbed by what she'd just witnessed. Like Maurice, Edna acted as if nothing had happened.

Trevor ran out through the rain to get the overnight bags from the car, then Maurice and Edna showed Trevor and Karen to their room. Everyone prepared to settle down for the night.

As soon as Maurice and Edna were out of earshot, Trevor turned to Karen and exclaimed, in a loud whisper, 'The most incredible thing happened to me!'

'Me, too!' Karen replied, shocked as he was, while making a similar effort to keep her voice down.

'When I went out for a pee, Maurice cornered me and told me he thinks Edna is trying to poison him.'

'Edna told me she woke up the other night with Maurice's hands round her neck.'

'Do you think it's true?'

'I didn't doubt it at the time, but now I've heard what you've told me, I don't know. What about you?'

'Maurice couldn't produce any evidence when I asked him. Maybe it's true, maybe they're making it up, maybe they're deluded – how would we know?'

'What should we do?'

'I don't know that there is very much we can do tonight. We'll just have to hope they don't kill each other…or us.' He caught her eye and burst out in nervous laughter. 'Jesus, of all the places we could have picked, we would end up in an isolated farmhouse with two homicidal geriatrics!'

'You don't think they'd do anything to us, do you?'

'I doubt it.'

'Do you think we should put something against the door, just in case?'

As quietly as possible, they pushed a heavy chest of drawers against the door, aware at the same time of how absurd their actions would have looked if there'd been someone else in the room observing them. They didn't bother with their pyjamas. They just took off their top layer of clothes and climbed under the bedcovers. Karen couldn't stop shaking. Her mind was going round and round in circles, with the night, Maurice and Edna, the kids… Trevor wasn't much better than her by this stage. They went to sleep with their arms around each other – for protection, love or both – like they hadn't done in years.

In the morning, when they woke, the whole house seemed unnaturally silent and still. It was a beautiful morning, without a trace of the previous day's fog. The rain had stopped in the night and a bright sun now shone out of a cloudless, blue sky. The paddocks surrounding the house sparkled like they'd just been washed. 'Everything looks brand-new,' thought Karen, raising the blind and looking out the window. Cockatoos and magpies could be heard squawking, screeching and gurgling at each other in the gum trees close to the house. But inside the house…nothing.

'I don't like this silence,' Karen said. 'It's not right. Do you think Edna and Maurice are OK?'

'Maybe they're not up yet,' Trevor suggested. He was still lying in bed with the covers pulled up to his chin.

'Don't be silly,' Karen replied. 'They're a farming couple. They should have been up hours ago. Not everyone keeps the hours you keep.'

'Come back to bed!' Trevor patted the cover beside him, feeling suddenly naughty, like a teenager, when his parents are away.

'No, Karen turned him down, sharply, irritated by his immaturity, his lack of grown-up concern. 'I want to go and look for them. Then I want to get out of here as fast as we can.' As usual, her thoughts were with the kids back in the city.

Trevor reluctantly got out of bed and joined her. They put their top layer of clothes back on, quickly returned the chest of drawers to its accustomed place in the room, opened the door and stepped out into the chilly, dimly lit hall. A bathroom tap dripping very loudly and distinctly was the only sound in the otherwise oppressive, alarming silence. They strained their ears for some indication that Maurice and Edna were up.

They walked down the hall to Maurice and Edna's bedroom, which they knew, from the night before, was at the front of the house. They both had a slightly sick feeling in their stomachs. Outside Maurice and Edna's door, they stopped and looked at each other nervously. Karen knocked, very quietly and timidly. There was no answer. Karen hesitated then knocked again – a little more firmly, this time. Still no answer.

'Hello. Is anybody there?' Trevor called, his voice sounding unexpectedly loud and shaky in the echoing hall.

Nothing. They looked at each other. As if in response to an unspoken agreement, Karen put her hand on the door and pushed it gently open.

The room was empty. Karen stepped in first and looked all around. There was the bed, which had obviously been slept in. The covers had been hastily pulled up. There was the cardigan Maurice had worn the night before, with holes in the elbows, thrown over the back of a chair in the corner. His slippers, with holes in the big toes, peeked out from under the chair and his stick leaned up against it. Edna's dress and cardigan – very plain and simple, and really quite elegant, Karen noted – hung on a clothes hanger from the wardrobe door. But there was no one there. The room itself was starting to grow cold, like the hall outside, as if no one had been there for some time. Trevor followed Karen in. They stood inside the open doorway and stared, both of them perplexed and increasingly worried.

'Well, maybe they're in the living room…or the kitchen…playing "no speaks".' Trevor attempted a jocularity he didn't feel.

They closed the bedroom door and walked back up the hall, past the bathroom with the dripping tap, to the living room at the far end. Trevor felt it was incumbent on him to take the lead this time. As he and Karen already suspected, there was no one there. The ashes of the previous night's fire still smouldered in the grate, but this room, like the other, was starting to grow cold.

That left the kitchen beyond. They both stared at the door, breathlessly imagining what terrible sights might lie behind it. Trevor was forced to take the initiative once again, as Karen was now quite clearly hanging back, urging him on from behind. He stepped up to the door and pushed it open. Nothing. That is to say, no sign of Maurice and Edna. But there were the makings of breakfast laid out on the table – some cereal, milk, sugar in a bowl, bread, butter, jam and a toaster. A handwritten note was propped up against the toaster. Trevor picked it up and read it. It said simply, in large, crude letters, HELP YOURSELVES.

Breakfast and the note aside, there was no indication as to what might have happened to Maurice and Edna, or where they might be. Their car could be seen out the window, parked in the garage at the end of the side drive, beyond Trevor and Karen's. A blowfly buzzed in the window, banging against the glass. Nothing else moved; nothing else could be heard – even the birds that had earlier been so loud in the trees had gone silent.

Trevor and Karen surveyed the scene, baffled and really quite scared now.

'God!' Karen exclaimed. 'What do you think's going on?'

'Well,' Trevor suggested, without believing a word he was saying, 'they could have gone out for a walk.'

'Sure!' Karen gave the idea short shrift.

'Then I'm buggered if I know!' Trevor declared, decisively. He'd reached the absolute limit of his interest in the situation. 'And I'm buggered if I'm going to hang around here and find out.'

'Do you think we should go?'

'Yes, I do.'

'Do you think we should have breakfast first?'

'No, I don't. We can always pick up McDonald's somewhere along the way.' A momentary flicker of the previous night's nervous laughter rose up inside him. 'Besides, this lot might be poisoned.'

But Karen wasn't amused. 'Come on, let's get going right now!'

They turned and ran like children back to their bedroom to pick up their overnight bags, then out to the car, pulling the chipped and scratched front door shut behind them. They jumped in the car, reversed out of the drive and headed back down the road the way they'd come yesterday in the fog as fast as safety – and what was left of their middle-aged dignity – would allow.

Some minutes down the road, they suddenly collapsed in hysterical laughter. Trevor had to pull over to the side of the road so they could recover.

'God,' screamed Trevor, 'what was that all about?'

'Who knows?' Karen screamed back at him. 'But we're better off out of it.'

They both laughed so much, their ribs were sore. They laughed until the tears ran down their cheeks. Then, unexpectedly, they felt like crying.

'There should be a signpost, somewhere close by, which will tell us where we are.' Trevor struggled to regain some control. 'We can find our way to the highway from there.'

'I hope it doesn't take too long. I can't wait to get back to the kids.' As she thought of Brigid and Quentin at home in the city, Karen began to regain some control over herself.

Trevor put the car in drive and they headed back out on the road. The whir of the tyres comforted Karen as the car carried her further away from the strange events of the night and morning, and ever closer to their home.

She reached out and touched Trevor's hand, where it rested on the console between them. 'We won't let that happen to us, will we?'

'I hope not.' Trevor patted her hand, reassuringly, concentrating hard on the road in front of him and trying not to consider the question too deeply.

Karen adjusted her seat, lay back and let the beautiful, sunlit morning landscape slip effortlessly past her.

Climbing the Mountain

Sitting behind the wheel of his car, Peter watched his father move across the front yard. His father moved with an easy confidence through his world, in spite of his age. It was a confidence Peter had always envied, never having particularly felt it himself, even in his own line of work, at which he was very successful. When he was a child, he loved to watch his father work with animals and machinery around the farm. He had the same, seemingly absolute sureness of touch with both and he was rarely proven wrong. To Peter's childish eye, it gave his father an almost godlike aura of infallibility which he'd never been able to get over – not that his father had done much to encourage him in that. His father liked to rule the roost in his own little world, and he still treated Peter very much like a child within it.

Of course, Peter had come to recognise that Bill – his father – was very much a fallible human being, all the same. In fact, he was at his most vulnerable now that the farm was being sold up and he had to leave his world. This was a cause of bitterness between them, because Bill had always hoped that Peter would follow in his footsteps and take over the farm, which Peter had never wanted to do. Instead, encouraged by his mother, he'd pursued an education and a career in the law, which had taken him far away from the farm, first to the city and then overseas for some years. He'd only started coming back to the farm very recently – and now it had to be on this sad occasion.

His father's face loomed, almost accusingly, in the open driver's window. 'Hello, Peter.'

'Hello, Dad.'

'You've come to take me somewhere?'

'Yes, Dad.'

'And where are you taking me today?'

'I thought we might take a little time, while we still have the opportunity, and go to the top of Mount Wales. Have you ever been there?'

'No, I haven't.'

Mount Wales was the mountain which dominated the view from the farm. Peter knew very well that Bill had never been there. Bill, in fact, had never been anywhere. He'd always been too busy working. Peter wanted to give him one last chance to step outside his familiar world – on this day of all days – to see things a little bit differently. It might be good for both of them, he felt. Peter wanted to show Bill, in some way, that he, too, had grown up, had a place in the wider world, did something which he was good at and people respected him for, and this might be a suitable place to start. Besides, he'd always wanted to go to the top of Mount Wales himself.

Peter noticed Bill was actually much slower than he used to be as he moved around the back of the car towards the passenger door. Up close, he was quite frail and almost doddery – a shadow of the figure of strength Peter remembered from his childhood years.

Out of the corner of his eye, Peter saw his mother, Marg, coming out the front door of the house, towards them.

'Now you take care of him,' she said, coming up to the driver's window. 'He's not as strong as he used to be!'

Peter wondered if this was code for something else that he should be seriously concerned about. But that brief moment of concern was overcome by the feelings of love and admiration he always experienced for his mother, who'd driven him on and refused to let him settle for a life of physical hard work and minimal financial reward like his father's – something for which he was extremely grateful. It created a bond between them which his father had always resented.

'You will bring him safely back home now, won't you?' Marg's doting, old face peered in the window.

Much as he loved her, he noticed with some sadness that she was ageing too, though not as much as Bill. Her hair had gone completely white and the lines were deepening in her face. She was developing that faint fuzz of down that blurs women's cheeks in old age.

'Yes, Mum.'

Bill muttered and groaned as he lowered himself stiffly into the front passenger seat. Clearly, he didn't care for modern cars like the brand-new BMW Seven series which Peter was so proudly driving. He was always much more concerned with practicality than prestige when it came to machinery.

'Your mother fusses too much,' Bill grumbled.

Peter flashed an apologetic little smile to Marg, who stepped back and waved them goodbye. He put the car in gear and they headed down the dusty, tree-lined drive, out the front gate and along the narrow, tarsealed road that led to the nearby, very small town of Longbridge.

It was Peter's intention to call in at the pub for a drink there before they headed off on the long road to the mountain. Saturday morning at the pub had always been one of his father's favourite times when Peter was growing up. After Bill had done his Saturday morning chores, he'd call in at the pub to catch up with his mates. The public bar overlooked the main road and commanded a view through the front window of the townspeople's comings and goings. Bill and his mates would have a few beers, watch the Saturday morning activity, exchange news, commiserate or laugh, then head off on their separate ways again, while Peter took it all in, wide-eyed, perched on a high stool at the window table with a glass of lemonade. Bill seemed more in his element then than at any other time, except when he was working around the farm, and Peter was hoping a stop there would revive some of those memories. He wanted to share in that male world with Bill as a grown-up, away from Marg's dominating, female influence at home. She'd never liked Bill spending much time down at the pub.

Peter was aware of admiring glances as they pulled up in the BMW outside the pub. He checked to see if Bill had noticed, but realised there was very little chance of that. They entered the dim interior of the pub and sat in their favoured position around the window table. A few men Peter didn't recognise were standing at the bar, talking to a new publican.

'Would you like a beer?' Peter asked Bill.

'No, thanks,' Bill replied, to Peter's surprise.

'You don't want one?'

'Nah, it'll only make me tired for later on – probably send me to sleep. That's what I'm like these days.'

'You don't drink any more?'

'Nah. I'm just too tired all the time,' Bill smiled, ruefully. 'Nothing makes you tired like old age.'

'Do you mind if I have one?' Peter asked, suppressing his disappointment.

'You go ahead,' Bill said. 'We don't have to be anywhere, do we?'

'Not at all,' Peter laughed. He walked to the bar and got a beer. On his way back to the table, he saw one of Bill's old mates coming in the door. 'Archie!' he called out. 'Come and have a beer!'

'Mate,' Archie hailed Bill when he'd got himself a beer from the bar, 'how are you? I haven't seen you in a long time.'

'I've been around,' Bill responded, without much enthusiasm, 'just not down here.'

'What's the matter?' Archie asked. 'You not drinking any more?'

'As a matter of fact, I've stopped drinking. I'm just too old.'

'Nah, you stop drinking, you're tired of life.' Then, realising this might not be a very tactful thing to say, Archie lapsed into temporary silence, nursing his beer.

Bill broke the silence eventually – with some difficulty, it seemed. 'I'm moving out, Archie.'

'Whaddya mean, moving?'

'We've sold up, we're packing, we're going.'

'Where're you going?' Archie tried to contemplate the enormity of life without old Bill, even if he hadn't seen him that often in recent times.

'Retirement home.'

Another silence ensued. Some local's dusty, battered old station wagon passed, heading for the bush, which started a few kilometres up the road. A tourist's flash new four-wheel drive – of which Peter noticed there were more and more in the area – passed the other way, heading back towards civilisation.

'Well,' Archie declared, after long deliberation, 'we sure will miss you round here, Bill.'

'I'm gonna miss you, Archie.'

But Peter noticed there was something lacking in Bill's reply, as in his whole discussion of the topic – a premature resignation, a fundamental un-concern – which he found disturbing. He wondered if Archie had noticed it too.

'Stay in touch!' said Archie, finishing his beer.

'I will, mate,' Bill promised, not very convincingly.

Peter finished his beer and they walked out of the pub's cool, shadowy interior into the full heat and glare of the midday sun on the road. The little knot of drinkers around the public bar door parted to let them through. Once again, Peter was aware of their envious glances, connecting him with the car. He was also aware that Bill was either deliberately ignoring them or hadn't even noticed them. Either way, he didn't let this, or the dis-appointment of not being able to share a drink with Bill, get to him. It was a beautiful day and they were on their way to the mountain!

They took the back way out of town. At a certain point, they turned off the tar-sealed main road onto a metal side road that headed across country to the mountain. Flanked by gum trees, it ran through open farmland for some distance – at first very flat, then slowly rising as the land began to slope upwards to the foothills. The paddocks began to have more and more trees in them as they headed up into the foothills, until, gradually, the bush took over. Now they were driving between stands of second- or third-growth bush. Most of this country had been logged several times. Not many people lived there. An occasional house appeared between the trees and disappeared again, to be replaced by the rapidly thickening bush.

'How are Nicole and the kids?' asked Bill, suddenly and unexpectedly.

Peter knew that this wasn't an easy question for Bill. He'd never been comfortable with the fact that Peter had a French wife, whom Peter had met while he was working in the UK. Bill found Nicole's accent, foreign ways and strange beliefs challenging, though he genuinely loved the kids. Peter was touched that he'd even brought the subject up.

'Oh, they're fine,' he said. 'Maddy's starting school next term and Nicole's all in a fluster. And little Ben is…growing up. He's almost walking now – at the pulling himself up and falling down stage.'

'They grow up so fast, don't they?' Bill mused, in a rather unusual way for him. He wasn't normally inclined to wax philosophical, even at this basic level. 'Just like you did. Just like I did, I suppose. And we keep on growing all our lives, isn't that what's supposed to happen? I wonder what happens if we stop?'

The conversation lapsed into one of the protracted silences which were much more typical of Bill's communication. Peter didn't really know how to respond to Bill's questioning anyway. When he glanced over, on a rare, straight section of the road, Bill had fallen asleep. His head had fallen over towards his right shoulder. His eyes were closed, his mouth was open. He snored lightly, like a child. Peter felt touched and protective. It felt a bit odd, but not uncomfortable, to be the one who was in charge and taking care now as they drove along.

The road was long and winding. Bill slept and Peter drove, trying not to cut the corners too much and stay out of the loose metal on the side of the road. He peered into the long tail of dust in the rear-vision mirror for any traffic coming up behind them. He put his sunglasses on, for protection against the disconcerting flicker of the trees' shadows on the road as the sun began to slant, ever so slightly, to the west.

By mid-afternoon, they were high up above the bushline and well into the foothills. It was a long time since they'd encountered anything coming the other way. Peter could see Mount Wales looming larger to the west and ahead of him, but he was increasingly uncertain as to how to get there. He suspected, somehow, they'd ended up on the wrong road. Driving under these conditions was tiring and he needed a break. It was with some relief that he saw up ahead a very small town – much smaller than Longbridge, even – among the trees.

The town consisted of a house, a hall, a CFA station and a general store.

With a crunch of tyres over gravel, Peter rolled the car to a halt outside the general store. He yawned, stretched and looked over towards Bill.

Bill's mouth shut, his eyes opened confusedly and he looked around, almost in a panic, for a moment. He was clearly very unsure about where they were. Then he saw Peter and relaxed, remembering.

'Ha!' Peter laughed. 'Did you forget we're on our way to the mountain?'

'Phew!' said Bill. 'For a moment there, I didn't know where we were. I was dreaming…' But what had he been dreaming about? He didn't want to tell Peter, but he'd been dreaming about his childhood. He was back on the farm with his father, walking across the paddocks, bringing the cows in for milking. It was a cold, grey day and their breath steamed as they walked. The dogs ran on ahead, barking and nipping at the cows' heels. Crows circled in the otherwise empty sky overhead… When he woke up, he was caught between this and some place he'd never seen before, which seemed less real to him than the dream. For a long instant, he didn't even recognise Peter.

'I've got a horrible feeling we've gone a bit astray,' Peter told him. 'I'm going to ask how we get to the mountain from here.'

He got out of the car and walked across the wooden veranda into the store. The interior was dim and shadowy, like the pub. It took a little time for his eyes to adjust. He walked to the counter and banged on the bell. He heard someone stirring in the back room. The door behind the counter opened and a middle-aged man came out, wiping his mouth and adjusting the waistband of his trousers. The man had black hair, slicked back like an Italian gangster, and very distinctive, V-shaped eyebrows, slanting dramatically up his forehead. He screwed up his dark eyes, squinting at Peter, trying to see him more clearly, silhouetted against the light, coming in the narrow opening of the door.

'Hello,' said Peter. 'I wonder if you can help us? We're trying to get to Mount Wales, but I've got a feeling we've missed the way somewhere.'

'No,' the man continued to screw up his eyes, as if he were trying to focus, not so much on Peter, as on something beyond him, 'you're on the right road. It's just a very roundabout route. You're actually not that far from it here. But why do you want to go up there?'

'I grew up around here…' Peter started.

'Ahhh!' the man said, as if that explained something he'd been wondering about.

'…and I've seen the mountain all my life…'

'Ahhh!' the man said again, with the same air of understanding something that wasn't available to Peter.

'…but I've never actually been there. In fact, I don't know anyone who has. I've got my father with me and he's never been either. He and my mother are selling up and leaving their farm, so I thought this might be my last opportunity to do something I've always wanted to do…and I thought my father might want to do it too. He's outside in the car.' Peter concluded in a rush, wondering why he felt obliged to explain himself to this rather strange man in such a detailed way.

'Ahhh!' the man said, finally and opaquely. He paused, then added, in what seemed to be some kind of veiled threat, 'You know nobody much goes up there any more? The road gets pretty rough after this. But that shouldn't be too much of a challenge for a flash new car like yours, should it?'

In spite of the heavily sarcastic tone, Peter felt obscurely pleased that the man had noticed what car he was driving – though how he could have seen that from inside the back room was a bit of a mystery. Maybe the back room had a window which looked out on the road, somehow. Still, Peter wasn't about to turn down any recognition that came his way in the middle of this increasingly difficult afternoon, which was turning out so differently from anything he'd imagined.

'Thanks,' he said, and laughed – he hoped, modestly. 'So I just keep on going up this road?'

'That's right,' the man replied, continuing to concentrate hard on whatever it was he was looking at, which appeared to be located somewhere over Peter's shoulder, in the middle distance, outside the door. 'It'll take you right there.'

Peter left the man still gazing in the same, grimly preoccupied way at that spot in the middle distance. 'I wonder what on earth he thinks he's seeing out there,' Peter thought, but he didn't have the time, or the inclination, to pursue the matter any further.

Back in the car, Bill was sitting up and looking round. 'Jeez, there's not much here, is there?' he remarked.

'No,' Peter laughed. 'The man in the store was pretty weird.'

'What else would you expect in these parts?' Bill laughed in return.

'How are you feeling?'

'I'm OK.'

'Are you enjoying it?'

'Yeah, it's very interesting. I always wanted to come up here.' Bill was sounding a bit more enthusiastic at long last.

'What do you think we'll see when we get to the top?' Peter asked. 'Do you think we'll be able to see the farm?'

'We'll probably be able to see your mother packing.'

They both laughed again. Peter finally began to relax. Maybe the day would turn out all right after all.

But, as the man had said, the going got a lot tougher from there. The road was little more than a farm track. The BMW's suspension wasn't really made for roads like this and it had some trouble coping with the deep ruts. The scrub closed in at the side of the road, obscuring the view, so it was like they were driving through a dark tunnel. They were quite high up now and the road got steeper all the time as it wound around the side of the mountain.

Peter looked over at Bill and saw, much to his surprise, that Bill had fallen asleep again. His head had fallen back against the headrest this time. Though his face was turned upwards to the roof of the car and his mouth was wide open, the breath that came out was feather-light, like a baby's. A thin trickle of saliva slid out the side of his mouth. Peter, however, was anything but repulsed. He looked at Bill fondly and smiled to himself. Then, going round a bend, the car slid in loose metal, and he had to focus on steering them out of trouble.

When he looked back, Bill's head had fallen right forward on his chest.

Something looked very unnatural about it, hanging there so loosely, bouncing around in a way that couldn't possibly be comfortable for someone asleep. Bill's colour wasn't right, either. His face was purple – suffused with blood. His eyes were wide open, though they obviously weren't seeing anything; his mouth was open too, but there was no sound of breath coming out at all now.

Peter slammed on the brakes. The BMW skidded to a halt at the roadside in a cloud of dust and a shower of stones. Peter looked more closely at Bill. He reached a hand across to feel for the pulse in Bill's neck, but, even before he'd touched him, he knew it was useless. Bill was dead. Peter knew it in his stomach, in the deepest part of himself. He knew it as surely as he'd ever known anything in his life. He knew, too, there was no point in struggling to bring Bill back. Bill had chosen his time and gone.

There followed a long, still moment. Peter watched the last of the dust settle. He saw the sky up ahead, which was starting to cloud over. He saw the dark, spiky leaves of the tea trees growing on either side of the road. He heard the birds calling, very clearly, through the silence. Slow, somnolent peace descended. They were alone, in the middle of a vast and lonely landscape, miles from home, miles from any other human being.

Peter stepped out of the car. He left the car door open. It was warm outside. In the afternoon air, he could smell the eucalypts which grew further back from the road. He turned and leaned on the roof of the car. He stared at the wall of scrub on the downhill side of the road. He thumped the roof of the car, as hard as he could, with the side of his balled-up fist. 'Goddamn!' he yelled. 'We'll never get to the summit now!' He was filled with sudden, overwhelming rage against Bill. This was his father's final evasion, his final refusal to give his own son any recognition, to do anything his son might want, to move even a little out of the world which he knew and over which he had power – his final act of frustration.

'You bastard!' Peter thought. 'Well, we'll get to the top yet. I'll take you there with me, whether you want to go or not.' He bent down to get back in the car. He was just about to lower himself into the driver's seat when he realised the foolishness, the irrationality of what he was doing. Tears filled his eyes. He lurched away from the car, around the back of it and over towards the scrub on the passenger side of the road.

He pushed blindly through a gap in the scrub. Branches whipped his face and eyes. He came out in a clear space on the other side. From there, he had a view right back down the mountain and across the plain. He could see the winding route they'd followed through the afternoon. The sensation of space was enormous. He felt like he was flying high above the plain. It seemed to him that he could see all the way back to Longbridge and the farm. In his mind's eye, he could see his mother finishing her packing and coming out of the house to welcome them home. 'What will she do now?' he wondered. From the vantage point where he was standing, he could feel the pain of her loss begin. He saw her face breaking up with the realisation. He wanted to hold her, to stop her from falling apart, but she was too far away.

He got back in the car. Bill was there, his head hanging forward, as silent and still as if he were carved out of stone. It was clear he was never going to move again. Peter lowered the passenger seat under him, as gently and tenderly as if he were putting one of his own children to bed. He tightened the safety belt around him, to stop him from sliding around. He tried to remember where the nearest hospital was. Slowly, carefully, he turned the BMW around and began to drive back down the mountain.

Where the River Ends

They parked the cars below the bridge, by the side of the dried-up riverbed. They took the picnic things out of the cars and began to walk up the riverbed towards the place where they were planning to have their picnic. There were eight of them, spread out in a line – four adults and four children. There were Mike and Ursula and their children, Matt and Andrea, and Nick and Delia and their children, Dave and Nettie. Delia was carrying the newest addition to her and Nick's family – the baby, Danielle – on her hip.

It was the middle of the day and it was very hot. The children complained as their feet slipped on the hot stones.

'Ouch, Mummy! I've twisted my ankle,' Dave complained. He hadn't been very happy since the arrival of the baby.

'It's so hot!' Andrea moaned, echoing Dave. 'How far is it?'

'Oh, Andrea,' Ursula reproved her, tartly, 'we've hardly started walking!'

'It's not far now,' Nick said, in a slight understatement. The picnic was really his idea, because he wanted to show Mike and Ursula this beautiful spot. The new house might not have been particularly impressive, but he wanted them to appreciate the beauty of its surroundings. 'It's a real mystery…' he continued, trying to whet everybody's interest, 'where does this river go? It's quite a big river, but it rounds the bend just below the swimming hole, flows into a big pool, slows to a little trickle on the other side, then just disappears…'

He saw the young children's faces turned to him with fascination. 'Aha,' he thought, 'I've got them!'

'It just disappears.' he repeated, for extra dramatic effect.

The children fell silent, thinking about this natural wonder. Everyone walked on silently for a while in the heat.

Redgums, willows and poplars lined the banks of the river. Massive clumps of blackberry grew down to the river's edge. The thick, tangled blackberry canes were covered with dusty, ripe fruit, protected by vicious-looking thorns. Summer flies buzzed around the blackberries – and every-body's heads and shoulders as they walked – giving the children another thing to complain about.

'I'll put insect repellent on you when we get there,' Ursula promised, wondering why Nick hadn't mentioned this problem before they started.

The heat was stifling. Just to move was a major effort. They all retreated into their own shells and concentrated on the simple act of walking. Sweat gathered on their foreheads and began to run down into their eyes.

'This place had better be worth it!' Ursula thought, suspicious, as always, of Nick and his bright ideas.

Delia grunted and shifted Dani from one hip to the other. She would've liked to hand her over to Nick, but he was carrying the picnic basket and the rug. The sky overhead was a clear, intense blue. The startling cries of whipbirds erupted from the bushes on either side.

The first time Ursula heard one, she stopped in a panic. 'What on earth is that?' she asked, her hand on her heart.

'It's only a whipbird,' Delia said. 'Well-named, isn't it?'

'God, it gave me such a fright! I thought for a minute someone was shooting at us.'

'Boy, I'd hate to go into real wilderness with you!' Delia thought, and sent an amused glance in Nick's direction.

Typically, he wasn't looking, but Mike was. He caught her eye and smiled wryly. He knew what a panic-merchant Ursula was.

The stones beneath their feet reflected the heat. Rising, it burnt their ankles and lower legs. The stones were amazingly smooth, shaped by the movement of water over centuries. At first, they appeared uniformly large, grey and rounded, but closer inspection revealed many different sizes, shapes and colours. The children stopped and picked up specimens that attracted their attention. There was one shaped like a finger and another shaped just like a heart.

In places, the river divided around bush-covered islands. As it curved around the islands, it looked uncannily like it had been frozen in motion. They seemed to be walking more and more slowly – especially the younger children.

'When are we going to get there?' Mike wondered. He was now leading the party, in spite of his burden of picnic things. He would've liked to take charge of the expedition himself, knowing it had been organised in Nick's normal, lackadaisical manner.

'Is it far now?' Matt asked. The oldest of the children, he'd been trudging along stoically, brushing the flies out of his eyes.

'We're just about there,' Nick replied, using his familiar, jollying tone, though it sounded like even he was beginning to have reservations, by this point. He knew what the other adults would be thinking. 'There goes Nick again, dashing off on one of his harebrained schemes. He wouldn't have thought it through carefully enough and everybody else will end up paying for his lack of foresight.'

Delia had already raised her concerns with him, before they left home. 'Do you really think this is such a good idea?'

'Yes, yes. It'll be cooler down by the pool and it's beautiful there…you'll see.'

'Are the kids going to be able to cope with the walk?'

'It's a longish walk, but they'll be all right.'

'God, you are such an optimist!' But, as usual, she'd gone along with his latest enthusiasm.

As they rounded another bend in this endless river of stone, Nick noticed, for the first time, the telltale signs of damp at the base of the stones. 'Look!' he said. 'You can see it here. You see how these stones are a bit wet at the bottom? Well, this is where the river reappears. No one knows where it disappears to. The locals say it goes underground, but who really knows? In a minute or two, you'll see running water, then we'll be at the pool.'

Sure enough, just up ahead, they heard, then saw, the cooling trickle of water running over stones. The children were delighted. They ran forward, bent down and put their hands in the water. They cupped their hands, splashed it over their faces and drank.

'Is it all right?' Ursula asked anxiously.

'Well, I drank it last time and it didn't kill me.' Nick's manner wasn't exactly calculated to put her fears to rest.

The water ran for a short distance through a narrow channel on one side of the wide riverbed. The rest of the riverbed consisted of heaped-up stones which made a kind of island with willows growing on it. They pushed through the willow fronds and saw the long-awaited pool. It was huge, as Nick had described it – long and shallow, taking up the full width of the riverbed. Its dead-calm surface mirrored the surrounding trees and sky. Other than the calls of the birds, there was nothing to be heard around them. They all gasped at the peace and beauty of the scene.

'Oh, good!' exclaimed Matt, preparing to lead the charge into the water.

Nettie wasn't far behind him.

'Is it safe?' Ursula queried anxiously once again.

The other adults looked at her, barely suppressing their longing to throw themselves into the water with the children.

'I think so, yes…' Nick temporised. 'It's only shallow.'

Mike cast a cursory glance over it. 'It's OK,' he confirmed, as if Nick's word weren't quite enough.

'Well, don't go out too far!' Ursula called.

'Hooray!' the children shouted and plunged in, clothes and all.

The peace was disturbed by their shrieks, first at the coldness of the water, then as they chased and splashed each other. Beads of water flashed through the air, glinting in the sunlight. The adults protested laughingly, as water splashed on them and the lunch they'd started to spread out on a picnic blanket.

When lunch was ready, the adults called the children. The children came running back, soaking wet and dripping like dogs on the hot stones.

'Come on, now, dry yourselves off!' Ursula commanded, handing round towels and taking changes of clothes out of the bag she'd brought with her.

'Lucky she thought ahead!' Delia thought, busying herself giving Dani a feed.

The children, as usual, were fascinated by the sight of Dani frantically sucking at her naked, swollen breast, though Matt, Delia noticed, seemed to be growing out of it. He turned away, discontented, and looked off down the river as if there were something of more interest to him there. Nettie, too, was divided between her childish fascination with the feeding and her growing desire to join Matt in whatever he was planning.

The children were dried, changed into new clothes, and covered with sunburn cream and insect repellent. The older children helped the younger ones while Ursula supervised. Delia put Dani to sleep in the shade. Nick and Mike discussed which of several bottles of wine they'd open first. Then they all sat down to eat.

The food was delicious. Everyone ate rapidly. The adults drank one bottle of wine, then another, growing steadily sleepier with the effects of the food, the alcohol and the heat. The children went back to playing in the shallows nearby.

'Jeez, that food was nice,' Mike said, always quick to express his appreciation of anything Ursula did.

'Delia helped, too.' Ursula hastened to share the credit.

'We should open a little bistro down here,' Delia said.

This was a recurrent fantasy, which they all knew was highly unlikely to happen. Mike and Ursula were making far too much money with their own extremely successful catering business back in the city.

'And this is a very beautiful spot,' Mike continued, knowing this would please Nick, who needed a bit of cheering up, with all the difficulties he was facing, trying to support a young family, plus pay off house and land, on a single primary teacher's salary.

'We've had some great picnics together over the years, haven't we?" Nick reminisced, feeling vindicated and a bit expansive. He was lying with his head on Delia's surprisingly taut stomach, from which Dani had so recently emerged.

Dani herself slept peacefully under a piece of mosquito netting. For a brief moment, everything seemed right with the world.

The adults all fell silent, thinking over times they'd shared. For Mike, Ursula and Nick, that extended right back to their childhoods.

Nick felt a powerful sense of intimacy with Delia. His head rose and fell with the breath in her stomach, only inches away from her sex. He swore he could smell its familiar fragrance rising towards him, like lying in bed after making love. He looked over, between sleep-heavy eyelids, at Mike and Ursula. They lay, by contrast, uncomfortably far apart. He wondered how things were with them these days. Ursula was always a rather stiff and difficult lover – not in the act itself, but afterwards, he remembered. For her, the intimacy of love was always more difficult than the intimacy of sex somehow.

He and Ursula had been boyfriend and girlfriend at school, and lovers at university, in spite of being such opposite types. In fact, their contrasting personalities might even have added excitement to the relationship. Mike had been best friend to both of them. When they broke up, Mike had asked whether it'd be all right with Nick if he started a relationship with Ursula. Nick said it would. Mike turned out to be much better suited to Ursula than Nick had ever been, and Mike and Ursula had been together from then on.

Nick was very happy with Delia, but he still remembered what Ursula was like as a lover. Apart from her desire to organise him non-stop, which she'd transferred quite happily to Mike, he remembered the youthful hardness of her body and the way she used to press herself against him while, at the same time, refusing to let him go any further. He also remembered her joyful cry when he finally entered her, as if her virginity were something, in the end, she was profoundly glad to be rid of. They celebrated afterwards with a bottle of cheap champagne. They were too different to last, but they had a lot of fun and they'd remained good friends ever since.

Delia had trouble with their history at the start, but, after getting to know Ursula, she'd come to accept it. It became something she and Nick hardly thought about, much less talked about. It was just there, a given in their relationship, like many others.

'Are we going to open that last bottle of wine?' asked Mike.

'Why not?' said Nick.

'You older kids look after the younger ones and make sure they don't wander off!' Ursula called. 'And no one is allowed to go in deeper than their ankles!'

Delia knew how Nick valued Mike and Ursula's friendship. But she also knew how the contrast between their success and his comparative lack of success pained him. She knew even a little of their money would make an enormous difference in his life – not that he would've asked them, of course. For their part, she was sure, they must have wondered why he was so lacking in initiative, why he'd never realised, as they were always saying, that people made their own opportunities.

'So how much did that house end up costing you?' Michael asked Nick. He thought the house was fine, if a bit small, and the setting was very beautiful, but he was curious as to why Nick and Delia had made such a choice at this stage in their lives.

'More than we could afford,' Nick admitted. 'It's eaten up most of our savings. But it's worth it,' he added.

'It certainly is,' Mike responded, approvingly. But he was really thinking, 'Why? It's just another example of the impulsiveness that's dogged you, all your life.'

Mike looked over to Ursula for tacit confirmation of his common sense in such matters, but she was asleep, for once, lying back in the shade, her mouth slightly open, snoring gently. He was feeling tired too. That last bottle of wine was making his head swim in the hot sun. Perhaps just a very quick nap… Nick and Delia were still awake, even if Nick looked tired and flushed. No harm could come to the kids playing in the shallows, although they did seem a bit further away than they were before…

Nick lay back. The day was working out much better than he could ever have planned. It went to show things did work themselves out, if you let them. You just had to have faith. That's how it was with the house. To most people, this might not have seemed the right time but he and Delia knew, in their hearts, it was absolutely the right thing to be doing at this stage of their lives. It was the natural expression of their love… His eyelids were getting heavier. His ears were full of the sounds of running water, and the children splashing and calling out to each other, though that seemed to be getting more distant as his eyelids finally closed…

Delia, too, felt the heat of the afternoon overpowering her, even though she hadn't been drinking. She checked on Dani, who was still soundly asleep under her piece of mosquito netting. She was such a good baby, feeding heartily and sleeping regularly – she loved her so much. She was a reward, Delia felt, for the other ways in which their lives were hard, such as the constant lack of money. She raised a corner of the netting and kissed one of Dani's silky-smooth, baby-smelling cheeks. The tiniest breath touched her like an angel's wing, like fairy dust… She wanted to curl up beside Dani and share her baby dreams, just for a minute. Those other kids, playing in the distance, would be all right, just for a little while…

Delia was woken by the sound of Dani crying close to her ear. She picked her up automatically and held her over her shoulder, patting her. As Dani quietened, Delia noticed there was silence all around them. There were no birds singing in the stifling heat of mid-afternoon, not even the whipbird's alarming cry. More significantly, there was no sound of the children playing.

The other adults, returning to consciousness, also noticed the uncharacteristic silence around them.

'Where…where are the children?' Ursula struggled to keep down the rising note of panic in her voice. 'What's happened to them?'

'Dani just woke me up with her crying,' Delia told her, 'and I noticed they were gone.'

'We can't have been asleep for long.' Mike tried to calm Ursula down. 'They can't be very far away.'

'Which way do you think they would've gone?' Delia asked.

'Well, they couldn't have gone far this way.' Nick indicated the wide expanse of the pool barring the way in front of them, surrounded by thick bush growing right down to the waterline.

'They must've headed back in the direction of the car.' Mike tried to sound as confident as he possibly could under the circumstances. 'If we head back now, we shouldn't have any trouble catching up with them.'

'Let's give them a call first, just to see if they're round here,' Delia suggested, calm and practical as ever.

'Bless her!' thought Nick, who didn't want any of the blame for this coming back on him.

So they called from the little stone beach at the tip of the island. Their voices echoed in the silence and stillness, rebounding from the bush-clad slopes around them. But no other voices come back to them, no matter how hard they strained their ears. Ursula began to whimper.

'Come on, then, let's start walking!' Mike urged them.

They packed up as quickly as they could. Once again, the men carried the picnic baskets, Delia carried Dani, who'd quietened now, and Ursula, out of respect for her upset state, carried nothing.

'I wish we'd never…' she burst out, hand over mouth, barely repressing a sob, as she pushed past Nick to take the lead.

Nick knew what she was going to say. 'Yes,' he thought, 'I'm going to take the blame for this. It's started already.'

He studied Ursula's rigid back, as she stalked along in front of him, radiating indignation. His eyes followed the undulating outline of her buttocks, through the thin material of her dress. Her long, slim legs strode out, determinedly, beneath. Like Delia, she'd preserved her figure, amazingly, after childbirth. She was as trim now as when they'd been lovers. In his imagination, he saw himself taking her from behind, gripping those lean buttocks firmly as he used to all those years ago. Somehow, she was always ready for him. He was surprised as much by the intensity of his desire as by its inappropriateness. Had the basis of their attraction been, he wondered, that there was so much tension to overcome between them? He could, quite literally, feel some of that old excitement returning now.

Mike had moved up beside Ursula. He was clearly taking charge. The straightness of his back, too, seemed to suggest that only he and Ursula were capable of dealing with the true seriousness of this situation. Delia had fallen behind a little, struggling with Dani on her hip.

'Go on,' she said, seeing Nick turn and wait for her, 'I'll catch up with you!'

He hurried to catch up with the others. 'Do you think they could've gone off on the side?' he asked.

They stopped and considered a worn-looking path leading to the top of the bank through a massive clump of blackberry. It made a rough hole through the blackberry, which a child might have been able to negotiate, at a squeeze. But the adults all stood and stared, hopeless in the knowledge they'd never get through. The vicious thorns would have cut them to pieces, let alone what snakes might have lurked within.

'Kids!' they called, in desperation. They felt themselves increasingly cut off, not just from their children, but from their shared pasts as well.

'Boy,' thought Mike, 'I don't think we'll ever do anything like this again! And if anything really has happened to these kids…'

'Where are they?' Ursula sobbed, caught between the panic she felt and the need she recognised, intellectually, to retain control. 'Bugger you, Nick,' she thought, 'you really have done it this time!'

Even Nick was starting to worry now, realising that something might be seriously wrong. 'But why would the kids suddenly take off like that?' he asked, attempting to shift a little of the responsibility away from himself.

'Who knows? They're kids. That's what they do,' Mike replied. He was feeling increasingly apprehensive about Ursula.

'We should never have gone to sleep like that,' Ursula said. At the moment, she hated Nick, Mike and all men, equally. Why had she ever agreed to come with them in the first place?

By this time, Delia had caught up with them. 'No luck?' she asked, adjusting Dani on her hip.

'None at all,' Mike responded, grimly.

'Well, they might just have gone back to the car, like you said.' Delia tried to stay calm and logical. She didn't want Ursula panicking, any more than Mike did.

'Bless you!' thought Nick again.

'Yes, but they're so small,' Ursula began to cry, 'and it's so far!'

'Matt would know how to find his way back to the car.' Mike cut her off.

'And so would Nettie,' Nick chimed in, behind him.

'But what about the little ones?' Ursula continued, in the same stricken tone. 'How would they keep up?'

'Well, we'll just have to trust.' Mike tried to console her. He wished Ursula would pull herself together, be more like Delia. 'Bloody Matt!' he thought. 'If they really have gone back to the car…'

Nick was happy to take the lead once more. 'Come on,' he rallied the others, 'it's not that far!'

The heat was truly oppressive now. The only things moving, besides themselves, were the omnipresent flies, which surrounded them in black clouds. They trudged on through the heat, waving the flies away, slipping and slithering on the stones. Sweat combined with the sunburn cream and insect repellent, stinging their eyes. Big drops, from their noses and chins, splashed on the stones and evaporated instantly. Their tops were soaked. Ursula bristled. Mike's thighs chafed, which added to his general level of annoyance. Delia shifted Dani more frequently from hip to hip. It was surprising how much a baby could weigh in a situation like this. They called out to the kids periodically, but there was no reply.

They rounded the final bend and there was the bridge, with the cars parked beneath it.

'Thank God!' Mike exclaimed.

But there were still no children in sight. They approached the cars in an awful silence. The ground around the cars was flattened and bare. If the children had been there, they would have been plainly visible. The adults looked up and down the river. Heat shimmered off the stones. Everything was calm, still, beautiful and absolutely empty, in either direction.

'Where can they be?' wondered Nick, now genuinely worried.

'I knew this would happen…' Ursula said, the panic taking control of her voice.

Nick felt the ground beginning to slide from under his feet.

'Now, Ursula,' Mike tried to prevent a scene, 'it's no one's fault…'

'I knew this would happen…' Ursula repeated. 'I knew we should never have come on this expedition. It's a typical of you, Nick – no preparation, no forethought. I had a bad feeling about it from the start. Why didn't I follow my feelings and stay back at the house with the children? When are you going to change, Nick? When are you going to grow up and accept the normal responsibilities of adult life, like the rest of us?' She faced Nick, unable to contain her anger any longer. 'What are we going to do now?'

Nick could hardly bear to look at her. He wished at the same time he didn't feel quite so excited by all this emotion, as if it somehow gave him power over her. Mike, standing alongside, felt – as he sometimes still did around Ursula and Nick – excluded, after all this time.

As for Delia, she was torn between her desire to protect Nick from Ursula's rage and her wish that the children would turn up soon, so she could get back to taking proper care of Dani. 'Ursula,' she pleaded, 'we need to stay in control. We need to organise ourselves so we can look properly for these kids.'

'Noooo…!' Ursula's voice ended in a scream. She was hysterical.

Delia and Mike tried to figure the best way of handling her. Nick was temporarily paralysed by the strange, uncomfortable mix of emotions competing for dominance inside him.

Just at this moment, they heard a giggle from the bushes on the edge of the cleared, flattened area where the cars were parked. They froze in their various postures, then all turned, suddenly – almost violently – to look in that direction. A small, tousled head peeked out. It was Matt, a lopsided grin all over his face. The others appeared behind him: Nettie, bravely backing him up, and little Dave and Andrea, following loyally, if uncomprehendingly, behind them.

'Surprise!' they said, as they'd heard adults do in such situations.

The adults simply stared at them, astounded. 'Where the hell have you been?' demanded a shocked Mike, the first to recover. 'Don't you know how worried we've been about you?'

The grin froze on Matt's face. He was seized by the sudden suspicion that things were about to go seriously wrong.

'Answer your father!' Ursula demanded, furiously. 'Go on, why don't you? Don't you know we've been worried sick about you – or was that part of the idea? Why else would you take off with two younger kids and just disappear in the middle of the day, leaving us to imagine all the terrible things that might have happened to you? You nearly drove us frantic. Then you turn up here and act like it's all a big joke. Well, I can tell you, it's not. This is extremely serious and you're in a lot of trouble, Matt!'

'Ursula!' Mike tried to protect Matt. He could see that Matt was regretful and hugely embarrassed.

But Ursula completely ignored him. 'You're a bad boy!' she was saying. 'You're a bad boy for even thinking of something like this, let alone doing it! What about your responsibility to the younger kids? What would you have done if anything had happened to one of them? You'll catch it when you get home, I promise you!' It was all she could do to restrain herself from hitting Matt right there and then – something she'd never done before. Her anger finally rendered her speechless. She spluttered into silence and found, unexpectedly, that she felt like crying. She would have liked to promise the same punishment to Nettie. Delia, she knew, was much too easygoing to give Nettie more than a mild reprimand. Ursula suddenly felt very alone in her adult sense of responsibility. Even Mike, who was normally her strongest ally, now seemed, for some reason, to want to protect Nick, on whom she would have liked to pour the full force of her rage.

The other adults stood round, embarrassed, not knowing what to do. Ursula was silent, struggling with her tears. Matt stood with his head down, humiliated. Nettie tried very hard not to catch her parents' eyes. The younger children were just confused.

'Why are we all standing round like this?' Mike finally broke the silence. 'Come on, let's get in the cars. Let's go home.'

'Yes, let's do that!' Nick followed his cue gratefully.

Children and picnic gear were rapidly packed into cars. At the end, the adults confronted each other, standing between the cars.

Nick was anxious to get back to normal, as fast as possible. 'Will you come back to our place? Come and have a drink before you go!' he offered, as a peacemaker.

'I don't think so.' Mike turned him down shortly. 'We'll go straight home from here.'

The adults opened car doors. There was a distinct awkwardness between them – none of the usual kisses and hugs goodbye.

'We'll be in touch,' said Mike.

Mike and Ursula left first. Nick and Delia followed them more slowly.

Even in the car, Ursula couldn't let Matt's behaviour go. 'What did you think you were doing?' she demanded of him, furiously.

'We wanted to surprise you.' Matt responded to her inquisition as truthfully as he knew how.

'Surprise us? I'll say you did!'

'Oh, leave him alone!' said Mike. 'He knows what he's done. He's not proud of it. It was a joke which misfired. Why did you have to talk to Nick like that?'

'He deserved it,' Ursula replied. 'He never plans anything. He always does things that way. It's time he grew up, like I said.'

'Jeez, you'll be lucky if he's your friend for much longer!'

'Oh, he'll be all right. It's not like it hasn't happened before.' Ursula was feeling more sure of herself by the minute as they travelled away from Nick and the peculiar ability he still had to unsettle her.

Matt slouched down in the back seat, sulking. In his mind, he revisited the exhilarating burst of freedom he'd felt, starting down the riverbed, leading the others. Andrea gazed out the window, unconcerned, happy they were going home now, with the air conditioning on.

Nick, meanwhile, was musing on the strength of the desire he obviously still felt for Ursula. It surprised him – even shocked him a little.

'You really shouldn't let her speak to you like that.' It was almost as if Delia could read his thoughts. 'It's not right.'

'Oh well,' said Nick, 'it's all in the context of our relationship.'

'Well, most people wouldn't put up with it, I'm sure.'

'Maybe they wouldn't. But maybe they haven't known each other as long as Ursula and I have.'

'Or as intimately,' Delia wanted to say.

'It's all part of our friendship.' Nick concentrated on the road ahead of him, with the same degree of intensity as, earlier, he'd watched the swinging of Ursula's hips. 'Friends can say those sorts of things to each other. We'll see each other soon enough.'

Delia stared at this man she loved, but sometimes barely understood. She wished, for the umpteenth time, they had a car with air conditioning that worked. She checked the kids in the rear-vision mirror. Nettie and Dave looked hot, tired and thirsty, but quietly pleased with themselves after their little adventure. Dani – bless her! – was sound asleep in her baby seat.

'I like Matt,' Nettie volunteered, suddenly. 'I hope we see them again soon.'

'Yes, darling,' Delia sought to assure her, 'we probably will…'

Grass

'Why don't you ever help me in the garden?'

'I do! I mow, I weed. I do what I have time and energy for.'

'But you never do what I want to do. I have such a vision of this garden. I want it to be garden beds with lilacs and roses up the front, and fruit trees and natives up the back, and paths so you can walk around and lose yourself in nature, in the middle of the city, but this damn Kikuyu grass keeps getting in the way… Why won't you help me with this grass?'

'I do. Like I said, I do what I can.'

'But you don't really want to help me. If you really wanted to help me, you'd help me get rid of this grass forever, not just for the next few weeks, until the next time you mow.'

'We've tried and it never works. The grass always grows back. It's easier to keep it under control with mowing and trimming the edges.'

'That's because you won't try. You have to keep it up week after week, until it's all gone – not just do it once and hope that'll do the trick.'

'Look, I'm happy to help you, but I can't do the impossible…'

'I hate this grass! It's driving me crazy! It grows everywhere…it never stops. I can't make a garden when it keeps taking over all the time and I can't get the help I need to get rid of it, for once and for all. You don't want me to have a garden. You don't want me to be happy here!' And so saying, Nerida turned and ran into the house, where she stood in the uncompleted kitchen, shaking with anger and frustration.

Lance continued mowing the lawn, because this was what he knew how to do. This was what he'd done all his life, since he was quite small. He was hoping one day his young son, Brian, would replace him and take over the mowing in his turn. Lance saw mowing as being the quickest and easiest way of dealing with the problem of the grass as he tried to balance out the competing demands of his full-time – or close to it – house-painting job, renovating the kitchen and doing general maintenance around their large suburban block.

But what he didn't understand was all the new ways Nerida kept coming up with to eliminate the grass altogether. This week, it was some method of spreading cardboard to kill the grass, then covering it with mulch to make the ground fertile, which she'd seen on television. It seemed like a lot of work, to combat what seemed, to him, a necessary evil – something they were just going to have to put up with if they wanted to have a garden. Besides, they never seemed to work, these methods of hers. They only seemed to encourage more growth, which cost him even more effort to control in the long run. Lance swallowed his mounting irritation with the whole situation and concentrated on pushing the roaring mower up and down the back lawn in neat rows.

Nerida could hear the two children, Brian and his sister Queenie, playing in the front room. She hoped they weren't aware their parents were fighting. She desperately wanted them to be happy, but that was getting more and more difficult when she and Lance weren't getting on very well. She felt alone, trapped in a situation which was far from anything she would have wanted, or even imagined, for her and Lance's marriage. It was at this moment that her phone rang.

'Hello,' she said, wiping her tears away and straining to hear over the noise of the mower.

'Nerida…' said the voice at the other end of the line. It was her older sister, Beatrice – she recognised the voice immediately.

'Bea!' she exclaimed. 'What's up?' Bea led a very busy and successful life as a corporate executive, interstate, and it was rare for her to ring Nerida, unless it was important.

'Nerida…' Bea repeated, in a tone which said, 'Brace yourself!' 'Grand-dad's dead.'

'Oh, no!' Nerida gasped. The news hit her hard. She loved her grandfather. As the youngest child in her family, she felt a special relationship with him. He was a very quiet and gentle man who loved to garden. She sometimes thought her love of gardening came from him.

'Nerida, are you all right?' Bea was, as usual, taking charge of the situation. This was how she'd deal with her grief, by running around and looking after everybody else.

'Yes,' Nerida replied, 'it's just that it's so sudden.'

'It was very sudden,' Bea agreed. 'He wasn't ill, but you know he was very depressed for a long time, especially since Mum died.'

'Yes,' Nerida said. She did remember – first, their mother dying while she was still very young, something which worried Nerida in relation to her own children, then their grandfather, who was already very depressed as a result of his war experiences, sinking even further into depression at the loss of his beloved daughter – a double blow. 'How do people stand such unhappiness?' she wondered. How did Bea?

'Look, I'm coming down for the funeral,' Bea went on. 'We'll all get through this together. It won't be easy, but if we support each other…'

'Good old Bea,' thought Nerida, 'still believing life comes with some sort of user's manual! There must be a right way – an efficient way – to handle every situation.' But, of course, she didn't say that. She just said, 'Yes,' as she did to Bea on almost every occasion.

It wasn't until she put the phone down that it really hit her. She felt devastated, weak and even shakier than before. As she walked to the back door, tears began to flow. That's how Lance saw her, standing at the top of the steps, shaking with silent, helpless tears.

That night, Nerida dreamed about the grass. In her dream, it spread itself across the back garden, making a soft, hissing noise until it smothered everything. The whole garden was covered in a knotty, tendrilled, green carpet which continued to reach out, entering the house through the back doors and windows, snaking across the polished boards of the interior, out the front door and windows and into the street, wrapping itself around cars and lamp posts, devouring everything in its path. It seemed that it would never stop and that living people, too, would be part of its fabric. She woke in a panic, her heart pounding, to find Lance sleeping beside her, his right arm draped heavily over her, his breath whistling in her ear, their bodies so close it was impossible to say whether it was his sweat or hers between them – far too close for comfort, despite her many requests to him to stay further away – so overpoweringly close that she felt she had to get away… She lay awake, staring at the darkened ceiling, until she felt calmer and was able to go to sleep again.

The next few days were taken up with her grandfather's funeral and Bea's visit for the occasion. The funeral was a quiet affair, held in the local church of the small country town where her grandfather had lived, attended mostly by family and a few old friends. Her grandfather was a shy, retiring man who didn't go out much and hadn't cultivated many friends, especially since his wife and his daughter died. Nerida, much as she loved him, had always thought there was a guarded quality about him, as if he were protecting some wound which wouldn't heal. Or maybe he just wasn't hard enough to live in this world, as she was beginning to think she wasn't either.

Bea was all right. Nerida, in her role as younger sister, just let Bea's super-efficient but well-meaning manner wash over her. It was the way it had always been between them and she didn't see any reason to change it. Even so, she – along with everyone else – breathed a sigh of relief and relaxed when Bea left. It was in this more relaxed mood that she went out into her sunny back garden at home, on the morning of the fourth day after the funeral, and found her grandfather, standing under the big, old Christmas plum tree by the side fence.

He came out of the shadow, under the tree, towards her. 'Hello, Nerida,' he said. His voice, as in life, was very quiet and gentle.

'Granddad…!' Nerida cried. On one level, she was startled – shocked – to see him there. On another, she accepted it quite calmly, as in a dream.

'I came back,' he said. 'I had to come back.'

'It's wonderful to see you,' she replied, and meant it. She'd been feeling so lonely, especially since he died. He was the one person, she thought, who might really have understood her.

'It's a beautiful garden you have here.'

'Well, it would be, if I could just control the grass.'

'That will come,' he said, with a quiet assurance which somehow gave her relief. 'We all have our problems, you know.'

This seemed like a cue. She paused for a moment, a little uncertain as to how to continue – or even if she should continue. In the end, she took her courage in her hands. 'I know you were never very happy yourself.'

'I was at the start – before the war – when I was young, riding my bike round the countryside in search of work. And I was happy when I met your grandmother…the happiest I ever was, probably. But, after the war, things were never the same again. The kids made a difference – your mother included – but not enough, I'm afraid. It was like I lost something in the war, some vital part of myself, and I could never fully enjoy life after that. Part of me was always back there in the jungle, running from the Japanese, and in such terrible fear…so much fear I can't even begin to tell you, Nerida!'

She wanted to reach out and touch him, to comfort him, as she would've done in life, but she found herself strangely unable to. Something held her back. He looked so tired, so frail, as if he might shatter at a glance, let alone a touch. It was as if he was barely there, and she didn't want him to go away, not now he'd come back to her. Just then, she heard Lance walking through the kitchen, returning from the shops with Queenie and Brian. She turned round to see them coming out onto the back porch. When she turned back, her grandfather had vanished. The shadow under the plum tree was empty and absolutely undisturbed, as if no one had been there.

'What's the matter?' asked Lance.

'Nothing…why?'

'You were looking very preoccupied when I came out here. I thought, for a minute, you might have someone out here with you.'

'No. No one.' Nerida wasn't quite sure whether she believed what she was saying. 'It's been a quiet morning. It's been nice, actually, having some time to myself.'

'Well, we've got most of the things we need,' Lance told her, referring to the shopping. 'We shouldn't have to go out again for a while. And the kids were really terrific.'

'Good!' Nerida said, her mind entirely elsewhere.

That night, she dreamed about the grass again. This time, it was in their bedroom. It grew with the same light whispering sound around the walls, across the floor and over the bed, where it entombed her and Lance. Lance moved closer to her, mumbling something in the dark. Their bodies rubbed together, like grass stalks rubbing in the wind. He was becoming excited now. His hands were all over her, grasping, touching. He was much too close. She wanted to move away.

'Don't!' she protested, struggling up out of sleep.

'You never want to make love any more!' he exploded angrily. 'What's wrong with you?'

'There's nothing wrong with me. I just don't want to.'

'Why not?'

'I just don't feel like it, that's all.'

They passed the rest of the night unhappily, lying as far apart as they could, on opposite sides of the bed.

The next day, she went for a walk by herself along the local creek, which ran through parkland at the bottom of the hill where they lived. The creek itself was a brown, polluted mess, surrounded by a detritus of plastic shopping bags, drink bottles and containers of all descriptions, many of them left hanging in the branches of trees after floods. But she found it – with its mute reminder of the natural world and the natural order of things – oddly comforting, even so. She was walking past an area where the creek widened into a muddy, sluggish lagoon, overhung by weeping willows, when she became aware that her grandfather was walking beside her.

'As I said,' he started, continuing the conversation at the exact point where he'd left off the day before, 'we were terrified. The Japanese shot the men who decided to stay behind and throw themselves on their mercy out of hand. Then they hunted the rest of us down through the jungle, like animals. The ones they caught, they shot. Often they tortured them as well. We lived for three months in the jungle, on the run, starving, in fear for our lives every minute. We could only sleep when we were completely exhausted…otherwise, any little sound woke us up. Our hearts would be pounding, we'd be shaking uncontrollably, imagining the Japanese behind every tree.'

'Why didn't you ever talk about any of this?'

'I couldn't. It broke my heart really. I wouldn't have believed life could be like that. Nothing that I'd experienced prepared me for it. It was like a nightmare, every waking minute. And when I came back, I just couldn't tell people about it, whether they wanted to hear about it or not. I didn't have the words – or even the interest, somehow. It was like the most important part of me had died, or been lost back there in the jungle, with the dead men and the heat, the mud and the insects, the never-ending fear and the exhaustion… and whatever was left didn't matter very much, to me or anybody else.'

They were looking at two people fishing in the lagoon, which, to Nerida's surprise and disbelief, people quite often did. They never seemed to catch anything; they just stood there, holding their fishing rods, lines bobbing up and down in the dirty water, with that air of quiet optimism she associated with people who fish. 'They must be true believers,' she thought, 'if they're prepared to wait so patiently.'

'I love the water,' her grandfather suddenly remarked. 'When I came back from the war, that's all I wanted to do…work with water. I was a hydrographer, you know.'

'I know,' Nerida replied. She'd heard this many times from her mother while she was alive.

'I had a great job. I used to go up in the mountains with some other men and measure the level of the water in the creeks and rivers. We used to stay out for a week at a time. It was so quiet and peaceful up there. I felt much more like myself there than I did anywhere else. And the other men left me alone. We all had things we were trying to forget, so soon after the war. No one got out of that lightly. So everybody understood, if you wanted to talk, you did, and if you didn't, you didn't. No one forced you. It made me feel much better. It helped me to cope. Of course, it was hard on your nan and the kids, me not being around very often. But I think your nan understood I needed time on my own too. Then I got that job working at the weir. That was better for your nan and the kids, because I was closer to town. I could come home every night after work. I missed the peace and quiet of the mountains, but I loved the weir for other reasons. It was a beautiful spot, it was important to the town, it made me someone around the town – someone people knew and looked up to a little bit. I was starting to feel like I belonged again, but when I went for that promotion and they turned me down, it broke my will somehow… I went back into myself and never really came out again. That made things very difficult between your nan and me for quite a while, and I didn't get on too well with the kids either. I just felt so disappointed and hurt by life, and I wondered if it was ever going to get any better.'

The two people who'd been fishing were packing up and getting ready to go. Once again, they hadn't caught anything, but that didn't seem to have deterred them. They joked and laughed as they packed up, happy to come back and try again another day.

'But I still loved water. And I loved growing things. That's when I got so involved with the garden.'

Nerida remembered her grandfather's garden. It was a beautiful place – a haven of shade and coolness in a hot, dry, dusty country town. She loved to play in it as a child. It was full of enchanted nooks and crannies where she was sure fairies and other magical creatures lived. It was a garden to make children dream and adults relax, forgetting, for a moment, their busy, fraught lives – the kind of garden she wanted to create herself.

'No matter what happened, I always had those two things: the water and the garden. That's how I survived. That's how I found some peace and satisfaction in the end.'

The people who were fishing had gone by then. There was no one else on the shadowy, tree-lined path behind them. Nerida looked up ahead to where the sun was setting on the far side of the main road. Rush hour traffic roared over the bluestone bridge that crossed the creek. When Nerida looked back, her grandfather was gone. She started home along the path alone.

'Where the hell have you been? It's getting late. I've been worried. The kids have been worried. What's the matter with you lately?'

'There's nothing the matter with me. I went for a walk, that's all.'

'You went for a walk? You've been away for hours. It's nearly dark outside. The kids and I were genuinely worried. What are you trying to do to us? And what are we going to have for dinner? Jesus Christ, Nerida, I've been at home working my arse off, and you've been enjoying a nice walk along the creek! I know this has been a hard time for you, but you've got responsibilities here too, you know.'

Nerida knew this was true. She could see Lance had finally begun work on the kitchen. His tools were spread out on the kitchen floor, along with bits of ripped-up floorboard and splintered panelling. Queenie and Brian, who'd been watching him working, clung to his legs as if for protection, looking at her with enormous, reproachful eyes. She wished he wouldn't talk this way, in front of them.

'I know. I'll try harder. I promise I will,' she managed to say, though, in truth, everything at home felt much too difficult for her to cope with at the moment.

'Good!' Lance didn't sound particularly convinced. Then he had an apparent change of heart. 'Look, love, I don't want to hound you, but it is hard on me and the kids, you know.'

'I know. I'm sorry.' Nerida wished she could feel what she said more deeply, but she just didn't seem to have time or energy for anything other than her own concerns right then.

'Good! Lance clapped his hands together, as if everything had been resolved satisfactorily anyway. 'Now what's for dinner?'

That night, Nerida dreamed about grass for the last time. In this dream, the grass covered the whole world in a thick, green web. Nothing could live or breathe under it. It was heavy, hot, dusty and dry…so dry it was taking all the water from the world. She woke. Lance was much too close to her, his arm around her once again. The heat he generated was fierce. She felt like she was dying of thirst. She shrugged him off, sat upright on the side of the bed and drank the glass of water on her bedside table in a single gulp.

A few days later, she was sitting in a coffee shop just off the main street of the local shopping centre. The coffee shop was a converted fire station, decorated retro style, with an amazing assortment of old furniture, amateurish paintings and posters sticky-taped to the red brick walls. She was sitting there, staring through the big, multi-paned glass doors at the street outside, when her grandfather came up and sat down beside her.

'Yes,' he said, 'the water and the garden. Those two things got me through. My relationship with your nan and the kids improved. The garden even became quite a talking point locally. People used to come from all over the neighbourhood to look at it. Do you remember?'

Nerida wanted to nod 'Yes', but she felt vaguely embarrassed, sitting there, in full view, at a window table in the coffee shop. Of course, she remembered. No one could resist the enchantment of that garden.

'I was happy then, for a while…' her grandfather continued, 'until your mother died.'

Nerida had been dreading this moment. She'd always known he'd get to it, sooner or later – the unexpected, early death of her mother.

'It just broke my heart all over again,' he was saying. 'I didn't know how I could go on after that.'

'I remember,' Nerida nodded in acknowledgement. 'It hurt all of us very deeply. I miss her still.'

'She was so young, so full of life. It just didn't seem possible that death would come and take her like that, so long before her time. How could any of us have known she had a weak heart? There was no indication, no warning.'

'You know that's what I'm afraid of?' Nerida interrupted.

'What?' Her grandfather looked at her, quizzically.

'Of dying young like that. Of leaving Lance and the kids. I don't think Lance could cope. Not like Dad did. Things are so different now. I can't bear to think of the kids growing up without a mother – or with someone else for a mother but all the time missing their own. That's my worst nightmare. Sometimes, when I lie awake at night, that thought goes round and round…'

'But it won't happen.' Her grandfather cut her off.

'How do you know?'

'I just know,' he said.

He looked at her and his eyes had the same calm certainty she remembered from when she was a child, walking with him in his garden, back when they were both happy, before her mother died. She felt oddly comforted to be back in that time. It was as if they'd come full circle with those words.

'That's why my garden is so important to me now,' she told him. 'It's kind of my protection against that fear. I feel happy – or, at least, not so full of worries – when I'm there. That's why it's so frustrating to me when Lance won't help with the grass…'

'Forget the grass!' Her grandfather cut her off once again, with the same air of calm certainty, but, at the same time, with an underlying urgency, as if he were trying to make every word – every second – count. 'That's not important. Remember, the water and the garden – they're what matter. Put your faith in growing things, not destroying them…'

He seemed to be fading away before her eyes. She looked through the panes of the door to the bright street outside, then back into the gloom inside the coffee shop, and she could hardly see him. All she could see in any detail were his eyes, which were pleading with her. She felt he wanted to hold on to her – where once she hadn't wanted to let him go, he now wanted to stay. Suddenly, she knew what she had to do.

'Look,' she said, as gently as she could. 'I love you, but you have to leave me now. I have to get on with my own life. I've been away too long. Lance and the kids are missing me. I need to get back to them.' She wondered if anybody was watching, if anybody could see the struggle she was going through as she sat in the coffee shop window looking out into the street. The sun flashed blindingly off the windscreen of a car going past. She looked down into the dark sediment at the bottom of her coffee cup. When she looked up, she found she was sitting on her own. She knew, with some sadness, but, at the same time, with something that felt almost like celebration, that she'd never see her grandfather again.

'I'm taking the kids and I'm going to stay at Mum's for a few days until you get yourself sorted out!' That's what Lance said to her, when she returned home. He was standing in the half-completed kitchen, surrounded by his tools. He was furious but trying hard to control it.

She could recognise the signs, however – the red face, the tears starting in his eyes. She hated to see him like that. She knew how confused and hurt he was by the way she'd been behaving. But she was willing to take responsibility for what she'd done and wanted him to understand that she'd changed. 'I'm sorry,' she replied. 'I know it's been hard for you and I'm very grateful for the way you've supported me through this. I'm aware I've been spending a lot of time on my own, and I've been neglecting you and the kids, but I'm over it and I'm ready to be part of this family again. Just give me a chance!'

'Give you a chance! What about me? Don't I count in all this?' His voice rose, indignantly, in pitch and volume. 'First you get this obsession with the grass. It's not enough for me to control it. You have to get rid of it completely. Nothing that I do about it is remotely good enough. Can you imagine how that feels?'

'Forget the grass! It really doesn't matter now…' she said, remembering her grandfather's advice.

'Then you completely ignore me and the kids,' he continued, unable to stop himself even if he'd wanted to. 'You're hardly ever here and, when you are, you drift round like you're in some kind of a dream. The kids are desperate for you to pay some attention to them and you act like you don't even see them. You haven't had sex with me in months. For Christ's sake, Nerida, what do you want?'

'I don't know,' she admitted, honestly and painfully, baffled by her own experience. 'But I do know I've been through a hell of a rough time lately. Granddad's death affected me a lot more than I thought it would. It brought up a whole lot of other things, like Mum's death, that made me feel very unhappy. In fact, it made me realise I haven't been particularly happy for a long time, and that's something you and I need to talk about. I'm sorry if I've made things hard for you and the kids. You know, as well as I do, how much I love them and I would never do anything to hurt them…or you.

But I had some things I had to get sorted out. I've done that and I'm feeling much better now.'

'Well, that's a pity because, the way I'm feeling at the moment, you might just have left it too late. You take some time and think, carefully, about what's happened. Then, if you're sure that you really do want to be part of this family again, you give me a call and we'll discuss it. Maybe we'll get back together or maybe we won't. It's up to you!'

And Lance was gone. She heard him collect the kids from their bedroom down the hall, heard the front door slam, the car start and drive down the street. She was left among the tools and debris of the uncompleted kitchen – which Lance was finally doing something about, after all those months of her asking – clinging to the bench for support. A final, brief flare of the setting sun lit up the kitchen as if from within. Normally, this was a moment she loved. But now she just felt hollowed out with disappointment. She'd come home with such high hopes, such a belief that things would really change. 'I should have known,' she thought, 'that things never turn out like we expect, but this is a very hard blow.' As the light died in the kitchen, she realised she'd never felt so alone. She knew she'd have to fight her way through the next few days – and after that? From where she stood, she could hear the grass grow.

Autumn in the Orchard

'This afternoon, I want you girls to rake up all the dead leaves and twigs in the orchard. Afterwards, you can have a bonfire, with some damper to cook in the ashes. Would you like that?'

'Yes, Mum!'

Alice and I love this time of year. We love bonfires and damper. We even love raking up all the dead leaves beforehand. It's more like fun than work. We do it every year. We look forward to this time of year so we can do this job.

Alice is two years younger than me. We both love winter, too, because you can wrap up warm and do winter kinds of things. So it's a sort of celebration for us – summer's over and winter's coming on. Mum knows it too. That's why she gets us to do this job. It's like a big game with us that she can join in too. Sometimes she and Dad – if he comes home early from the paint factory – come out and join us. Sometimes they bring sausages as well, and we have tea outdoors sitting around the fire before it gets too cold and we have to go in.

Alice and I race out to the toolshed, so we can get started right away. We pull the door open, check carefully for spiders, then take the rake and a big basket we use for putting the leaves in, and race to the orchard. We have a big orchard at this place. It's behind the house, in the back garden leading down to the creek. Alice and I counted once and we reckon there are at least forty trees in it. We have plums, apples, nectarines, peaches, figs, apricots, oranges, lemons, passionfruit and gooseberries…you name it and it's probably there. We eat fruit all summer and then, when autumn comes, we clear up the leaves.

We get started straight away, because we want to get to the bonfire fast. We take turns raking, then scrape the leaves up with our hands and put them in the basket. One of us takes the basket to the end of the orchard and makes a pile of the leaves, while the other continues with the raking up. It's a big job and it'll take us most of the afternoon – with breaks, of course, when Mum brings out cordial to quench our thirst.

We're just getting started, when a head of bright red hair pokes itself up over the hedge between us and next door. It's Mattie, as we call her – the older one of the two sisters who live there. 'Hi, Soph!' she calls out. 'What are you and Ally doing?'

That's pretty stupid really, because she can see perfectly well what we're doing. It just means she and her younger sister, Issy, have nothing to do, as usual, and want to join in with us. But I play along anyway.

'Um…we're raking up the leaves,' I say, like I just realised it myself.

'Yes, I can see that,' says Mattie.

She knows as well as I do what's going on, because she and Issy came over and helped us last year, not that Issy was much help. She's way too young to do anything useful.

'Mum says that we can have a bonfire, with some damper at the end, if we do a good job,' I add, even though I don't need to, because Mattie knows all this already. She and Issy stayed for the bonfire and the damper last year. I don't want them to come over again. Mattie tries to help, but she just gets in the way really. And Mum doesn't like them being here. She tries not to be nasty, but I know what she thinks. They don't wear very good clothes, they're often dirty and, sometimes, they even smell a bit.

'They're common!' I heard Mum say to Dad once when she thought I wasn't listening. I didn't know the word, but I understood what she meant from the way her voice sounded.

But even with all that – somehow – I can't help myself. I feel sorry for them and I have to invite them over. 'Would you like to come and help us?' I hear myself asking them.

'Oh, no!' Alice moans behind me. I can just see her, rolling her eyes and pulling a face.

'Yes, I'll go and ask Mum,' Mattie replies, and her red head disappears.

Of course, her mum will say yes. Their mum never has anything for them to do. They're bored over there with her. That's why they're always trying to come over to our place. I know, from what Mum and Dad have said, I'm not really being fair to her – because she's a single mum and everything – but it's true.

'What have you done?' Alice hisses at me.

'You know how it is. I had to say something.'

'No, you didn't. You could've told them we were sick. You could have told them we had the flu and were highly contagious.' She turns away from me, annoyed, and starts raking leaves really hard.

Suddenly, there's a burst of noise at our gate. Mattie and Issy come running through the front garden. Issy, as usual, trails behind Mattie, but she's running as fast as her stubby little legs can carry her. They're both very grubby and barefoot – something our mum would never allow. We always have to put shoes on, or at least sandals, before we go outside.

Issy is eating an apple as she runs. She has a cold and the snot is running straight down her upper lip, getting all mixed up with the apple. 'Mattie, Mattie, wait for me!' she calls out, through a mouthful of snot and apple.

'You hurry up!' Mattie calls back to her. 'I always have to wait for you.'

'Oh, no!' Alice complains, under her breath.

Watching her raking furiously, I can imagine her arching her back and bristling her fur, just like our cat.

'Couldn't we…?'

But it's too late. They've reached us already.

'How can we help?' Mattie's all smiles and happiness at having something to do.

'You can run around and pick up leaves with your hands and bring them back here,' Alice suggests. She's hoping, if we make it hard enough for them, they'll go away.

'Sure,' Mattie agrees, eager to fit in.

She and Issy rush off. Or at least Mattie does, with Issy following along behind her, munching on her apple.

We work for a while. It's going well. Even Alice is starting to cheer up. Mattie tries really hard, as she always does, even if she doesn't know what she's doing, but Issy just plays with the leaves between bites of her apple. She seems a bit distracted today – even more distracted than usual.

'Mattie,' I say, 'you can use the rake. You and Issy keep raking up the leaves, and Ally and I'll start making the bonfire down the end of the orchard.'

I give Mattie the rake. She's very pleased to have it. Now it's like she's doing real work. Alice and I take the basket and empty the leaves in a pile at the far end of the orchard. We add any sticks or bits of bark we can find. The pile's quite big already and it looks like it's going to burn really well. We walk back and see that Mattie's still working, but Issy's sitting down, crying.

'What's happened to Issy?' I ask Mattie.

'She's upset because our nan's in hospital,' Mattie says. She's nearly crying herself.

'What's wrong with her?' I ask. I know how much Issy loves her nan. She spends a lot more time with her nan than she does with her mum.

'She's got cancer.' Mattie's voice is hardly there, like she's got a great big lump in her throat.

'Our mum says she's very sick and she's going to die!' Issy wails. She breaks into huge, uncontrollable sobs.

From the kitchen, Mum hears her crying and comes running out to see what's wrong. 'What is it? What's happened?' she calls out before she's even in sight. She runs into the orchard like she's expecting the worst, like one of us has fallen out of a tree or something. She sees Issy sitting there and stops. 'What's going on?' she asks, in a dangerous tone of voice. She thinks Alice has been picking on Issy again.

'Issy and Matty's nan's in hospital,' I explain very fast.

'Oh!' says Mum, startled. 'I hope she's all right.'

'No, she's not.' Matty's still very upset. 'She's got cancer. Mum says she's dying.'

'Oh, that's terrible!' says Mum. 'You poor girls and your poor mum – how are you all coping?'

'Mum's very sad,' Mattie tells her. 'She stays in bed a lot and only gets up when we go to the hospital.'

'I see.' Mum doesn't sound all that surprised. She's got a pretty good idea what Mattie and Issy's mum's like, even if she doesn't have a lot to do with her most of the time. 'Have you had any lunch?'

'No,' Mattie replies. A single tear starts to trickle down her cheek.

I'm seeing a side of Mattie I haven't seen before and I'm sure Alice is too. She's much braver than I thought.

'Well, Sophie and Alice's dad is on his way home from work with some sausages we were going to have for tea. Why don't we add them to the damper and you stay for tea with us?'

'Yes, please!' Alice pipes up, being kind to Mattie and Issy for once.

Even Issy calms down and starts to brighten up with the thought of sausages and damper for tea.

'Would you like to come inside with me, Issy, and help me make the damper?' Mum asks.

Issy looks at her and nods. Her cheeks are completely wet. A river of snot is running out her nose. Much to my surprise, Mum takes Issy's wet, snotty hand in her own and leads her slowly back into the kitchen.

'Well, we'd better finish this before Dad gets home,' I say, feeling very big and responsible. 'Mattie, can you keep on raking the leaves, while Alice and I build the fire?'

Mattie looks at me, gratefully, and nods.

'Yeah, Mattie, you're doing a really good job,' Alice adds, to encourage her.

I look at Alice in surprise, but I see she's smiling and really means it.

We work until the leaves are all raked up and we've built the fire. The sun's setting by this time and it's quite dark in the orchard. We hear whistling and the front gate banging, which is Dad coming home. Alice, Mattie and I go into the kitchen to meet him. I'm glad to see that Mum's cleaned Issy's nose. Issy has a fresh apple and she's looking much happier.

Dad puts the packet of sausages on the bench and listens silently while Mum explains the situation to him.

'Mattie and Issy,' he says, very seriously, when she's finished, 'I'm really sorry to hear your nan's in hospital, but that's the right place for her to be.

I hope she gets better. They can do amazing things these days. You keep going to see her and give her all the love that you can. And give some to your mum too. She sounds like she needs it at the moment.' He gives our mum a serious, grown-up look as he says this. 'And now,' he opens his arms wide and speaks in a deep, important-sounding voice, like he's acting in a play, 'let's go and eat these sausages!'

We take the food and go out into the orchard. The sun has just set. The sunset clouds are red. The black shapes of the poplars down by the creek stand up tall against the yellow sky. The birds are going to bed.

Because they've been so good, Mattie and Issy are allowed to light the fire. Issy holds the box of matches and Mattie strikes the match along the side. She puts the match to the leaves and they blaze up straight away. The fire makes a bright spot in the darkness under the trees. Dad puts a couple of big, dried-out branches on it, so it'll burn longer and hotter, while we cook the sausages. We stand around the fire in a circle, all thinking our own thoughts, watching the flickering flames.

Jack-o'-lantern

I had that dream again last night. My wife was sitting looking at herself in her dressing table mirror. At first, the reflection showed her face. Then it showed a skull – a naked, disgusting skull, with hollow eye-sockets, a hole where the nose should be, and rows of teeth locked together in a never-ending grimace. I woke up sweating profusely, gasping for breath, my heart pounding so hard I thought I was going to have a heart attack. At the same time, a voice was saying in my head, 'She was here!' There was a kind of wonder in that, along with the horror. I reached over to the other side of the bed, in a gesture of hope, but there was nothing there. It was as cold and empty as ever.

In the darkness, I listened for any sound from my son, David, but there was nothing there either. He'd apparently slept completely undisturbed through what had been a night of horror for me. I muttered a little prayer of thanks – to whom, or to what, I don't know – that this should be so, turned over on my sweaty, rumpled side of the bed and tried to sleep again. Eventually, sleep did come as dawn began to creep into the room.

I was up early this morning, even so, partly on account of David and partly because I don't really sleep that much any more anyway. Every time I do go to sleep, it always ends the same way, with that dream of my wife, or something very similar. I went out onto the front lawn to greet the morning before David got up and saw my neighbour standing on the driveway in front of his garage.

'Those bloody kids!' he exploded as I walked up to him. 'I left the car out last night, because I wanted to start work on it early this morning, and the kids have stolen it!'

My neighbour, I should explain, has an old bomb he's always tinkering with as a way of filling in his time now that he's retired. The neighbourhood kids had certainly interfered with it before, but they'd never gone off with it.

'How do you know it's the kids?' I asked.

'Of course, it is,' he said. 'They've nicked it and gone off joyriding in it. Look at the date! It's just the time of year for that kind of behaviour.'

I had to admit he had a point there. It was coming up to Halloween and the neighbourhood kids were definitely showing signs of restlessness. Even David was pestering me to be allowed to go trick or treating this year. Some of the older ones were obviously graduating to more serious activities.

'It's still theft,' said my neighbour. 'Halloween or not, I'm going to ring the police!'

Much as I agreed with him, I doubted the police would take it very seriously. The kids had probably pushed it halfway round the block and left it there…pure nuisance value, that was all.

When I went back inside, David was up. He was sitting in the kitchen, waiting for breakfast.

'The neighbour's hopping mad,' I said. 'He thinks the local kids have stolen his car.'

David hardly appeared to notice my remark. At the age of six, the neighbour's old bomb of a car didn't really mean that much to him. 'Dad, please can I go trick-or-treating this year?' he started asking straight away. 'You promised I could.'

'Well, I didn't exactly promise,' I replied, 'I just said I'd think about it.' Truth to tell, I was reluctant. He still seemed a little young to me – even if I went around with him – and then there was the issue of honouring his mother's memory to consider.

Carolyn had been strongly opposed to what she saw as imported, highly commercialised customs like that. 'It's not traditionally Australian, Angus,' she used to say to me. 'They brought it in from the States and they really only use it to sell a whole lot of merchandise. I don't want him eating all of that sugar.' (Carolyn fought hard to keep him on a healthy, whole food diet.) 'And I don't want him being traumatised by all those stupid horror stories, or believing in a whole lot of primitive superstition either.' Carolyn had very strong views about a lot of things, which she was prepared to defend fiercely, although in the long run she could usually be talked into loosening up and having a bit of fun,

Thinking about Carolyn – especially with David there in front of me – brought back, as it always did, memories of the night she died. The memories were confused, which – in some ways – made them even more terrible. I can remember waking up and smelling smoke. I can remember hearing David, who was much younger then, screaming down the hall. I can remember leaving Carolyn lying in our bed – she appeared to be waking up, but more slowly than I had – and running down the hall to David's room. There was thick smoke everywhere, although I can't remember seeing any flames at that point. It was hot as hell and there was a terrifying roar coming from the roof. I scooped David up from his bed. He'd gone quiet under the heavy pall of smoke, and I was gasping for breath myself. I couldn't think of anything except getting him outside safely.

I ran up the smoky hall again, with David in my arms, across the living room and out through the front door. As I made it onto the front lawn, the house literally exploded into flame behind me. Flames were coming out the roof, the windows and the door, along with that thick, black smoke. The neighbours had already called the fire brigade, which arrived very quickly. I laid David down on the lawn. I was exhausted, shaking, weak, close to passing out myself. Someone began CPR on David to get him breathing again. Fortunately, they were able to do so fairly rapidly.

I turned to go back inside to see how Carolyn was doing. At that point, a section of the roof in the centre of the house, over the kitchen and our bedroom, fell in, sending a huge cloud of sparks up into the night sky. I was crying and screaming that I had to go back in, but some of the neighbours, assisted by firemen and the police – who'd also turned up by this time – restrained me. They wouldn't let me go – they forcibly held me back. I had to stand and watch as the firemen fought to bring the blaze under control until, finally, someone could go in…

David, luckily, was too young to remember much of that horrific night, but he certainly missed his mother, as I did, every day from then on. There wasn't a day spent around him, with everything he said and did, that I wasn't reminded almost constantly of her. It was like I was still sharing his growing up every step of the way with her. And at night, there were those dreams.

I was haunted by a dreadful sense of guilt. I wondered why I hadn't taken more care of her, made sure she was out of bed and all right before I set off down the hall for David. I wondered why I hadn't been able to get out of the house more quickly so I could have turned around and gone back in to rescue her. These thoughts, and many others like them, tormented me night and day. I felt I was living in an afterlife where nothing was quite real. I travelled back and forth between a shadowy, dreamlike place where I talked constantly with Carolyn – excusing myself, justifying myself, telling her how much I missed her and how lost I was without her – and the real world, which was dominated by David and his developing needs. Somehow, he and I survived, we made it through, but I still felt deeply divided between the world I had with him and the one I'd lost with Carolyn. One way or another, I told myself, I'd make it up to her for the way I'd let her down, the way I'd failed her.

And now, here David was, sitting in front of me, wanting to be allowed to go trick-or-reating for silly, bloody Halloween, which his mother would never have approved of. For a moment, I was tempted to say a flat 'No' – no more discussion, no more argument – but then something came back to me.

'Do you remember those pumpkins we harvested in the autumn?' I checked with him.

'Yeah…' David replied, a little uncertainly.

'Why don't we go out to the shed, pick one and carve it into a Jack-o'-lantern? That's one thing people always used to do for Halloween.'

'Yeah, let's do that!' David was considerably more enthusiastic once he heard the mention of Halloween. But he still seemed puzzled. 'What's a Jack-o'-lantern?' he asked after a short pause.

'You hollow the pumpkin out and carve it with a skull face. It has holes for the eyes and mouth and sharp, pointy teeth with gaps between them. Then you put a candle inside it and light it up. It looks very spooky and you can use it for a lantern – a light in the night-time, to guide the trick-or-treaters to your house.'

'Oh yeah, I'd love to do that!' David was completely convinced now.

We ate our breakfast in a hurry and went out to the shed. The pumpkins were lined up on a shelf at the back of the shed. I use the shed as a backyard workshop. It's got a good roof, a concrete floor and it's lined. It stays cool and dry year round. The pumpkins were well-preserved – as bright orange, round and firm as when we harvested them from the old compost heap at the end of the garden the previous autumn.

From the moment I opened the shed door, I had the strongest sense of Carolyn being with me. It was like she was standing right beside me. I could feel her, hear her, smell the perfume that she used… In reality, there was only David, but it was like she was standing between us, with her arms around both of us, enveloping us with her presence. I wondered if he could feel her too.

Carolyn used to make pumpkin soup and pumpkin pie with the pumpkins we grew at our old place. I'd made pumpkin soup with them since we moved in here, but not pie – I wasn't much of a baker – and certainly never a Jack-o'-lantern. I wondered if Carolyn would approve. I almost asked her, 'Is this all right?' except in front of David I suddenly felt foolish about speaking to thin air. But I got a feeling that she was coming around, that she was slowly warming to the idea of a Jack-o'-lantern, in spite of her very strong views on Halloween.

I took the biggest pumpkin down from the shelf and put it on the workbench. David and I had brought a spoon and a sharp knife with us. I cut the top off the pumpkin and he began to scoop out the interior. The seeds came first, then the stringy flesh surrounding them, leaving a layer of firm flesh around the walls. I inserted the knife and carved out an evil-looking, triangulated eye. David did the same on his side, revealing skills with the knife which were at least the equal of mine. He carved another triangle for the nose. The teeth were more of a problem. We drew them on the side of the pumpkin with a marker pen, then cut out the triangular gaps between them as best we could. I left him to shape the tips so they looked as sharp as possible, and stepped back beside Carolyn to admire him working.

I could tell she was deeply moved and extremely pleased. She slipped her hand into mine as we stood there, looking down at him. When he finished, he looked up at us with such an expression of contentment on his face that she gave my hand a squeeze and whispered, 'Kiss him for me, will you?' I bent down to kiss the top of his head and it felt like someone else took over. I kissed the top of his head once, twice, three times, four… I buried my nose in his hair, like I was drinking him in. When I stopped, Carolyn had gone. There was silence, emptiness once more, where she'd been.

'That'll do,' I said. 'You've done very well. Are you happy with that?'

He nodded his agreement, silently, wide-eyed in awe of his own handiwork.

'We'll put that big candle from the table on the deck in it and light it tonight to welcome the trick-or-treaters…' I continued, 'and we'll put some fruit and nuts out for them, too. I don't think your mum would've approved of us putting out lollies for them. That might be going too far. But I know she would've been very proud of you and what you've done today. And next year, if we can work the lolly thing out, we might just take you trick-or-treating. What do you think?'

'Yes, please!' exclaimed David. 'Can I light the candle?'

'Of course you can,' I said.

Falling Off the Edge of the World

When George Mellford broke up with his wife, he went to live in their country place in the little town of Longbridge, a long way from the city. George wanted to bury himself in the countryside and allow time for his bruised spirit to recover. He felt battered by the long drawn-out decline of their relationship. Since they had no children, the division of property was simple. The country place was his and she kept the place in the city. George had no further interest in the settlement than this, though friends told him he should have fought for a share of the city place much harder than he did. All he wanted to do was heal.

And he was sure he would heal in the clean country air. The country had always been his special pleasure. Janine had never spent much time there. It was boring, she thought. She liked the restaurants and theatres and art galleries in town – the kind of superficial, trendy, middle-class lifestyle that George abhorred. He could think of nothing worse than having a coffee sitting at a pavement table, surrounded by the hot press of crowds and the stink of traffic-infested roads. He liked the calm, clear Longbridge nights, with the stars wheeling over, the slow, solemn passing of the seasons and that feeling of sinking his roots deep into the earth of home.

Income was no problem, since George was a successful writer, though it was a long time since he'd published anything. He was half-afraid his public might have forgotten him, they'd waited so long for the follow-up to his first, extremely popular novel. In fact, one of the causes of the break-up of his marriage had been that Janine felt he wasn't doing enough. She felt he was resting on his laurels when he should've been out there creating and networking like Dave, their very successful friend, who resembled, as Janine said, a whole publishing industry in himself.

George had his doubts about Dave. He was undoubtedly highly productive and conspicuously ambitious, but George had always been suspicious of his interest in Janine. George sometimes suspected that he'd been cleared out of the way so Janine could get together with Dave, although it was too soon after the break-up of their marriage for anything like that to have happened. Still, that wouldn't have surprised him, as he felt he hardly knew who Janine was any more. She'd become a stranger, and not in a way that was interesting or exciting to him, but in a way that frightened him. He was lost. He couldn't recognise any of the once-familiar signposts in his life. He desperately needed time to recover.

Longbridge was the perfect setting for that. It was a scruffy little town in the shadow of the Great Dividing Range. It would never be fantastic real estate, but it did provide the advantages of quiet and solitude, which was what he needed for his spirit to heal. The house itself, located in the middle of an empty paddock on the outskirts of town, was built above a river flat and commanded an uninterrupted view of the mountains.

Day after day, that immemorial range sailed on into eternity, sometimes green, sometimes blue, sometimes covered in cloud, sometimes completely clear. It was never the same two days – or even two minutes – running, yet it was always there. George had only to lift his eyes up from the desk where he was working – or attempting to work – and there it was. 'I will lift up mine eyes unto the hills…' George remembered the psalm from the Bible, although he wasn't the least bit religious himself, and he felt as inspired by his view of the mountains as the long ago writer of that beautiful verse had been by his hills. Here at last, living all on his own, far from the city, working (sort of), eating and sleeping entirely according to his own needs and nobody else's, he entered an oddly timeless zone as his spirit began to rest and heal.

When he first shifted in, he found a cut crystal ball in one of the bedrooms, which he'd brought back from Tasmania once for Janine. He hung it in the window, where its facets filled the room with rainbow shards of refracted light, like a beautiful promise, like the hope he'd lost so long ago, he'd practically forgotten it… Seeing the beautifully coloured fragments of light dancing around the room, he came as close to tears as he had at any time since their break-up. That was why he'd set his desk up under that window and tried very hard to work there.

But the words wouldn't come. Day after day, they stubbornly resisted him. He forced himself, against his own rapidly growing reluctance, to bend over the desk for long hours every day, waiting for the voice in his head to speak, waiting for the flow to begin which would unburden him of all the sadness he was feeling. But the voice wouldn't speak; the flow had dried up as completely as the stony creek bed which ran through the river flat between him and the mountains. The page – or rather, the screen – of the flashy new laptop he'd bought himself, in anticipation of his return to creative output, remained an achingly unsullied white, as dazzling as it was disappointing.

In this situation, George started sleeping a lot through the daytime and waking up at night. He felt increasingly out of kilter with the rest of the small town he could see around him, which got up every morning and went about its appointed work, made money, friends, returned home at night to dinner, a program on TV, perhaps a late-night cup of tea, a warm bath or shower, and bed. George's became a world of darkness – except for those great, bright Longbridge stars – in which he felt completely alone. He began to think he might be going mad.

It was about this time too that he started to notice some activity in the beautiful old Victorian farmhouse next door, which, up till then, had appeared completely empty, if not abandoned. Someone was coming and going late at night, with the sound of a car engine running, lights on in the house, doors banging, sometimes voices…then silence. Curious, George began to spy on these comings and goings, using the binoculars which were nominally for birdwatching to peek through a gap at the bottom of the Roman blind in the darkened upstairs bedroom.

He could see two figures. One appeared to be a thick-set, middle-aged man, the other, a beautiful young woman – aged, he thought, in her early twenties – with long, blonde hair. They seemed to be together, but the young woman didn't look happy about it. The middle-aged man bundled her out of the four-wheel drive, into the house and, some time later, back out to the four-wheel drive again. The young woman didn't exactly resist, but she certainly didn't go willingly. Once, when the middle-aged man tried to kiss her under the front porch light, she turned away. George could see her face clearly through the binoculars. She was on the verge of crying.

If George had felt bad about the situation of his own life, he felt much worse about the girl's situation. He developed a strong desire to rescue the girl from the clutches, as he saw it, of the middle-aged monster. He cast about for a plan, but none occurred to him.

As it turned out, he didn't need one. He was up early one morning – after having been awake all night – when he noticed that the young woman hadn't, in fact, gone off with the middle-aged man. There was smoke coming from the kitchen chimney at the back of the farmhouse, and the young woman could be seen quite plainly out the front moving around in the early morning sunlight. George decided to go for a walk to inspect the boundary of his property.

As George walked along the fence line in the direction of the big, old river gums that grew in the corner of the paddock near the road, the young woman saw him. She waved to him, acknowledging his presence. He waved back and motioned her over. To his surprise, she came. She was even more beautiful in the flesh than she was through the binoculars. Her beauty up close took his breath away.

'Hello,' he said, hoping he sounded more confident than he felt. 'I'm George Mellford, your neighbour. I've heard you coming and going late at night, but I've never actually seen you,' – here he took a deep swallow, feeling very self-conscious and more than a little foolish – 'so I thought I'd introduce myself.'

'I'm pleased to meet you,' said the young woman, in a pleasantly straightforward manner. 'My name's Crystal.'

Crystal! George hated that name. It sounded like a character in a soapie, or a bad American TV show from the 1980s. Why did she have to be called that? But the woman was so beautiful, and her manner so trusting, that George almost immediately overcame his dislike of the name. In fact, it began to sound almost romantic and charming to him.

'Does this place belong to your family?' George asked.

'No…I mean, yes,' said Crystal. 'Actually, it belongs to my uncle.'

'Your uncle!' George was astonished.

'Yes, he lets us use it.'

'So you're not down here by yourself?'

'No…yes, I am. My uncle was down here last night, but he left this morning. I'm here by myself at the moment.'

'It's a beautiful place.' George attempted to cover his confusion.

They both stopped for a moment to admire the beauty of the farmhouse in the early morning sun, with its carefully tended rows of vines out the front (though George had never seen anyone tending them) and its long, curving, poplar-lined drive.

'Would you like to have breakfast with me?' he asked, recovering a little of his poise. He felt inspired – emboldened, even – by the beauty of the scene and the warmth of the sun.

'Why, yes…yes, I would,' said the woman, as much to her own surprise, as to George's.

And so it was that George and Crystal came to be sitting down in his kitchen, a few minutes later, listening to the kettle boiling and inhaling the warm smells of toast rising from the toaster. The time they spent together didn't end with breakfast either. Since both of them were temporarily at a loose end, they spent the whole day together…and many days after that. They got on very well, despite the age difference between them, and their time together seemed to pass in an enchanted haze.

They did things like swim in the nearby rivers and lakes. One day they went to the beach, swam some more, picked up some seafood on the way home, and had a feast at George's place – just the two of them. Another day, they went to the mountains, ate lunch at a pub that was strangely decorated in the style of a cattleyard, swam in the river behind the pub, stopped at a vineyard on the way home, and descended through a long, hot, golden afternoon to the plain again in time for dinner.

These days were perfect, except for one thing. George – who was slowly but surely falling in love with Crystal – would beg her to stay the night, but she'd always refuse.

'I don't want us to be like that,' she'd say. 'I'm happy with us the way that we are.' Then she'd rapidly turn the conversation towards some other topic, like George's Englishness, which fascinated her. 'You've got an English accent, haven't you?'

'I was born in England, but I came out here when I was very young,' he told her. 'My parents are both English. I feel like I belong in both places, but I belong most here.'

Her evasiveness of course caused George great frustration. Every night, he would have to put up with Crystal returning to her house across the paddock, then hear the four-wheel drive pulling up out the front. He couldn't sleep till he heard it pulling out again, crunching the gravel, in the early hours of the morning, while he turned restlessly, tormentedly, in his bed.

Finally, this became so much of a problem for him, he decided to confront Crystal about it. 'It's so unfair,' he said to her, over breakfast the next morning. 'You constantly turn me down and yet you go home every night to this man you hate. Why do you do it? You know that I love you and he doesn't. Why do you put him ahead of me?'

Her eyes glistened with held-back tears. 'Because I have to,' she said.

'For God's sake, that's the most absurd thing I've ever heard. Why?'

'It's a story that goes back many years. You have to understand the relationship between him and my father. There was never much love lost between them… Basically, my father owes him a lot of money and I'm the price that has to be paid for it.'

'That's not just absurd – that's disgusting! You have to do something about it!'

'No, please, you have to understand!'

'What is there to understand? A major injustice is being done to you. If you don't do something about it, I will!'

'No, you mustn't do anything! If you interfere, it could have terrible effects on my father's life and health. He's not well. He needs money for treatment. I know it's hard for you, but you must leave everything exactly as it is.'

'Including us?'

'Including us.'

George stood up from the breakfast table, fists clenched. 'I'd like to kill the bastard!' he exploded.

'You must promise me you won't do anything of the sort, or you won't see me again!' she pleaded with him.

He saw the desperation in her eyes. 'I promise,' he said, though his anger and extreme reluctance to do so were tearing him apart inside.

They continued much as before. The days rolled by in a timeless round of simple pleasures. On the surface, George couldn't have been happier. Deep down, though, he was terribly unhappy. He didn't feel he'd had time to fully recover from his break-up with Janine and now he was wrestling with a whole lot of horrific, apparently insoluble, problems in his relationship with Crystal.

The weather grew hotter and muggier. Thunderclouds gathered over the mountains. At night, lightning played around their peaks.

One day, George went out by himself to the local shops and, while he was out, he noticed plumes of smoke rising from three large fires up in the mountains.

When he got back, he pointed them out to Crystal. 'Look!' he said. 'There are fires up there. They must have been started by lightning strikes.'

The fires continued to burn for several days. Gradually, the smoke haze hid the mountains from view. The smoke spread from the mountains across the sky and formed a dome over the whole plain. The sun took on a brassy, bushfire glare at noon. The sunsets were spectacular. People began to talk fearfully about the possibility of strong northerly winds.

The winds finally arrived midweek. The temperature that day was feverish, at the end of the heatwave. Around the middle of the day, the sky suddenly became much darker, like an artificial twilight. The birds flew home to their nests, settled down and went to sleep. An unnatural silence fell.

George, who'd already done his preparations – such as they were, in the midst of everything else that was going on with him – was worried about Crystal. He crossed the paddock to her house and knocked on the door. There was no one there. He ran around the house, peering in the windows, calling out to Crystal and banging on the glass. The house was empty, abandoned, like it had never been lived in. George was furious. He howled, he swore revenge on Crystal's uncle. In his imagination, he smashed his fist into the uncle's reddened, drinker's face, he smelled the foul smoker's breath Crystal had told him about, just before he laid the uncle out on the ground and beat him senseless with a big, old gum branch he found lying around. But the fantasy brought him no satisfaction. Crystal was no longer there. She'd vanished, as completely as if she'd never existed.

George returned home. He listened, with increasing alarm, to the bushfire reports on the radio. Through the afternoon, the voices ringing in became more clamorous, more hysterical. By three o'clock, it was pitch-black outside like midnight in the middle of the afternoon. Longbridge was under threat of ember attack from the north. The smoke closed in until George could no longer see the boundaries of his property. He felt islanded on the tiny patch of land immediately surrounding the house, and completely alone in the universe, except for the couple over the road, who'd chosen this particular moment, it seemed, to get drunk and have a fight – every word of which was carried to him, with an extraordinary loudness and clarity, through the unnatural silence. Black leaves began to rain down out of the sky.

At six o'clock in the evening, the grass around the house turned blood-red, from the reflected light of the fires. Shortly after, the wind finally went around, bringing relief to everybody except the poor citizens of Longbridge, who were now, they were informed, under threat of ember attack from the south. Wearily, George went outside to confront the new threat.

He stood at the back of the house, looking at these new fires in the south, when he saw a giant, red cloud rise on the skyline. The cloud seemed to have a life of its own. It sailed up the sky as if under its own power, directly towards George. The sky overhead was completely dark, except for the blood-red cloud. George stood there, clutching his water bucket and a damp, knotted towel, as the cloud sailed towards him. He thought about his life's journey, which had brought him all the way round the world from England to Australia, to this particular place and time. He fingered the medal his mother had given him to remind him of his childhood home in England, which he wore round his neck. Janine and Crystal seemed equally far away from him and equally irrelevant. He wondered, idly, if he would ever write again. He looked down and saw, as if in close-up, tiny ants crawling through the roots of the grass. He knew, in that moment, exactly what it felt like to be one of those ants, confronted by a gigantic, hostile being towering above it. The red cloud came closer – ever faster, larger and lower down, it seemed. George braced himself and prepared to fight the fiery breath.

Long Shot

Far from the city and its famous harbour, the sun rises over the open sea. It's the beginning of another hot summer's day. The sea is almost flat, dimpled only very slightly by what would be waves if there were any wind, which there's not. The sky is completely clear, with the pale, eggshell blue of the very early morning, like a clean sheet of notepaper, an unwritten page. The sun is a brilliant, blinding disc which presides over an absolute silence – there's no wave crash or bird cry, no thump or chug of passing vessel. Time seems to stand still, suggesting not only is nothing happening now, but nothing is ever going to happen. It's a perfect image of deep and abiding peace.

At Sydney airport, by contrast, all is noise and bustle. The early morning flights are getting ready to leave. A reporter is interviewing an up and coming young Sydney film director, Michael Anthony, and his leading actress, Monique Levy (who is, perhaps, better known for her participation in soaps), before they leave for New Zealand to shoot some scenes for their next film. The director and the actress have that slightly complacent look of a newly established couple. They seem very pleased with themselves.

'What's your film about?' the reporter wants to know.

The director replies in a determinedly artistic manner, without wanting to give too much away, 'We're making a film about time, ambition and a journey back to the source.'

The reporter bravely swallows this and continues, 'So why are you shooting in New Zealand?'

'Because I come from there,' the director replies.

The actress dimples a smile, the photographer's camera flashes and catches the actress and the director flush with anticipated success at this moment of their setting out.

The director's wife, Moana, stands nearby at a large view window over-looking the tarmac. She takes no interest in the interview and doesn't share in its celebratory, self-congratulatory air. She prefers to watch the planes taxi and take off in a dazzle of flashing lights and a roar of jets, from behind the glass, in silence.

They fly into Auckland, over mudflats and mangroves. The airport is larger and more modern than Michael remembers it. He and Moana separate from Monique (with some reluctance on Michael's part, Moana thinks), catch a taxi to their hotel, rest up for the afternoon, then catch another taxi over the Harbour Bridge to the North Shore. In the light of the setting sun, the harbour is even more beautiful than Michael re-members it, with the white boats bobbing at anchor in the marina, the dark cone of Rangitoto flanked by the islands beyond, the shadow of the bridge on the water far below them, and the Shore disappearing in a smoky haze ahead – a fitting rival to the more famous harbour they left earlier in the day.

'We won't stay very late, will we?' Moana asks, anxiously.

'No,' Michael assures her, 'but I do want to see the old bastard again. I haven't seen him for quite a few years.'

'I'm very tired, that's all,' says Moana with an air of resignation. She knows how Michael and his father drink when they get together. She snug-gles closer to him and puts her head on his shoulder as if she were going to go to sleep there in the back of the taxi. Once, Michael would have put his arm around her to comfort and protect her. Now it seems like a feeble at-tempt at intimacy which Michael ignores.

After dinner, they sit at a garden setting outside Michael's father's study. Michael and his father, whose name is Mallory, are still drinking, which wor-ries Moana. She knows how drunk they can get, even if, at this stage, they're only getting started. The study is lined with books on all four walls, and has a set of French doors which open out onto the garden. There's a small area of lighted lawn, where they're sitting, then native bush, which Mallory cultivates, looming darkly beyond. The night is loud with crickets chirping, and dense with summer insects flying into the outdoor lights and dying.

'So what's your movie about?' Mallory pours another shot of whisky for Michael and himself. 'Moana?' he asks, proffering the bottle.

'No, thanks.' She stands up and goes back inside to wander round the study, looking at the books. Mallory really has the most fascinating collection.

'It's about living with a permanent sense of exile and a memory of the time when we were happy,' says Michael, when Moana has gone back inside.

'You're not happy any more?' Mallory lowers his normal, booming tone, sympathetically, so Moana won't overhear.

'We haven't been for some time,' Michael replies tensely. 'She doesn't like my lifestyle, she doesn't like living over there. She wants to come back. But what would I do?'

Moana settles down on the chaise longue in the far corner of the study with a book to help her get through what is obviously going to be a long night.

Mallory pours Michael another whisky, even though they're barely halfway through the one they have already. They show no signs of stopping anytime soon. As they drink, their voices get louder and more aggressive, continuing an ancient (for them) conversation.

'An artist has to be responsible,' Mallory, who's quite a well-known writer himself, declares. 'He has a responsibility to create for a wider audience than himself, to address the issues that are relevant to the wider society, to use his gifts to promote social change. Otherwise, what use is his art, to himself or anybody else?'

'But art must start with the personal and move out to the universal.' Michael mounts the opposing argument. 'Otherwise, how are we going to know if we're telling the truth…unless it's grounded in personal experience?'

And so on and so forth, their voices rising in volume proportionate to the amount of whisky consumed, half with love, half with loathing, until Michael finally says, in tones which apparently brook no contradiction, 'I'm a better artist than you!'

His father (who's always held his drink very well) seems to have the sense, or good taste, not to respond. Moana, as the only sober one there, calls a taxi, which takes her and Michael away. At the front door, Michael and Mallory virtually have to be forced apart, locked as they are in embrace or conflict – or maybe simply for balance.

The next day, Michael and Moana fly out by seaplane to Waiheke Island, where some of the scenes are going to be shot. There, they are reunited – fairly reluctantly, in Moana's case – with Monique, who's overjoyed to see Michael again and to be starting work finally.

Filming goes well for the first few days. The island is beautiful – as beautiful as Michael remembers from earlier days – and the weather is good, which is, of course, every film-maker's dream. They're shooting approximately five minutes of film each day, which is practically unheard of. The crew murmurs that it can't last, that surely some catastrophic reversal is coming.

On the third night, Moana wakes in the early hours of the morning from a difficult and disturbed dream. Her agitation also wakes Michael, which isn't good, because he has a six o'clock start scheduled.

'What the hell is it?' he demands, trying to be sympathetic but unable to mask his irritation.

'Oh, it's nothing.' She feels hopelessly confused. She wonders how Michael can possibly understand, with so much on his plate at this time, and the two of them not communicating – drifting apart, in fact – given his preoccupation with the film and increasingly, she thinks, with Monique. 'It's just…'

'Yes?' he prompts her, once again, more curtly than he intended.

'Do you remember when we went to see that guru in India?' she asks.

'Yes,' he replies tersely, bored with the subject already. Can she really have woken him up in the middle of the night to talk about this?

'I so wanted something to happen,' Moana goes on, 'but all he did was mouth platitudes. I was so disappointed. I was hoping he would say something which would…I don't know – light up my life, give me some direction, give me some hope for the future. I feel like I'm just hanging on your coat tails. Do you remember when we used to be partners? I don't feel like I figure in your life at all now. I need a life of my own. I need a change. I need things to be different.'

'I know what you mean,' says Michael – he hopes as sincerely as possible. 'Look, I sympathise with what you're going through, but can we talk about it tomorrow night? I've got that early start tomorrow morning and, if I don't get some sleep, I'm not going to function efficiently, and things are going so well, I want to stay on top of them… This could be the film that makes it for us.'

'I know.' Moana, as always, accommodates his every need. She lies awake in the densely dark room as he goes back to sleep, staring up at where the ceiling should be and listening to the waves dumping on the beach across the road.

In the morning, they start filming in the Tunnels, at the far end of the island. The Tunnels is an underground complex, built during World War Two, to support artillery which had been placed on top of a hill to stop enemy ships entering the harbour. It's a massive development, featuring what seem like miles of interconnecting corridors, all linked to a central storage depot, which resembles an enormous cave, buried deep in the centre of the hill, impregnable to attack from the air and difficult to attack from the ground. There are no lights now, if there ever were, so miles of lights and cables have to be run to make the location safe before filming can even begin.

When Michael and Moana arrive, the lighting techs are still running cables, so there's a considerable period of waiting around. Even with the lights that have been set up, large areas of the complex remain unlit and off-limits. The black of those areas is the black of absolute darkness and everyone's warned not to go anywhere near them.

As soon as they arrive, Monique comes up, whisks Michael away from Moana and monopolises him. 'Michael,' she says, 'I'm worried. This location is spectacular, but it scares me. What will we do if the lights fail? It's so dangerous. Oh God, I hope no one gets hurt! I've been feeling so vulnerable lately…about myself, about my performance… I couldn't bear it, if anything were to happen to anyone. There's so much riding on this for me. Do you think my performance is really all right?'

'Yes, of course it is,' says Michael, for the umpteenth time, used to the ways of actresses. 'I have complete confidence in you. I wouldn't have cast you otherwise.' He has no choice but to listen and reassure her. After all, she's the leading actress. The film has been financed on the basis of her reputation, such as it is. He doesn't want to go back to another dreary round of funding applications if he can avoid it.

While Michael and Monique are talking, Moana wanders off on her own. It seems the appropriate thing to do. Moana, like every film wife, knows there are long periods when her husband doesn't want her around – in fact, hardly knows she exists. She's grown used to this, along with other things, over the years of their marriage, so she obliges by quietly removing herself.

Michael and Monique continue talking intensely for quite a long time after Moana goes. Then the lights and cameras are ready, so they start filming. All in all, it's mid-morning before they think of her again.

'Moana! Has anybody seen Moana?' Michael asks at the end of a particularly difficult shot which has been engrossing everyone. He looks around. No one's seen her.

They search the lighted corridors and the central storage depot, flashing their torches down the side corridors and calling out her name, which echoes, amplified, through the vast space. There's no sign and no reply. People are sent to search outside, while others in teams search the side corridors. The side corridors are dangerous because they're in such a state of disrepair and have many deep holes which people could fall into. When word comes back from outside that Moana is nowhere to be seen, the search inside becomes more and more desperate. Panic begins to set in.

Michael struggles to maintain control of himself. It's important for everybody else's safety – and most of all for Moana's – that he does so. But he's filled with conflicting emotions. On the one hand, he can't quite bring himself to believe that something serious has happened. Moana has often wandered off by herself, but she's always come back. On the other, this location is so dangerous that anything could happen. He's angry that she went off without telling anyone.

On top of that, the filming was going so well. They only have limited time in the location and they were well ahead of schedule. Now they're falling behind, wasting precious time on this search. But suddenly, he feels a pang of sympathy for Moana. She hasn't been happy lately. It's true that they're drifting apart, for reasons he thinks are largely unavoidable, but he does love her – even if they're no longer 'in love' – and he hopes, sincerely, that nothing horrible has happened to her. He can't bear to think about her suffering. He knows, if he loses her, he will lose an important part of himself as well.

His PA and assistant director are at him to call the police in. They're terribly afraid. Not only are the Tunnels themselves dangerous, but the whole area is surrounded by high cliffs. It would be all too easy for someone to slip and fall, either onto the rocks at the base of the cliffs, or into the sea, which breaks on the rocks with astonishing ferocity, sending clouds of spray high in the air.

Monique comes up to him. 'Oh, Michael!' she says.

He looks at her in wordless need. She opens her arms to him and they cling to each other. Michael senses the comforting warmth of her body through her clothes, which – to be perfectly honest – he's already imagined in other contexts.

The police arrive. They set up a command post and search the Tunnels and the clifftops exhaustively. They make launch and helicopter searches of the surrounding sea.

At the end of a long and harrowing day, which goes on well into the night, Moana is declared missing. Privately, the police tell Michael and Monique (who stands supportively at his side during the television and press interviews) to prepare for the worst.

Michael turns more and more to Monique in the next few days. She's always there, unobtrusive but dependable, right by his side. Somehow, she's able to bridge the gap that had grown up between him and Moana over the last few years. He'd never thought he'd be this close to somebody else again – or not so soon anyway.

One night, after another day's fruitless searching, he unburdens himself to her. 'I've been so lonely.' he tells her. 'My relationship with Moana really was going nowhere…had been for a long time. It was a long way from anything either of us wanted when we started out. It made me sad and angry, because it was such a waste. But, realistically, things like that happen between people, I suppose. We grew apart. Our lives went in separate directions. I could accept that. But now she's disappeared, I'm left in a kind of limbo and I don't know what to do. I try to imagine a future – for her, for me, for any of us – but I can't. And there's the pressure of the film on top of all that! I can't function like this, where nothing is resolved…' He's on the verge of breaking down.

Monique listens like the good friend she is, but with an understanding that goes beyond that as well. She's got to know Michael first of all from working with him, then from having been through the last few days with him, and now she knows what he really needs.

'Michael, I know it's been hard for you, but I'm here for you now. You can count on me. Things will turn out all right, you'll see…' she murmurs as she takes him, once more, in her arms.

That night, they become lovers.

Michael feels renewed, able to go on. Everyone remarks on the change in him, though he and Monique are necessarily discreet. No one else knows about their relationship, though some have their suspicions.

After a few more unsuccessful days, the police call the search off. Moana, they say, has disappeared without trace. There's no evidence of foul play. Neither is there any evidence of suicide. It's simply one of those mysterious events which occur from time to time for which there is no apparent explanation. Maybe the mystery will be solved eventually – maybe not. The currents in that area are notoriously tricky and can carry a body straight out to sea. In the absence of any definitive proof, there's nothing more the police can do.

Michael and Monique call the cast and crew together. They talk about the terrible time they've all been through. But there's no other choice, they say, except to complete what they came here to do.

'Moana would have wanted that,' Michael declares. 'Let's finish this for her!'

Cast and crew erupt into spontaneous applause. Many have tears in their eyes. They settle down to the hard task of catching up the time they've lost, with more determination than ever.

Shooting on the island wraps within a few days. Michael and Monique are in a curious mood – still overhung by the sadness of Moana's disappearance but in a mood to celebrate their new love and the progress they're making with the film, which they believe is looking very good. It brings back to them the feeling they had on leaving Sydney.

That night, they take a ferry from the island to the city. They've been invited by an old friend of Michael's to a party in Ponsonby. When they get there, Michael finds, in fact, that he feels a bit odd about introducing Monique into a circle of friends most of whom remember and associate him with Moana. He feels odd, too, to be off the island, which has been like a separate, self-enclosed space for him and Monique, and out in the world again. He feels suddenly exposed, uncertain, adrift.

The party is loud and crowded. Michael gets very drunk and stoned. Monique is left standing on the sidelines as he sinks into a sea of familiar – and some less familiar – faces. There is one woman there he hardly knows but who seems very attracted to him. Monique is completely forgotten as Michael and this other woman talk.

'And what do you do?' she asks him.

'I'm a film director,' he replies, full of the boldness that comes with being drunk and stoned, but not yet completely out of control. 'And a very good one, too.'

'Have I heard of you?'

'Probably not. But you will.'

'Are you working on anything at the moment?'

'Yes, I've been shooting scenes for a film I'm making out on Waiheke. But we've finished shooting there and we've come back to town to shoot a few more scenes here.'

'Oh, I heard about that…' the woman exclaims, then realises she's about to commit a terrible faux pas.

'It's been tough,' says Michael. He and the woman, whose name is Moira, get on like a house on fire. It's a relief, he realises, to be talking to someone who's not intimately associated with the film and his tragedy. It absolves him of responsibility, makes him feel like he could be someone else for a night and leave all the complications of his life behind, even if only for a short time – a feeling he could never have with Monique, for instance, in spite of the invaluable support she's offered him.

Somehow, he loses sight of Monique in the blur of the night. He assumes she's found some entertainment of her own – after all, they're not tied together. Eventually, Moira invites him back to her place in Parnell, and he accepts willingly.

She drives a convertible. He lets his head lie back on the thickly padded, tan leather headrest and looks up at the stars. He wishes the sky would open and swallow him up, that he could be anyone from anywhere and no longer burdened by his own sad, confused self.

He and Moira aren't so far gone that they can't make love several times, enthusiastically, before dawn. Then he sleeps the heavy, drugged sleep of total forgetfulness. When he wakes, he feels terrible. His head hammers; he feels nauseous, exhausted. It's as if everything he's experienced in the last while has come down on him at once.

He excuses himself from spending the day with Moira, saying life has been so busy and traumatic lately, he desperately needs to spend time on his own. She's worried about him, but lets him go. He buys her off with the vague promise that he'll ring her sometime soon, which, of course, he has no intention of doing.

He staggers downhill to Parnell Village. It's still comparatively early Sunday morning, and there aren't many people about. He orders a coffee and sits, nursing his throbbing head in his hands. Monique has been trying to reach him on his phone. He messages her, to let her know where he is.

'Hold on. I'll come & get u. I luv u, Monique,' she messages back.

He's too tired to run away any more.

She arrives half an hour later. She steps out of a taxi, looking radiant. The Sunday morning crowd, which is slowly gathering, parts to let her through. They don't know who she is, but they think she must be some kind of celebrity, looking like that. She makes her way over to Michael.

He feels thoroughly ashamed, but oddly defiant, too. After all, this is his life. No one else can tell him how to live it.

'How are you?' she asks.

'I'm all right,' he mumbles.

'Do you think this makes any difference to us?'

'No, I suppose not. That's up to you.'

'No, it's not. It's up to both of us. Michael, I care about you. I realise you've been terribly hurt. I'm trying to reach you.'

'Well, we'll have to see.'

'And what about this film?'

'What about the film?'

'Are you going to be able to finish it?'

'I'll finish it.'

A year later, Michael is sitting in an office high above Sydney Harbour talking to his producer and a group of his investors.

'What is this, Michael?' his producer's saying. 'You've brought in a film which starts out with one story that never gets finished, then it starts another and that doesn't get finished either. Does this film have an ending and is it anything that anyone else can understand?'

'Michael,' one of his investors asks, anxiously, 'we can appreciate that you've been through a terrible time, but we did place a trust in you and what we want to know is, who is this film aimed at? What kind of audience do you expect for it?'

'I've made the film I set out to make,' declares Michael, who's feeling stronger all the time now, 'and I didn't let anything stop me.' He says that with a growing sense of pride, as well as the pain that's accompanied him through the past year. 'I think it will find its own audience.'

'But what kind of audience will that be?' asks another of his investors. 'After all, we have to market this film.'

'Anybody who's interested in the problems of modern life – how we feel about each other, the limits to knowledge, the absence of meaning, the apparently random nature of existence…of life anytime, I suppose,' Michael replies, aware that no one's listening to him.

The others are much too preoccupied with their own problems to take in what he's trying to say.

'Yes, but is it finished?' cries his producer, in exasperation.

Michael looks out the window. He can see clear to Sydney Heads and the ocean beyond. The harbour is a mirror this morning. Summer is nearly over. The risen sun shines a blazing path on the water underneath the bridge and right out to sea. There are times now when he begins to understand Moana and that strange, terrifying decision she made. 'Will I ever feel like that?' he wonders. 'Will I ever be able to walk away from all this?'

The harbour has no answer for him. Its surface doesn't move and nothing moves on its surface either. After everything he's been through, nothing's changed. For the first time since Moana's disappearance, he feels the beginnings of peace coming over him – not a deep and abiding peace, but peace nevertheless. He longs to take out his notebook and start scribbling again.

'It's finished,' he says.

A Man Adrift

Daniel Diver stood up to his waist in the sea. It was a beautiful day. The sky was bright blue, with fluffy white clouds blowing over in the slight wind. The sea was bottle-green. The offshore wind held the sea up in small waves, each capped by its white mantle of breaking foam. Seagulls squawked and swooped above him, and little children screamed and ran from the waves, or tried to surf them, all around him. The waves broke around Daniel's middle and splashed up onto his chest, which recoiled in shock from the sudden cold to which his nether regions had already succumbed. He knew, sooner or later, he would have to immerse himself totally in the frigid water but, as yet, he lacked the courage to do so.

It was just at that moment that he saw something white and solid roll over and flash between the waves further out. At first, he thought it was a large fish – maybe a dolphin or a shark – although the colour was wrong and there was no fin. Then he realised, with a rush of horror that made him feel sick to his stomach and breathless at the same time, that it was a man. When it surfaced again a little further in, he could see, quite plainly, the man's head, with its mop of greying hair, lolling above his shoulders. The eyes were closed and the expression oddly peaceful, as if the man were relaxing there, buoyed up and down by the waves. For a moment, Daniel thought it might be just that – someone relaxing, floating on his back, who had somehow drifted out there and who, in a moment, would realise where he was and come swimming back in. But then he knew, with the hard, cold impact of reality, like a wave breaking over him, that the man was dead and what he was seeing was a drowned body washing back to shore.

Other people began seeing it, at the same time.

'Look! What's that?' people were calling out, and then, 'Uuuurgh!' – in shock and disgust – 'He's dead! It's a drowned body! Look, out there!'

And suddenly, Daniel found himself moving, swimming out through the breaking waves, hardly conscious now of the water's temperature, towards the incoming body. He bumped into the body, or the body bumped into him, he wasn't sure which. It was solid, heavy and very, very cold. He seized it by an arm, then attempted, by a hand cupped under its chin, to tow it in to shore on its back the way he'd been shown in childhood to rescue a drowning person. But the body was large and awkward, made even more so by the waterlogged T-shirt and board shorts with which it was clothed, and progress was very slow. Fortunately, by this time, other people had arrived and they all trod water around the body, holding it up until the surf skiff came. The lifeguards loaded the body onto the skiff and paddled the skiff back to the beach, surfing the waves into the shallows.

On the beach, the lifeguards worked on the body in vain until the ambulance arrived. The man was dead and obviously had been for some time. In front of the silent crowd, paramedics loaded the body into the ambulance and drove away. The whole event cast a pall over the afternoon, like a heavy, dark rain cloud replacing the fluffy white clouds and overshadowing everything beneath. But within ten minutes, everyone – especially the children – had forgotten about it and gone back to enjoying themselves in the sea and sun.

Everyone except Daniel Diver, that is. He couldn't forget the beauty of the day, the horror of his first sighting of the body, swimming out to it through the waves, its size, its weight, its lifelessness… He couldn't forget it then and he couldn't forget it for a long time afterwards either. He went on and on thinking about it, wondering who the dead man was, how he'd come to be in that situation, who his family and friends were and how they were handling this shocking turn of events.

Daniel had recently been laid off from his job, divorced from his wife of many years and separated, as a result, from his growing family. He was washed up in middle age, loveless and jobless. When he touched the dead man, he identified a kind of numbness, a deadness, inside himself.

'It could have been me,' he thought, over and over. 'Why wasn't it me? What is it that makes the difference between those who die and those who survive in life? Is it just luck, or is it something more than that?'

From the media, he learned that the dead man was a well-known painter, Clive Montgomery, who'd gone missing from his home the day before. That might have quieted his mind had it not said at the end of the article, 'Police are investigating'. Investigating what? Surely this wasn't a murder? There'd been no signs of violence on the body. Was it a suicide then? Why would a successful man like that – a man who apparently had everything to live for – commit suicide?

Things became a little clearer over the next few days. Social media, radio, TV and the papers all carried items reviewing Montgomery's life and career. They talked about his early success, about how he'd defined the image of the coast in people's minds, about how his images had become iconic or emblematic (these were new words to Daniel in this context) of the way sea and land meet all around this great island continent of ours. They hinted, too, not necessarily at a lessening of powers, but of depression towards the end. Finally, the coroner came to a verdict of death by misadventure following a fall, but left it open as to whether it was suicide.

Daniel took this very personally. Because he was the person who'd found Montgomery's body, because of the way he'd touched him and identified so closely with the deadness of the body, he felt personally implicated. He knew it wasn't rational, but he experienced the dead man's betrayal of life, as he saw it, as if it were his own. 'Why did he do it?' he wondered, over and over again. The thought was made worse by the fact that, as the media revealed, the dead man, like Daniel, had a wife of many years, though they had no children. 'How could he have done that to her?' Daniel wondered. 'And how's she feeling now?' These thoughts went round and round in his head night and day.

Eventually, to end the speculation and find some peace, he decided to go and see the dead man's wife. At the very least, he thought, he could introduce himself to her as the man who'd found her husband's body. He could offer her some sympathy. He wasn't sure how much he should tell her about his own situation and why her husband's death was so important to him – if that was appropriate at all. But he knew he had to see her.

Daniel found where she lived from her husband's website. He knew that he should call her, explain who he was and ask if he could come and see her, but somehow he couldn't. He was too scared, in fact, that she might turn him down. He felt if he could only see her in person, she'd understand and everything would be all right.

It seemed too far to drive all the way there and back on his own, so he travelled to her place by train and bus. Her place lay right at the end of the line. The bus finally pulled up at a remote spot in the middle of the afternoon. Past this point, the driver assured him, they could go no further. Daniel still had to walk for some distance along the road and up a dry, dusty track leading between pine trees which hid the house from view. It was a steep climb. The house was a long way back from the road, on top of a cliff. There were more pine trees behind the house, through which Daniel could dimly perceive the vast, blank ocean moving somewhere way below.

The house itself was big, modern, with picture windows to take advantage of the fantastic view, and very comfortable. It was obviously the house of someone very successful. It was also very quiet, sitting there in the afternoon heat like a big, empty shell. Nothing could be heard but the sounds of cicadas shrilling among the pine trees, and the cries of gulls circling in the blue sky overhead.

He stood for a few minutes in the shade of the pines, recovering his breath. He wiped the sweat from his forehead and surveyed the house. He didn't want to look too excited, or distressed, when he stepped up to the front door. He wanted everything to appear as normal as possible. He took a deep breath, told himself to stay calm, stepped up to the outsize, solid timber pivot door and pressed the buzzer.

The woman who answered the door was unexpectedly beautiful. He told himself he should have been expecting it. She'd been married to a very successful man…the artist's model and all that. But it did surprise him. In fact, it took his breath away. He felt even more confused and foolish than he'd thought he would.

'Hello…' he said, struggling to find the appropriate words. 'My name's Daniel Diver. I'm the man who found your husband. I know this must appear very unusual – and I'm sorry I didn't ring or anything – but I felt I absolutely had to come and see you. Somehow, I can't stop thinking about it and I was thinking…if I could just come and see you…maybe – I don't want to cause you any inconvenience and I certainly don't want to stir up any unhappy memories – but I thought, if I could just talk to you about it, it might just help me to get over it, which I don't seem to be able to do at the moment…if you see what I mean.'

He finished up and stood there, silent, helpless. The woman looked at him. Her beauty, which grew more striking with every passing moment, was enhanced by the distinctive gravity and stillness of her bearing. The cicadas shrilled; the gulls cried. A faint wind moved in the pine trees.

Then, to his immense surprise, the woman smiled, quite broadly, and said, 'Yes, of course I understand. Won't you come in?' She held the door wide open for him to enter.

He crossed from the brightness of the day into a cool, dark and very silent interior. He was acutely aware of his own hotness, sweatiness and general confusion as he passed by the woman.

'By the way, my name's Sarah…Sarah Montgomery.' The woman closed the door and held out her hand to him.

Her hand was very dry and smooth. Up close, she gave out a cool, silvery feeling, very soothing and relaxing, in contrast to his own clammy perturbation. It sent a shiver right through him. 'I recognise this,' he thought, without quite knowing why. 'There's something here I can learn from. There's something here that I need.'

'Pleased to meet you. My name's Daniel…Daniel Diver,' he stammered.

'What a nice name!' the woman said, and laughed. She had a lovely, liquid laugh, up and down the scale, with a slight hint of sadness, like a catch in the back of her throat. 'Diver Dan…your parents must have had a sense of humour.'

'Yes,' he acknowledged, sheepishly, remembering how he'd been teased endlessly at school about it. But he could feel himself relaxing at the same time. The woman – Sarah – was extraordinarily easy to be around. His initial nervousness was slipping away.

'Come through this way.' Sarah spoke and moved very graciously. She ushered him through the darkened entrance hall, towards a large, open-plan living and dining room beyond.

The walls of the entrance hall were painted deep indigo – the colour of the sea on a cloudless, sunny day. The hall had two pictures on the walls. One was an exquisite Tibetan thangka of a bright blue Buddha sitting on a lotus throne. The other was an enormous oil painting of the sea at night, painted, Daniel felt sure, from the top of the cliffs he'd glimpsed at the back of the house. The sea lay, like a clean, polished mirror, smooth and still, reflecting the light of the full moon riding above it, shedding an eerie glow. That was all there was in the picture, but it cast a powerfully disturbing spell. It was all dark blues – of the night sky and the sea – and the silvery white of the moon and its reflection. It was very beautiful but also, somehow, sad. It was filled, above all, by a terrible sense of loss, as if the person painting it were the last person left in the world, contemplating the scene, completely on his own. There was no consolation in the beauty, as one might expect there to be…just a terrible, aching loneliness and emptiness.

'Are you interested in that?' asked Sarah, noticing that Daniel had stopped in front of the seascape.

'Yes,' replied Daniel, though the word seemed to stick in his mouth. There was nothing else he could say, he felt so overcome.

'That's the last painting Clive ever painted,' Sarah told him. 'He was working on it when he died…though it looks pretty finished to me.'

'Yes,' Daniel agreed with her.

The painting did look very finished – absolutely complete. For a moment, they stood in front of it in shared silence, then passed on, into the open-plan living and dining room beyond.

This room, by contrast with the hall, was bright, warm and comfortable. It had ochrey walls and floor-to-ceiling windows which looked out onto a view of the clifftop, the pine trees and the vast sea far below stretching to the horizon.

'He painted it from just out there,' said Sarah, pointing to a spot on the clifftop.

'Yes, I thought he might have. I could see the view, coming up the path,' Daniel replied.

'Won't you sit down?'

'Thank you.' Daniel sank down into an enormous, cushion-covered couch positioned to take full advantage of the view.

'He liked to spend hours out there, just looking at the sea,' Sarah went on. 'It was his favourite thing to do. He painted a lot of daylight views from there, but only one at night… Would you like some coffee?'

'Yes, please.'

While Sarah busied herself in the kitchen, Daniel took stock of himself and his surroundings. He felt quite calm, which was good. He didn't want to ruin his chances of discovering what there was to be discovered here. There were no pictures in this room. Clearly, the focus was intended to be the view. And it was breathtaking, if so vertiginous as to make it more than a little disturbing.

'Many years ago, Clive and some friends built a swing out there,' Sarah remarked, coming back into the room with a steaming pot of coffee and two cups on a tray. 'You can sit on it and swing right out over the cliff edge. You can look down and see the sea breaking on the rocks way down below. Or you can look up and see nothing but sky. It's the closest thing to flying. It's still out there. Clive liked to go and swing on it, right to the end. In fact,' she went on, very reluctantly, but with a feeling that she had to say it, 'there's some suggestion that's what he might have been doing…the morning that he died. There's some suggestion that he might have lost his grip… that it might have been an accident. But I doubt it somehow. There were too many other signs.'

'Like what?'

Sarah put the tray down on the coffee table in front of them. She hunched forward while she poured the coffee into the cups. 'Like the fact that he had long since ceased to feel very involved with his painting. He still did it – obsessively almost – but he said he felt like he was just going through the motions, in search of some lost inspiration. Except for that last one. With that one, he was suddenly involved again. Only, there was a feeling with that one that it was much too powerful for him. He'd gone from one extreme to the other and he couldn't handle it. He said it was tearing him apart.'

'What did he mean by that?'

Sarah handed Daniel his coffee. 'I don't know,' she confessed. 'He said a lot of strange things in the months before he died.'

'So why did he do it?' Daniel was astonished to find he had the courage to ask the question so directly. But there was a quality of openness about Sarah which made it easy for him to do things he couldn't have remotely imagined doing otherwise. He felt like he'd known her for a long time, rather than just met her. 'Why would a man as successful as he was do something like that?'

'I don't know,' she repeated. 'But I do know that he'd come to the end of something. Painting had been his life since he was very young. Painting had been like a lifeline for him…something which helped him to get through every day. He used to say he got through life from one painting to the next. It gave him some purpose, some meaning, as well as an identity, of course – the person who became the famous painter. When all that collapsed, when it didn't work for him any more, he felt like he had to confront the emptiness behind the canvas… At least, that's how he explained it to me.'

'What did he mean by that?'

'Again, I don't know. He was a very insecure man deep down – although you wouldn't have thought it on the surface. From an early age, I think, he used painting to cover any deficiencies he might have felt. It was like a gamble he took with life. And when that didn't work any more…'

'But what about you? Didn't you count in the scheme of things?'

'I had done once, I guess, but not any more. Our relationship hadn't been much good for years. Not having any children didn't help, of course. He was very lonely man, right in the centre of himself. He didn't know how to let other people in. He had his painting – and me, for a while, of course. But eventually, we drifted apart. Then painting let him down and he was left with…nothing.'

There was a silence in the room when she finished. Daniel's coffee was all gone, leaving behind a hint of its delicious aroma and the swirl of black grounds in the bottom of the cup. The mid-afternoon sunlight was beginning to slant over the pine trees.

'Would you like to go for a walk?' Sarah asked, suddenly, setting her cup back down on the tray.

'Yes,' Daniel replied, surprised but grateful for the invitation. There were so many questions he still wanted to ask her.

Sarah slid the centre windows back, and they stepped out of the house into the view. Russet needles crunched underfoot and yielded up their sweet, dusty scent. The faint wind made the trunks of the pine trees creak and the branches sigh. The fresh, green needles rustled together, like they had some secret they wanted to tell. The cicadas were very loud, up close, but Daniel could still hear, between their deafening trills, the sound of the sea breaking on the rocks below.

'So how did you feel,' asked Daniel, 'when he…did what he did?'

'I was absolutely devastated.' Sarah spoke slowly, wrestling with the emotion which threatened to overwhelm her at every point. 'We'd grown apart…but that didn't mean that I didn't still love him. I felt terrible that he'd go ahead and do something like that and not tell me how bad he was feeling. I knew he was depressed, of course. That'd been obvious for years. But it seemed like he was becoming more involved in his painting again, like he was coming back to life, like he might even come back…eventually…to me. So it felt like some sort of ultimate betrayal – some ultimate rejection – that he wouldn't share how he was feeling with me. It made me think that there's always some room inside people that they keep shut from everybody else. Maybe they can't even open it themselves. Maybe it's the last, loneliest room where people are finally and irreducibly themselves, where they have no connection to…and no responsibility for…anyone except themselves. I think maybe he was locked in there and he couldn't – or didn't know how to – come out. And I feel very sorry for him because it must have been so painful for him…'

They'd arrived at the edge of the cliff. The booming explosions of the waves on the rocks below came up to them with a slight delay. Spray rose in clouds and vanished in mid-air. The broken waves sucked back from the rocks in a surprisingly delicate, lacy wash, then milled around, gathering strength for another surge. Seagulls screamed in their ears closer to hand. The wind was stronger here, too, with nothing to stand in its way. Sarah's expression was set as if in refusal to cry, looking out at the distant horizon.

'This is the swing.' She gestured to something on the other side of Daniel.

Daniel turned and saw a home-made swing – a smoothly polished log, with a long, thick rope tied around its middle, suspended from the gnarled bough of a huge, old pine tree, perilously close to the cliff's edge.

'Sit on it,' Sarah said.

Daniel did, feeling a little like he was in a dream.

'Try it out. See what it's like.'

He began to swing, slowly and ponderously, kicking his legs up in front of him like a child to try and gain some momentum.

'Pull it right back and take a run at it,' Sarah told him. 'Then you can jump up onto it. That's what Clive and his mates used to do. In fact, they used to throw it for each other. Sometimes they didn't even bother to sit on it. They just used to catch it and hold on.'

The thought made Daniel's blood run cold. Still, he slid off the swing, as she suggested, and pulled it as far back as he could. He held the log and the rope up high in front of him. Then he took off in a sprint, jumped up onto the log, jammed the rope firmly between his legs, held on for dear life and soared out beyond the edge of the cliff, into the void, suspended between sea and sky. He felt absolutely like he was flying. He felt tremendously exhilarated, as well as terrified. For just one moment, he felt released from all earthly confines; for just one moment, he felt free.

He returned to earth with a rush and a bump, running along the cliff top with a child's whirling footsteps, out of control, trying to slow himself down. Luckily, he succeeded, before taking the return journey, out into the void. He climbed off the swing, laughing shakily. 'Wow,' he exclaimed, 'that's quite a ride!'

Sarah waited while Daniel recovered. 'Now how about you?' she asked, when he'd caught his breath and gathered his scattered wits.

'Well,' he replied, glad to be back on solid ground, but still trembling with the excitement of being out over the cliff edge, 'there's not much to tell. I'm not an interesting person, like you…or your husband. I'm just an accountant who worked for many years for the same company, then got told one day that they were downsizing – rationalising, they called it – and, suddenly, I didn't have a job any more. I was too old, you see. They wanted younger men with flashy business degrees and big ideas who knew all the right buzzwords and could make the kinds of changes they wanted…not some old fogey who'd been plodding away quietly for years, just doing the job that he was paid to do, even if he was very good at it, as they constantly told me I was…'

'You sound bitter.'

'Of course I am. I knew more about the actual job than those young turkeys are ever going to know – and I cared about the company, too, which is more than they did. All those types care about is where their next promotion's coming from. It's all bullshit! There's no loyalty, no follow-through, no concern for the future or anyone else who might be involved. It's just me, me, me, all the way to the bank and, when they don't produce the results they were supposed to in that position, they just skip to another position. Just keep talking the fancy talk and don't let anyone, or anything, stop you…'

'It sounds awful.'

'It was.'

They walked back to the house. It felt warm and welcoming to Daniel after his experience on the clifftop. He was relieved to be safe inside and sitting on the enormous, comfortable couch again. 'I feel happier looking at that view than being part of it,' he remarked.

Sarah laughed. 'You're not the first to have said that. So what happened next?'

'Well, my wife, to whom I'd been married for many years, decided that she was going to leave me…taking the kids – who were almost grown – with her.'

'Why did she do that?'

'She said she was tired of the way I gave in so easily. She wondered why I didn't ever stand up and fight for myself. I suppose she wanted me to be more like one of those younger men – one of those cocky, young bullshit artists at work – who only thought about themselves and how they were going to get ahead in the world. But I couldn't be like that, so…in the end…she left me.'

'And what happened then?'

It was getting well on into the afternoon by this time. The sun was sliding down behind the tops of the pine trees. Their lengthening shadows reached out towards the house. Daniel began to imagine the night, the seascape that Clive Montgomery had painted, his plunge into the abyss…

'Then I started drifting. I felt like I didn't have a will of my own any more, like I couldn't do anything…just roll with the tides of life, wherever they took me. And – predictably – they didn't take me very far. In fact, after a while, I felt less like I was drifting than that I was stuck. I felt like I was stuck, like a brick in a wall…on the side of some street…and that people, walking along the footpath, would just pass me by…and not see me. It was like I'd ceased to exist for anyone else – I was even ceasing to exist for myself.'

Daniel was astonished to find himself talking like this with such an attractive woman who, only a couple of hours before, had been a complete stranger to him. These were thoughts he'd hardly dared articulate to himself, let alone anybody else. And yet, there was something about her that was so familiar, so consoling. He felt like he could share his deepest secrets with her and that, somehow, she'd understand him and – more importantly – she wouldn't betray him. He peered out into the growing darkness under the pines.

'So that's how I was when I found…Clive.' He felt awkward, using the dead painter's name like that, in front of Sarah, but he also felt, very strongly, this was something they now shared.

There was a long silence when he finished. Sarah, too, was staring into the pines. She'd been listening to him, but not looking at him. Daniel noticed that her cheeks were wet, though she gave no other sign of emotion.

'I'll make dinner,' she said, wiping the tears from her cheeks, impatiently, with the palms of both hands. 'Would you like to stay for dinner?'

The shadows of the pines were reaching inside now, darkening the room. Daniel wasn't sure how he was going to get home if it got late; he hadn't thought that far ahead. Even so, he found himself replying, 'Yes, I would, thank you,' surprised, once again, by the kindness of her offer and the alacrity of his response. But he was feeling a growing confidence. They were getting on so well. 'Everything is going to work out,' he thought to himself, for the first time in ages. 'Everything is for the best. What do minor details like how to get home matter?'

And so they talked on, while Sarah made dinner. By the time it was ready, it was well and truly night. They ate the meal, which was delicious. They drank a bottle of wine with it, then opened another, because the first was so good and they were still talking. They discovered they had many things in common, in spite of the superficial dissimilarities of their lives. They each had fresh insights, new understandings, changed ways of looking at the world and doing things, which their losses had brought them. They had a coffee, then another wine, and finally they started to feel tired, with the end of the evening approaching. Any thought of going home had long since vanished from Daniel's mind. Besides, did he really have a home to go to, any more?

They finished up in front of the painting in the entrance hall.

'It's beautiful, isn't it?' said Sarah, sipping from the glass of wine she'd brought with her.

'Yes, but it's sad, too,' Daniel responded a little uncertainly, unused to giving his opinion in artistic matters and aware he was on very personal ground. But he was aware, too, of the trust that had been established between them. 'I think it's the loneliest painting I've ever seen.'

'Yes, it is, isn't it?' Sarah seemed to understand perfectly what he was saying. 'I think he was painting that final loneliness I was talking about earlier. The whole night seascape is like the locked room inside him…or that emptiness he was talking about beyond the canvas. I always feel immensely sad when I look at it. I sometimes wonder whether he was seeing me as the moon and himself as the sea – one's so dark and the other's so bright, and there's such a distance between them. Or, maybe, it's the other way round and the moon is like a cold eye, looking down – I don't know…'

'So why do you keep it here, if it causes you such pain?'

'Because it's so beautiful and it's like a last message – almost a challenge – from him to me.'

'It is a challenge.' Daniel couldn't have explained exactly what he meant by that, but he was convinced, deep down, he was absolutely right. 'It's a challenge to all of us.'

Sarah took a long time to consider what he'd said, as if, once again, it made perfect sense to her. She stared deeply into the painting before she finally broke with it. She shook her head, dispelling its influence, then turned to him and asked, 'Well, what are you going to do now? It's too late for you to be going home. You'd better stay the night.'

'Where…?' Daniel looked around, momentarily disconcerted.

'We've got plenty of rooms,' Sarah laughed. 'I'll put you up in the guest bedroom.'

'Oh…thank you,' said Daniel.

'Unless…that is…you'd rather sleep with me.'

Daniel looked at her, startled – shocked, even – not sure he'd heard her correctly. But Sarah gave him a look of such openness, such vulnerability, in return that Daniel couldn't resist. He felt like he was seeing right into the centre of her, right into the depths of her innermost need.

'We wouldn't do anything,' Sarah hastened to reassure him. 'Just for comfort. I could certainly do with some comfort right now. Just the comfort of a warm body sleeping by my side.'

'All right,' Daniel agreed. He had that same dreamlike feeling he'd experienced earlier on the swing. It seemed Sarah could carry him along with her sometimes by the power of pure suggestion, almost as if he had no will of his own.

'Good!' Sarah concluded, very matter-of-factly. 'That's settled then. The bedroom's this way.'

They stopped at the door of the bedroom, looking in.

'Please excuse the mess.' Sarah waved an apologetic hand. 'No one else has been in here since Clive died.'

There was, in fact, very little mess. The room was quite plain – impersonal, even – rather like the living room, except for a sun-filled seascape on the wall, obviously painted in much happier times, and a photo of Clive beside the bed. Daniel experienced a distinct shock, being confronted with the dead man's face so clearly like that, after the blurred images he'd become used to from photos in the media. It brought back memories of that first day at the beach and the dead man's pale, bloated face rolling up out of the water. The Clive in the photo was good-looking, young and happy, but with haunted, dark eyes which seemed, even then, to contain a question for the viewer.

'I'll change in here,' Sarah indicated an en suite beyond the bed. She drained her glass, put it down beside the photo of Clive and vanished into the en suite, leaving Daniel in an awkward state of indecision.

He supposed he should take his clothes off and lie down on the bed. That would be the next step in the normal run of things. He stripped to his underpants and lay down on the cover. He vaguely wished that he were physically more attractive than he was – a greying, balding, middle-aged man with a spreading waistline – but he was sure, like Sarah, nothing would happen between them.

Sarah came back into the room, dressed in a nightie under which, it was clear, she'd kept her bra and pants on. She was very beautiful, with her long hair out and freshly brushed. 'Under the cover, silly!' she said to Daniel.

'Oh…sorry!' Daniel stood up and hovered self-consciously while Sarah turned back the cover, then climbed in with her, trying to stay as far on his side as possible.

'Sorry!' they cried out together, when their feet touched. Gradually, they settled down, backs to each other.

'Goodnight,' said Sarah, and turned off the light.

'Goodnight,' said Daniel. He lay, for a few moments in the dark, reflecting on the oddness of the situation. How had he, a middle-aged, di-

vorced, unemployed accountant, a person of absolutely no consequence –
or even expectation – any longer, come to be involved with this beautiful
woman and her famous, dead artist-husband, to the point where he was
now sharing a bed with her in the middle of the night, after having known
her only a few hours? It was a situation so far outside his normal experience
that he could make no sense of it; neither did he particularly want to. In
fact, he gave it only very fleeting consideration before sleep claimed him,
as it had already claimed Sarah.

Sometime later that night, they must have rolled over, found each other
in the middle of the bed, touched… However it happened, they started
making love, in spite of their earlier agreement that they wouldn't. They
were still half-asleep. Daniel felt exactly as if he were diving down out of
the sky into the sea, which everywhere surrounded him. He was not in the
sea, he was of it, as she was too. Their lovemaking was like the waves, which
buoyed them up and down, rocking them in a rhythm beyond their control. When they came, it was like a final wave breaking – an explosion of
cold, salt spray which threw them out into the air again and landed them
onshore, where they lay gasping. Even then, they didn't wake up. They separated eventually, went back to their own halves of the bed and continued
sleeping.

When he woke the next morning, their lovemaking during the night
was like a distant memory, or a rumour, to Daniel. He lay awake, staring
at the still-sleeping Sarah, hardly able to believe what had happened.
She was even more beautiful in sleep, if that were possible. Sleep drained
away the sadness and tiredness of her life and left her face as it must
once have been, the face of a beautiful young girl, full of hope and
dreams.

He found his underpants, got out of bed and dressed, taking great care
not to disturb her. Silently, he let himself out of the bedroom, then out of
the house. He took the path down to the road, walked back to the start of
the return bus route, opposite where he'd got off the day before, and waited.
The road was empty. There was no traffic in either direction. It was a beau-

tiful morning, very still and clear, with bright sunlight, no clouds in the sky and only the sounds of the birds around him – the first, he was sure, of many such mornings from now on in his life. He felt no desire to return to Sarah; neither, he was sure, would she feel any particular desire to see him again. They'd shared what they had to share; now they had to get on with their own lives, separate from each other. But he knew that neither of their lives would be the same from that point. The past was over, for him as for her, and the future lay ahead like that shining morning road, waiting for him to travel it.

www.ingramcontent.com/pod-product-compliance
Lightning Source LLC
Chambersburg PA
CBHW051223210726
48290CB00003B/772